Patrick Abbott. A tall, lan[l] out to become a U.S. Marine.

Jean Abbott. His brand-new wife, who wants to make the most of what time they have together before Pat reports for duty.

Ellen Bland. A calm, collected woman whom Pat knew in Paris and who brings out the protective instinct in most men. Jean distrusts her.

Louis Bland. Her nasty, controlling ex-husband who still exerts a powerful hold over Ellen and their children.

Dick Bland. Their 16-year-old son, already on the road to being an alcoholic.

Susan Bland. Their 18-year-old daughter, outspoken and youthfully self-absorbed.

Anna Forbes. Louis's former nursemaid, now the family housekeeper, a rude, sour-faced woman who despises Ellen but still adores Louis.

Hank Rawlings. A chemical engineer who's deeply in love with Ellen.

Mary Kent. An expatriate who fled occupied France. Ruthless and overbearing, she's considered a good match for Louis, who is expected to marry her.

Daphne Garnett. Another of the Blands' Parisian friends now living in New York. A seemingly silly woman, she's more perceptive than people expect.

Clint Moran. Another refugee, indolent and enigmatic and an inventive pianist. Flat broke, he lives in a flophouse. He and Louis go back a long way.

Bill Reynolds. Susan's fiancé, who's serving in the Merchant Marines.

Dr. Maxton Seward. The family physician, fat and sleek and opportunistic.

Patrolman Isaac Goldberg. Conscientious to a fault, he will never believe that Pat and Jean are really married.

Lieutenant Jeffry Dorn. A deceptively angelic-looking police detective.

Laura Gilbert. Hank's beautiful, dedicated secretary, in love with her boss.

Sarah Howe. The fussy old maid who lives across the hall from Laura.

Books by Frances Crane

Featuring the Abbotts

The Turquoise Shop (1941)
The Golden Box (1942)
The Yellow Violet (1942)
The Pink Umbrella (1943)
The Applegreen Cat (1943)
The Amethyst Spectacles (1944)
The Indigo Necklace (1945)
The Cinnamon Murder (1946)
The Shocking Pink Hate (1946)
Murder on the Purple Water (1947)
Black Cypress (1948)
The Flying Red Horse (1950)
The Daffodil Blonde (1950)
Murder in Blue Street (1951)
The Polkadot Murder (1951)
Murder in Bright Red (1953)
13 White Tulips (1953)
The Coral Princess Murders (1954)
Death in Lilac Time (1955)
Horror on the Ruby X (1956)
The Ultraviolet Widow (1956)
The Buttercup Case (1958)
The Man in Gray (1958)
Death-Wish Green (1960)
The Amber Eyes (1962)
Body Beneath a Mandarin Tree (1965)

*Reprinted by the Rue Morgue Press

Non-Series Mysteries

The Reluctant Sleuth (1961)
Three Days in Hong Kong (1965)
A Very Quiet Murder (1966)
Worse Than a Crime (1968)

Non-Mystery

The Tennessee Poppy, or, Which Way Is Westminster Abbey? (1932)

The
Pink
Umbrella
by Frances Crane

Rue Morgue Press
Lyons

ABOUT FRANCES CRANE

AFTER SHE WAS EXPELLED from Nazi Germany prior to the start of World War II, Frances Kirkwood Crane, recently divorced and with a daughter heading for college, needed to find a new way to make a living. The old market for her writing—primarily poking gentle fun at Brits from the point of view of an American living abroad—was suddenly out of fashion. Americans no longer wanted to laugh at the foibles of the English now that brave little Britain was engaged in a desperate struggle for its very survival against the forces of Hitler.

Up to that point, life had been relatively easy for Frances. Her husband, Ned Crane, was a well-paid advertising executive with the J. Walter Thompson agency, whose dubious claim to immortality was the Old Gold cigarette slogan, "Not a cough in a carload." Frances herself was a regular contributor to a new sophisticated humor magazine called *The New Yorker*. Many of her short sketches for that magazine were collected in book form in 1932 as *The Tennessee Poppy or Which Way Is Westminster Abbey?*

Back in the states, newly divorced and in need of money—living in the United States was more expensive than living in Europe—she had turned to the mystery field at the suggestion of one of her old editors who told her it was a "hot market." Not long after arriving in Taos, New Mexico, Crane, now around 50, heard about an incident involving a jewelry store in that artists' colony, which inspired her first Pat and Jean Abbott mystery, *The Turquoise Shop*, published by Lippincott in 1941. Although she changed the name of town to Santa Maria and even commented that it had not yet been spoiled in the fashion of Taos and Santa Fe, there is absolutely no question that it was based on Taos. In fact, Mona Brandon and her hacienda in *The Turquoise Shop* are loosely based on Mabel Dodge Luhan and her famous adobe home (now a bed and breakfast inn).

Jean Holly (she sounds terribly experienced and world weary, yet she's only 26) meets up with a handsome San Francisco private detective in that first novel. *The Turquoise Shop* was followed by 25 more books featuring Pat and Jean Abbott, who marry toward the end of the third book, all with a color in the title. Many of them take the Abbotts to locales across the United States and around the world, although they were to return to Santa Maria several times in the course of the series. While some contemporary critics weren't always kind to her books, readers loved them, and still do. The series was so popular that it spun off a radio program, *Abbott Mysteries*, which ran on the Mutual Network in the summers of 1945, 1946 and 1947.

Nor was Crane ignorant of the trends in contemporary detective fiction. She was extremely well-read in the field. Along with fellow women mystery writers

Lenore Glen Offord and Dorothy B. Hughes, she was one of the most influential mystery reviewers in the country, dwarfed in influence only by Anthony Boucher (for whom Bouchercon, the World Mystery Convention, is named). She relished her place in the literary world and numbered among her friends such literary lights as James Jones and Sinclair Lewis as well as her editor at Random House, the very urbane Bennett Cerf. Yet she realized she was not in that same league with these literary heavyweights, remarking once to Cerf that she was but a "minor light."

But all good things seemingly must come to an end. The Abbotts cracked their last case in 1965 with *Body Beneath the Mandarin Tree*. In the 1960s, Crane also wrote five stand-alone mysteries which were published in England but failed to find an American publisher. The last of these, *Worse Than a Crime*, appeared in 1968 when she was 78 years old, and though she would live another 13 years and enjoy relatively good health, her career as a mystery writer was over, and she settled into a well-earned retirement. Yet she had a better run than many women writers of her era, and, unlike most writers, male or female, she earned a good living at it. While many other female mystery writers who began in the 1930s and 1940s saw their careers end with the death of the rental libraries and the advent of the male-oriented paperback original in the early 1950s, Crane not only survived, publishing well into the 1960s, but endured, as any out-of-print book dealer who has ever offered one of her titles in a catalog and been overwhelmed with orders can testify. Her fans don't just enjoy her books, they revel in them, then and now.

She spent much of the last forty years of her life in her adopted New Mexico, mostly in Taos (though the "hippie invasion" in the 1960s drove her eventually to move to Santa Fe). She returned frequently to Lawrenceville to visit family. Three months before her 91st birthday, failing health forced her to enter a nursing home in Albuquerque, where she died on November 6, 1981. She made one final posthumous visit to Lawrenceville, a trip that many old-timers in that town still recall with amusement. The postmaster sent word to her nephew Bob, a local doctor, that a package had arrived for him from New Mexico. "Only," he explained, "you'll have to pick it up yourself. I'm not touching it."

The package was marked "human remains." Bob and other fellow family members scattered the ashes it contained on the family farm. Frances Kirkwood Crane not only came home, she did so in her usual unconventional style.

CHAPTER ONE

Patrick and I were strolling west on Fifty-fifth just west of Lexington and talking when we did talk about the queer beauty of New York in the artificial twilight called the dim-out. The air was warmish, tender, faintly veiled with thin haze, and full of the somewhat depraved smells which in the cities pass as springlike. There was no wind. The outlines of the old brownstone houses flanking this block and those of the looming apartment buildings ahead on Park Avenue were softened and blended oddly in the strange light. Sounds were distorted and intensified. Some of the most prosaic were furtive, almost menacing. The slow wheeze of a motorcar held mystery. The tread of a faceless pedestrian suggested some dire urgency. Across the street a shadow mounted shadowy steps on peculiarly sonorous feet.

"New York's spooky," I said. I pressed close against Patrick's overcoat sleeve and moderated my voice to the atmosphere. "That's the last thing I ever expected, in New York."

"It's only the dim-out," Patrick said.

"The dim-out isn't spooky in San Francisco. It's grand."

"The difference is in the air, dear."

"I don't want to know the difference," I said. "And I don't mind. Only it's not my idea of New York. I thought everything would be bright and scintillating and exciting. I like it better this way, only it's not what I expected. That's all. I really love this, Pat. The buildings all around us are so—so anonymous."

Patrick sniffed. "Whatever that is."

"We don't know anybody in them. That's what I mean. Not a soul. Isn't it wonderful, Pat? Just you and I, all alone, in a whole city full of dimmed-out people. Don't you love it, dear?"

Patrick doesn't like obscurity of any kind. But he made a friendly noise in his throat and pulled my hand so close against his side that I could feel the warmth of his body through his thick man's clothes.

Then a sad thought recurred to me as it had been doing all day long. Patrick had joined the Marines. We had, at last, got three days all our own and what had he done, first thing, but join the Marines, simply because it was his first chance to join the Marines. I was glad, proud, sad, and simply furious. Nothing nowadays makes sense.

We strolled on. Halfway along the long block a taxicab slid by and stopped before a tall narrow white house with white marble steps and black iron railings.

A long thin boy in a gray flannel suit and a porkpie hat got out. He propped his back against the cab and started feeling through his pockets. As we approached the short thickset driver came around the car, took the boy by one arm, and tried to propel him towards the steps.

"Be a pal, man!" the boy implored. His young voice was clumsy from drink. "My mother will pay. Only please don't make a fuss, pal. My father's in there. See?"

The driver didn't want to be a pal. He wanted his dough instead. He pushed the boy forward.

"It's a matter of getting to Mother first, pal!" Suddenly the boy stared at us. "Hello, Pat," he said vaguely.

Patrick left me near the railing which guarded the areaway and stepped forward. "Hello, Dick," he said. The boy and the man both gaped. So did I. "Supposed you were still in Paris, Dick," Patrick said. He took the hand the driver hadn't got and pumped the arm.

"What's the racket?" sneered the driver. "That meter says four dollars and fifteen cents. I'm going—"

Patrick took out five dollars. "Here!" he snapped. "Scram!" he added when the man fished hastily for change. The fellow went silky and jumped into his car and sped away.

I stepped forward. The Scot in me is always irked by Patrick's western carelessness with money.

The boy, unpropped while Patrick was paying the fare, had slipped into a heap on the bottom step. He stared up at me owlishly from big dark eyes in a good-looking face and then asked with exaggerated politeness, and a wave of the hand, "What is this?"

"This is my wife, Dick. Jean, Dick."

"For heaven's sake, Pat!" I muttered.

Dick's unblinking stare swung between us. "Wife? I thought you were Pat Abbott? He has no wife." He stood up. He swept his little round hat off and said, "Old Pat always could pick 'em, Wife. Come on in. Mother will love you, Wife. Shush!" He laid a finger on his lips. "Louis is here. It's not such a hot idea to come home oiled at this time of day, Pat. Louis is always hanging round evenings, same as in Paris. Now, we'll go easy. I've got my key. Shush—we'll sneak in, see?"

"Pat?" I said. With meaning.

Then the white door at the top of the white marble steps swung inward and a very slender woman in black was silhouetted against a gloomily lighted vestibule. I could see the triangular shape of her face and the upward sweep of her hair.

She slipped the lock's catch and stepped out and closed the door after her. I caught a whiff of her perfume, something sweet and fresh.

"Hello, Ellen," Patrick said quietly. She stopped short and clasped her hands together, then said, as though shocked with surprise, yet hardly lifting her voice even in excitement above its naturally low tone, "Oh, Pat! My dear!"

Patrick went up the intervening steps. They kissed. I felt a wild stab of jealousy.

"What a wonderful surprise!" the woman said huskily.

"Rather! How are you anyway, Ellen? Come and meet my wife. Jean, Ellen Bland."

"Wife?" Ellen said. I was standing quite still, at the foot of the steps. I was numb from my jealously. I couldn't move. She came down, took both my hands, and kissed me. "How wonderful!" she said. "I didn't know. But, of course, we lost touch." Her tone changed suddenly, as she spoke to Dick, "Go on in, darling. Go through the house on this floor and up the back stairs. Take a shower and change before coming down. Your father's here."

"So I deduced," Dick said elaborately.

"Go along quickly, Dick. The door isn't locked. Hurry!"

Patrick's voice held a note of bitterness as he asked, "Still standing guard, Ellen?"

"Just the same, Pat. Only more so. Won't you come in? I can't get over my surprise. Have you seen Hank? How did you know where we lived? But . . . come in! We've got so much to say to each other."

I made our excuses. We had yet to have dinner and after that we were seeing *The Eve of St. Mark*. We accepted an invitation to tea tomorrow afternoon. I said, "If Patrick hasn't already been snatched by the Marines."

We told her we were at the Rexley, which was only a couple of long blocks away, walked up the steps to the door with her, shook hands again and said goodbye.

We had started down the steps when Ellen Bland opened the door.

A man's sarcastic voice accosted her, as from a staircase.

"Do you often entertain on the street, Ellen?"

"I'm sorry, Louis," Ellen said.

"Who was that!" the voice demanded.

The door closed.

"Who was *that?*" I asked then.

Patrick growled in his throat, "That was Louis Bland."

"He sounds like a dilly," I said.

Patrick growled again, and tucked my hand snugly into the crook of his elbow. We walked on, arm in arm. The shadows loomed mightier as we neared Park

Avenue. But the charming anonymity of the dim-out was gone. Its spell was broken. We knew people.

CHAPTER TWO

At the corner of Park Avenue and Fifty-fifth we waited under one of the dimmed-out streetlamps for a green light.

"Let's not get involved, dear," I said.

"Involved?"

"With those people, or any people, for that matter. It isn't as though we've got a lot of time, or even know how much we've got."

Patrick knew I referred to the Marines. He put his arm around me and, just as though we were alone on some lone prair-ee, gave me a long tender kiss.

That was all right with me till I heard a sort of sly step behind us and to my right, and slanting a glance in that direction I found myself looking into two shiny beetle-brown eyes, which were part of a swarthy heart-shaped face that belonged to a policeman. The eyes were leveled on us suspiciously from a distance of about six feet. I murmured in Patrick's ear that this wasn't the Wild West and that you shouldn't kiss women on street corners in civilized places like New York. Patrick slid a look at the officer and promptly announced in a Wild West accent, for his benefit, "Poison does it the quietest, hon. Then we can get married."

The policeman coughed. The cough crawled with suspicion.

"Behave yourself!" I said to Patrick. The lights changed. We walked on. From the middle of the parkway I looked back and the policeman was staring after us, with one hand rubbing at his cheek. I giggled then and felt quite lighthearted, until Patrick said,

"It's a damn shame if Dick's no good after all Ellen has had to take on his account, Jean."

For politeness, I said, "He's a sweet-looking boy, Pat."

"Looks too much like his father for my taste. Though Louis is damn good-looking. Have to concede that. Funny running into them like this. Took it for granted they were stuck in Paris, didn't think they could even bomb Louis Bland out, frankly. When Paris moved to Biarritz or Cannes or Monte Carlo he went along, but no further. I met them there five years ago. Saw a lot of Ellen and the kids. The kids took a shine to me because I was a real live detective and I was pretty keen about Ellen." My jealousy started bothering me. Patrick had lived thirty-two years before we'd met and women didn't leave him exactly numb. I said "Kids?" sort of perfunctorily and Patrick said, "There's a girl. Susan. She's a couple of years older than Dick. Dick should be about sixteen. Sue was a nice fat, happy, brown-haired youngster, no trouble for her mother at all, but Dick always was a proposition. Poor Ellen. She's had punishment enough already, from Louis."

I did a little bridling. I've no patience with downtrodden women, unless they've got some hypersuperduper reason like a broken back or something, but I realized that Ellen was out of Patrick's romantic past, and indeed from that specially romantic time when he lived for a while in Europe. So I merely asked, "Why does she live with him, then?"

"She doesn't. They're divorced, have been for years. Louis just hangs around."

"But really!"

"You have to know Louis to appreciate it, Jean. He meddles, nags—generally contrives to be a chronic nuisance."

"We got laws, darling."

"Oh, sure. But Louis has all the money in that family. And they lived in Paris, remember, not here, which may have made some difficulties I wouldn't know about."

"He's still hanging around, dear. And they're here now."

Patrick let it pass. We had been stopped—a red light—at Madison. He said, "In France a married woman usually has the upper hand in the family because she controls the money. Ellen had no money of her own. That alone might have affected her chances in a French divorce court—but honestly, I don't know much about it, because they were already divorced when we met. All I heard was gossip. Trials of that kind are held privately in France, but of course people talked. Louis got the legal say-so about the kids. That gave him a whip over Ellen. She always was nuts about those kids." The light changed and we walked on. "He divorced her on an adultery charge. Ellen's friends said he had no real case, but that she let him get away with it because she wanted to get rid of him."

"It doesn't seem to have worked."

"Not entirely anyhow."

"Was there somebody?"

"There wasn't really. Not then." Patrick hesitated. "You heard Ellen ask if I'd seen Hank? He must be in New York. His name is Henry Rawlings. He was a friend of Ellen's. People said they weren't in love at all until Louis started prying and accusing. Louis named Hank corespondent, in any case, and neither of them confirmed or denied the charges, just let him get away with it."

"What happened then?"

"Well, then, later, they did fall in love and wanted to marry. Nothing came of it because Ellen wouldn't leave the kids. Seems that after Louis divorced Ellen and got the custody of the kids he didn't want the bother of them after all, so he fixed it up for them to live with Ellen. It was a funny setup. Ellen stayed on in a house they'd had for years on the rue de l'Université. Louis lived at the Ritz. But he and his gang were eternally at Ellen's. His crowd wasn't her kind at all." Patrick paused, then said, "There was a Mrs. Kent. Ellen thought that Louis would marry her. Maybe he did. For a time Ellen and I wrote now and then, but the war ended that. Ellen must be happy to be back. She wanted to have the children educated in

America, but Louis was so completely sold on France."

"Maybe he's changed," I said.

"Maybe," Patrick said.

Fifth Avenue was all in gray, a chasm of pearl-gray wedged between slate-gray spires and skyscrapers. Ruby-red taillights and dimmed amber headlights wove sleek patterns in the grayness.

We crossed, then crossed Fifty-fifth and after a few more steps were at our hotel.

There was a telegram in our box. My heart did double-time as Patrick picked it up, imagining it was an urgent summons from the Marines. Naturally, once they knew he was available, I was sure they would grab him at once. I watched him as he opened the yellow envelope, taking his time, performing the small action with graveness and precision. I thought suddenly of the first time I'd seen him, standing with those long blue eyes fastened gravely on a picture in the window of my curio shop in Santa Maria, New Mexico. Tall, lean, sunburned, easy-moving and easy-spoken. White teeth flashing in a brown face. Poker-faced like all good Westerners. A Stetson covering the back of his dark brushed-back hair and his long legs in corduroys belted low on lean hips.

He looked quite as well though less romantic now in a gray felt hat, a light overcoat, and a double-breasted navy-blue worsted.

His face didn't give a hint at the nature of the telegram. So I quaked till he handed it over.

It said: "After what you've been through here since war started don't wonder you picked a nice soft berth like the Marines. But remember the Pacific's your home ocean. Animals happy. Love to you both. Lulu."

Lulu was Lulu Murphy, Pat's secretary in his office in San Francisco. The animals were our black Persian cat Toby and red dachshund Pancho, in Lulu's care while we were away.

What Pat had been through since the war started was the spy business which had kept West Coast detectives super-busy since Pearl Harbor.

The telegram made me feel good because it called to mind our San Francisco, and because it didn't snatch Patrick right off to the Marine Corps.

We had dinner at 21, went to the show, arriving late, went to a nightclub called *La Vie Parisienne,* and got back to the hotel the next time at ten minutes past three. A slip in our box said that Ellen Bland had phoned at ten minutes before ten.

"I wonder what she wanted?" Patrick asked. He was at once almost gravely concerned.

I kept silent as a stone. I wouldn't have voiced it for anything, but I was glad we'd missed her.

She phoned again next morning as I was leaving the room. Patrick had gone down ahead, for cigarettes.

"Mrs. Abbott?" Her voice was stunning, really, one of the low authentic-sounding ones. I'm a sucker for voices, so I braced myself against her in advance. "This is Ellen Bland. I tried to reach you last night to ask if you and Pat won't come to dinner tonight?" Dinner? I felt panicky. Dinner would mean a whole evening. I said I was terribly sorry. It was, luckily, enough. "Oh, I am too," she said. A little too quickly, as though she had wanted to be refused. "Of course, it's such short notice. You *will* come for tea?" I said definitely, and she said, "That much of you is just an *hors d'oeuvre* but we'll have to make do, I guess. Dick will be here, I hope, and Sue, and perhaps her friend Bill Reynolds. They're so excited to be seeing Pat again. You've no idea!"

In the lobby I reported the call to Patrick—omitting, I'm afraid, the dinner invitation part. His face lit up. "For two bits I'd call her back and ask about Hank," he said. "Hank Rawlings. But I guess he'd be in the army or something, only from what she said, he may be just now in New York. I never knew Hank, though, like Ellen."

We had breakfast in the Alpine Grill, which we preferred to the formal dining room. As I tried to squeeze out of the pot a second cup of coffee apiece that never had been there to start with, Patrick lit our cigarettes and said, "I suppose that's all over long ago, but it was too bad they didn't get married. They made a swell pair. Hank's a chemical engineer. He was in Paris doing a little scientific prying into something or other and vacationing on the side. He painted, as a hobby. I guess he was a better engineer than artist."

Patrick grinned ruefully. I recalled his own suppressed desire to be a painter instead of a detective. There is always something, I thought, feeling sad. Things never work out entirely.

I sat feeling stricken for a while because of Patrick's wanting to be an artist but having to spend his life catching spies and other criminals and now serving with the Marines. Patrick himself went on wrestling with the Bland problems. Nice people, I thought, strictly to myself. The kid gets drunk at sixteen. The father's a louse. The mother's apparently a vine. There's a rich widow—or divorcée—in the offing. Why bother? What you can't unscramble you can't unscramble and the hell with it, I was thinking, while Patrick was saying, earnestly, "Her mistake is in dealing honestly with Louis."

Oh, I thought. Ellen! What hocus-pocus, really. If she loved this Hank, she should have married him.

I blamed her entirely, for whatever it was, and I never said a word.

CHAPTER THREE

After breakfast, Patrick started off to police headquarters to look at some new crime-detecting gadgets and I went shopping for a hat. We had flown east for

Patrick to make some sort of report in Washington, hadn't even expected to get to New York, and on leaving San Francisco, expected to take four or five days at the most for the trip. For clothes I had only the black suit I was wearing, a topcoat to match, a black cashmere sweater, some blouses, lingerie, and so on, two pairs of shoes, and only one hat, a skull cap of tiny canary-yellow feathers, perfectly adequate really, as anybody knows, but with the windows of upper Fifth Avenue and Madison simply seething with the most delicious spring hats I had got to the point where I simply had to have another hat.

I window-shopped for a while and then had the marvelous luck to find just what I wanted, a perfect dilly about the size of the palm of your hand and made entirely of emerald green violets, which would match to perfection my emerald engagement ring and the synthetic-emerald hoop earrings I was currently wild about.

Small exclusive-looking gold letters in one corner of the window spelled Chez Hortense. I hesitated. The place looked costly. After all, did I need this hat? I went Scotch on myself.

I considered the pros and cons. My husband could go indefinitely without a new hat. I walked on, rationalizing it. After ten or fifteen minutes of reasoning, I concluded that one hat you adore is worth a hundred you but semi-adore, so it would be really an economy to buy it. I hurried back to the shop.

The hat was gone!

A taxi was chugging away at the curb. I took hope. Perhaps it was only being shown, taken from the window to be tried by some customer from this taxi. She might decide against it.

Hope flickered again, faintly, as I opened the door to step into the shop.

A rather piquant voice was saying in English with a French accent:

"I knew I would offend you, Madame, but—"

An American voice cut in. It was an interesting voice, ragged and rather deep, a smoker's voice, maybe, but interesting, and cruel, too.

"I thought you were doing damn well, Hortense. I've told everyone to come here."

Hortense replied in a tone close to tears, "But, the competition, Madame! I think all the modistes in Paris escaped to New York. Please believe me, I would never have asked, but I am frantic, Madame."

"I told you you'd get it!" Madame snapped back.

She didn't take her eyes from the image of herself in the mirror where she sat trying the hats. The eyes were astonishing, very large round pale blue eyes set so flush with her cheeks they reminded you of plaques in a wall.

The Frenchwoman saw me then, hurried over to greet me. She brushed tears from her bright black eyes as she indicated a chair. "A tiny minute," she said. I spied at once my green hat, lying on a table at some distance from the customer, and sat down. I didn't mind waiting. Both Hortense and her plaque-eyed customer interested me.

The customer decided on a hat—a flowery bonnet which Hortense put tenderly with three others on a separate table—then got up, cruised about, indicated other hats with a gloved hand, and sat down again at the mirror. She handled her tall, lithe, broad-shouldered, slim-hipped body like a mannequin. She wore a blue wool dress, a mink jacket, and very smart low-heeled suede shoes in the same warm dark blue of the dress. Her gloves matched the shoes.

I tried to decide why she was attractive. Her straight yellow hair was touched up. Her face was too large, her mouth was too small, her chin too pointed, her forehead bulged a little, and there were those eyes. But she fascinated me, intensely.

She finally decided on six hats.

The green one was not among them so I lit a cigarette and relaxed.

Hortense added up the bill.

The customer waited idly in the chair where she had tried the hats. She opened her bag, which belonged with the gloves and shoes, took out a long beige-colored cigarette and a lighter, lit the cigarette, and returned the lighter to the bag. The movements were automatic, I mean performed in the manner of a real automaton.

Her face seemed really blank, seeing nothing, hearing nothing, thinking nothing. She smoked with deep inhalations like a genuine addict.

The sweetish tobacco smell soon pervaded the gay little shop.

Hortense offered the bill. The customer scrawled beneath the figures without looking at them and said, "Pack them up. I'm taking them with me."

"But so many boxes, Madame! I must send them instead."

"Do as I say! My taxi's waiting."

"Mais oui, Madame."

Hortense came briefly to me. "I shall fetch a girl to wait on you, Madame."

"I'll wait on myself," I said. "May I try that green hat?"

"But of course!" The Frenchwoman took a quick step and picked up the hat. The customer said, "That green hat was one of the ones I selected, Hortense. What ails you this morning? Put it with the others, and do hurry." She rose with a single lithe movement. "I'll wait in the cab. Now, hurry!"

She sauntered out, Hortense fluttering to open the door. Shutting it she exploded angrily, before her shop manners closed in on her again, "She will not even keep the green hat, Madame. She does not wear green. But I will have to put it in with the others or she will get in a rage and return them all." She remembered herself. "She is an old customer, from Paris," she said, apologetically.

She added, in her bright professional manner, "Ah, have you ever seen such chic, Madame? It would be a pleasure to dress her, for nothing."

Chic, I thought, furiously. Yes, that explained her fascination, but it was spoiled by her selfishness. I'd met people like her before. She hadn't wanted the green hat till someone else wanted it.

Hortense had nothing else that morning in true emerald green. It was the color for me, she agreed, with my yellow eyes and jet-black hair—her words—and my emeralds, and shouldn't she make me a copy? I didn't want a copy of that woman's hat. So I merely said I couldn't take the time. What a pity! Hortense said clasping her hands. She would love to design a hat for me specially. I was a type, she said. I was sorry, again the matter of time. "I shall do it," she said tenaciously but smilingly. "If you do come back, it will be here."

I left my name. I suspected she wanted to make the sale desperately so I bought for utility a very smart and inexpensive black felt Basque beret and took it away in a little green-and-white checked box.

I met Patrick for lunch at the Algonquin. He peeped dutifully into the box at my French hat. I told him hotly about the so-and-so snatching the green one, and he said she should have been shot but he thought he liked this one quite as well. Then he confessed that instead of going to police headquarters he had spent his time at an exhibition of modern French paintings. "Got somehow to thinking about France," he said. People at the table next ours were speaking French. Half the menu was in French. After lunch we went to more French art shows and lingered so long at an exhibition of Tchelichew portraits—painted in Paris—that evening was almost at hand when we got to Ellen Bland's. We had to wait a couple of minutes after ringing at the top of the stiff white marble steps. The day had held a pallid brightness but now the air was darkened and thickened and scented with a pall of coal smoke which was settling over the city. It looked purplish and un-healthy. I wished suddenly that we had not accepted this invitation. I rebelled against this narrow white house, with its tall second-story balconied French win-dows, its black iron urn-ornamented railings, its deep areaway. Not because I have a gift of sensing things to come. Candidly, I have never had an intimation worth the name. I merely resented this house because it was about to swallow an hour of our time. It would probably do even worse. Already a brief contact with this house had sent us scurrying about all day after things French. These people would impose memories, speculations, invite us elsewhere, we would invite them, our time would fly, what there was left of it, if any.

The white door opened slowly, inward. I surrendered myself with a reluctance which was not lessened by the fact that Patrick was stalking into this trap with an eagerness he made no effort to hide.

CHAPTER FOUR

An elderly stout round-faced maid, in a plum-colored uniform, opened the door. Her face was full of lines and tiny puffings until it looked finely quilted. She had small grim blue eyes and iron-gray hair drawn primly back into a bun on her neck.

Her voice, when she got around to using it, was gruff and sullen.

She closed the door after us in silence and still without speaking; in a hall gloomy from its own furnishings took our topcoats and Patrick's gray hat. In silence she hung them in the closet under the stairs and then ushered us up a longish double flight with a landing. She opened a door. We entered a long tall elaborate room.

"I'll tell her," she grunted then, her first and only words to us.

She backed out and closed the door. It was a silent door, on well-oiled hinges. We were alone.

"What a sourpuss!" I said. Again I felt critical of Ellen Bland, for keeping a disagreeable maid.

Patrick said nothing. He was examining this room with a nonchalance which in him tokened extreme interest.

"Isn't it a dilly, Pat!"

"It's something."

"It's a drawing room, darling. The real thing."

Patrick crossed to the middle of the three tall front French windows and lighting a cigarette looked into the street. I noticed polished ashtrays here and there. "It seems almost a sacrilege to use these ashtrays," I said. "People who really belong in this room must smoke after dinner in the dining room, or there will be a library, or a den, or they'd take walks, for smoking."

I chose for myself the best seat in the room, the fireplace corner of one of two sofas which faced each other across an open grate. The one I sat in faced the front of the room. It was not a room to expect an open fire, but one burned neatly, without a vagrant ash or cinder, in the polished grate. The room was long for its width. There were other windows, the sash kind, at the back. It was filled with quantities of ornamental furniture, made of satinwood, rosewood, and red mahogany, and embellished with fancy marble and brass filigree work. The walls were covered with paintings, landscapes framed with elaborate molded gilded frames. The woodwork was painted white. A piano stood in the back of the room where another white door led into what must be the same hall.

A silver tea service, set on a huge silver tray on a low table in front of the other sofa, humanized a place which, for all its grandeur, was as inhuman as a hotel parlor.

What a queer place! These things were old, the room must have been furnished forty or more years ago, but everything looked fresh and unused.

I started to light a cigarette and didn't, because of the chasteness of the ashtrays. At the same time I felt critical again. I detest overtidiness. I blamed Ellen.

"Come to think of it, this room would make a first-class morgue," I said.

Patrick remarked, "They built real stories when this house was built." I compared his tall leanness with the lean pearl-gray tallness of the window beyond him. It dwarfed even Patrick. "It's a long drop into the area from here," he said.

"Rather," Ellen Bland said.

I jumped. That silent door had opened. When? Had she heard my crack about the place being a morgue?

She closed the door. It made no sound save the faint chuckle of the latch.

She came towards me. I stood up. Patrick came from the window. We shook hands. She was not so tall as I, and even thinner. She wore black, a long black dinner dress with a plastic ornament at her throat. Her only ornament. She had elegance, and she was distinguished. Her eyes were very blue, her hair, save for two narrow white streaks, very black, her straight brows and eyelashes ditto, her nose straight and small, her crimson serious mouth lovely, with very white small teeth, but it was her manner, her way of carrying herself and looking at you and listening to you that gave her her quality. I resented it. I was jealous.

"She must be ten years older than I but doesn't look a day older," I thought. The gray in her hair was enchanting.

We settled, Patrick with me on the sofa, Ellen behind the table. She struck a match to light the alcohol lamp under the old-fashioned silver kettle. The water was hot already and started hissing after only a few minutes.

We talked about the house.

"It's rather an elephant, I'm afraid," Ellen Bland said. "Louis's father had it furnished for his mother when she came here as a bride. It belonged in his family before that, of course." Her straight black brows met for an instant. "Nobody likes it now except Anna. It's a pity. But she adores it, perhaps enough for all of us." She indicated a fat crystal box. "Don't you smoke, Jean? Please do. I don't, as it happens. Tell me all about yourselves—begin at the beginning, please."

"Who is Anna?" Patrick asked, first.

"The housekeeper. She let you in."

"She didn't seem too hospitable," Patrick said, smiling.

"It's just her way," Ellen explained. "She was here so long alone before we came back—"

"Did you ring?" that sullen voice said.

I felt startled again. Another door had opened silently, the rear one this time. Back there the light was now a thick dusk. The quilted face of the old servant, and her white clasped hands, stood out against the shadows.

Ellen answered easily.

"No, Anna. Thank you."

"I thought I heard my name." She had advanced into the room. "You'll want the curtains drawn while I'm here, I guess." She kept coming. She was being deliberately rude, no "Madams" or "may-I's" or "thank-yous."

"Leave them, Anna, please."

"It's close to dark. It will save me the steps again."

"We'll draw them, thank you, Anna."

Ellen's voice was perfectly firm. The woman went on a little further towards the windows, then wheeled and left by the front of the two doors, closing it with a crisp little slam.

It seemed a good time to answer the question about ourselves. I told Ellen, Patrick chiming in, about how we had met in New Mexico, got engaged in Illinois, and married in San Francisco.

Ellen busied herself with the tea. She measured it from the caddy into the silver pot, steeped it with the boiling water from the kettle, and poured it into the flowery Limoges cups, asking how I liked mine and remembering after five years that Patrick, when he took tea, had it plain with two lumps. Patrick reported his big news, the Marines. Ellen asked what I would do and I told her about the business course I'd taken since getting married, which would qualify me for a defense job.

Everybody was doing something useful, except herself, Ellen said, rather enviously, and I went touchy again thinking well, why didn't she? She seemed to sense my thought. She said, "I can't take a job,—yet—I'm afraid."

Why? I wondered. Patrick asked, suddenly, "How did you get away from Paris, Ellen?"

"Ran. Like any other refugee."

"Yes, of course. But—"

"You shouldn't say 'yes-of-course,' Pat. Our country was neutral then. Americans should have waited to be evacuated. It was silly of us to add ourselves to the confusion on the roads. It was a dreadful business."

"I'm surprised that Louis would leave Paris, under any conditions, Ellen."

Ellen smiled. "He thought we could stay in Biarritz for the duration. You would have been amused by our arguments at the time, Pat. I never wanted to live in Paris, as you know, but in that panic I refused to budge. Louis, who couldn't bear to leave Paris ever, got frantic to leave. He insisted that the children had to go whether I did or not. They thought escaping would be exciting, so in the end I had to give in." Her brows met. "He is so unhappy in New York that he thinks now he would prefer even a German-occupied Paris. By the way, he's getting married. Immediately, we think. Do you remember Mary Kent?"

"Yes. That ought to make a good match."

Patrick implied that they were two of a kind. Ellen's reply ignored it, was again almost super-cautious. "Most satisfactory," she said. "They have the same tastes. And Mary Kent is as miserable in New York as Louis is. They will go to South America right away and stay there till they can go back to Paris. Or so I'm told." She interrupted herself and said lightly, "But now for real news. Susan is in love."

Patrick protested, "She's not old enough, Ellen."

"She's eighteen, Pat. The boy's name is Bill Reynolds and he's serving with the Merchant Marine." She lowered her voice a little. "I'll tell you a secret. They are going to be married as soon as Louis is gone. I am so happy. Bill is just right for Sue, a marvelous boy."

Patrick said that was fine. "But what about you?" he asked.

I could see Ellen's face pinkening even in the firelight, and her voice came warmly natural.

"Funnily enough, that's all right, too. Hank and I have been seeing each other, when we could, on the sly for more than six years. Can you imagine anything more silly, Pat? At our age! And since neither of us are sly people, it's fantastic, for—"

Ellen's gaze shifted. Her teacup made a tiny shivering sound against its saucer. "What is it, Anna?"

Heavens! She must do it with mirrors. I'd make the woman wear a bell, or something.

Anna was already in the room and taking her stand between the sofas and the front of the two doors. Her face and her white apron singled her out of shadows now as deeply plum-colored as her uniform.

"I'm here to draw those curtains," she said.

"Leave them as they are, Anna. Please. But thank you."

"It is practically dark outside," the woman argued. "It don't look right to leave them open. We never have."

She took a step towards the windows. Ellen said, "Anna, that will do!"

The maid wheeled on her.

"I will tell Mr. Louis!" she screamed. "We'll see who's running this house! A divorced woman giving me orders, eh? We shall see!"

Ellen's voice cut in like a whip. "Anna!"

The maid shut up, shuffled out and closed the door rather shakily.

Ellen found her handkerchief and brushed it over her face. It was the only sign that she was left in any way disturbed. Her voice was exactly the same, low and even, as she said, "Anna gets in a state if any of her rules are interfered with. I suppose she can't help it. She has lived here since she was hardly more than a child. She came as a cook's helper, then became a housemaid, then Louis's nurse, then she was housekeeper, and finally when no one lived here any more she became the caretaker. She adores this house."

That explained, I thought, the drawing room—so looked after, yet so unused. But why should Ellen make such a point of the curtains? What difference if they were drawn or open, if it mattered so much to an old woman?

"I'm neglecting you," Ellen said then. "Jean, do let me have your cup."

Patrick asked bluntly, "But why does that woman hate you so?"

Ellen gave her head a little shake.

"I don't think Anna would have liked anyone who married Louis. She began hating me more, however, when we were divorced. She probably heard the gossip about me, at that time. Besides, she abhors divorce. She's a very prejudiced woman. She's been alone too much."

"I hope she didn't hear what you were saying about yourself and Hank?"

Ellen looked frightened. "Heavens, Pat! I hope she didn't. She runs to Louis with everything. I—I sincerely believe that Louis thinks that Hank and I have broken off. I think Louis has finally decided that I will never marry again. If he didn't, he himself wouldn't marry." She lifted her eyebrows. "How smug that sounds! But you know what I mean. Louis really gets such a lot of fun out of punishing me. He would lose interest in me if he could no longer hurt me."

My own curiosity about Louis Bland was reaching a pitch. It was soon to be partially satisfied, as it happened, for five minutes or so later there was a flock of footsteps on the stairs and the housekeeper ushered Louis, Mary Kent, a woman named Daphne Garnett and a man named Clint Moran, into the room. I had a faint shock at Mary Kent's being the woman who had snatched my green hat, and a second when Louis Bland turned out to be charming and handsome.

Anna closed the door behind them and sailed over and drew the heavy brocade curtains. She drew first the weights which operated the middle pair, then those on the right window, then the left. She straightened the hems against the thick Persian rugs and patted in the folds to her satisfaction and then stood off and beheld them triumphantly. She came over and picked up the heavy tea tray and, saying obsequiously to Louis that she would bring the liquors, sailed out of the room. She ignored Ellen entirely.

CHAPTER FIVE

Thinking back on Louis Bland I can see that he was not a complex person at all, but he seemed so that afternoon because he was so handsome he was almost dazzling. He was tall, well-proportioned though extremely slender, beautifully dressed in tails and a white tie for some affair he was to attend with Mary Kent. He had great gentle dark eyes, dark hair, and a small mustache. His hands were delicate and he used them like ornaments, and mostly, one thought after a while, for putting in and removing cigarettes from the long black holder he affected. With Louis about the ashtrays would quickly fill up. But Anna wouldn't mind. She adored Louis. I looked for a flaw, which might give his too handsome face a variation which is sometimes charming, and found it—his teeth were too long and slightly yellow. It was not a becoming or charming flaw, however. It marred his appearance. Soon, of course, there was to be proof that he was vain, selfish, insolent and indolent. I would know that his troubles were mostly self-made. He loved no one, except himself. He suspected everyone. His way with most women was rather European, I imagined, and he started right in trying to please me, a new woman, by sitting beside me, lighting my cigarette, hovering expertly, and saying very little. He rarely talked—I would soon discover—save to find fault.

Daphne Garnett was a plump, talky, dyed woman, fortyish, dressed in French clothes a little too small for her curves. She was not dressed for evening, but in a day dress and minks. Clint Moran was short, solid, loose-fleshed and greenish-eyed. He wore a baggy brown suit, none too clean.

Mary Kent was in a sapphire-blue dinner dress, and a dark fur wrap. The rich blue gave her eyes color. For ornament she wore only a large star sapphire on her ring-finger, and her long painted nails were gilded. She looked at me only when we were introduced but her round pale bare looking eyes gave no sign of remembering me from the hat shop. She had not even looked at me in the shop. She had no need to.

We got settled, Louis beside me, Daphne with Ellen, Patrick and Mary Kent in two chairs drawn up to complete the semicircle about the fire. Clint Moran lit a cigarette and went to the piano. He began playing in a limp nostalgic skillful fashion, a continuous medley of all sorts of music.

Daphne took a cigarette from the crystal box and after Patrick lit it for her started talking between determined puffs.

"We're not the same gay carefree crowd you knew in Paris, Pat. *C'est triste, mon cher.* We simply cannot adapt to this great raw New York after living such a time in Paris. We are really Parisians, Pat darling, we lived so long among them."

At the piano Clint Moran played "The Last Time I Saw Paris."

Mary Kent's strong ugly well-kept fingers stole into her gold mesh evening bag, filched a beige cigarette from some packet or case, and came out also with the lighter. Her face blank, she lit the cigarette and put the lighter again in her bag. She heard, saw, thought, apparently, nothing. Daphne talked on. Louis Bland ignored her, smiled down softly at me every time I did so much as stir. Ellen listened to her prattle and Patrick hung onto it with an owlish solemnity. "You look like Gary Cooper," she told him abruptly. "That is, in a way. I never go to American pictures, you understand, they are so inferior to the French, but somehow I know you do look like him, Pat."

Mary Kent laughed. "The great western type, Pat," she said.

Clint played a snatch of "Get Along, Little Dogies."

Patrick's eyes glinted slightly at Mary Kent. "I'm flattered."

"You should be," she said lazily. The words meant nothing. But they stayed with you.

Anna came in with another silver tray. It held glasses, bottles and a siphon. She set it on the coffee table, which she had already placed near Louis.

"Mix me a gin and lime, will you, Anna?" Clint called from the piano. The maid glanced at Louis, then left the room. Clint slouched over and mixed the drink for himself and carried it back to the piano. Nobody paid the episode any notice. That happens often, I thought.

"We've been here more than two years," Daphne was sighing. "Imagine!"

Ellen said lightly, "Pat has joined the Marine Corps, by the way. And Jean will have a defense job."

Mary Kent rested the eyes on me. "How horribly competent," she said.

I felt angry. I glanced at Patrick. He looked detached.

"Well, it really is," Daphne gurgled sedatively. "I wish I could do something, I do really. But what? That is the question."

"You could stop talking occasionally," Louis Bland suggested. At the piano, Clint slid into the Love-Death music from *Tristan*. In his peculiar way he seemed to be having fun. "Ellen, where is Dick?" Louis demanded peevishly. "I have to see him tonight, it is absolutely imperative." He leaned forward as though to wrest the information from her. "Where is he?"

"I don't know," Ellen said. "I expect him at any minute. He had some college entrance quizzes—"

"Don't make excuses, Ellen," Louis snapped.

"Oh, Ellen," Mary Kent drawled, "you should have been with us at the Stork just now. Hank Rawlings was there, with an utterly luscious brunette. I thought he was supposed to be in Washington?"

Louis sneered, *"Très appétisante*, Ellen—the one we've seen him with before, of course." Clint gave us another lovely bit from *Tristan*.

I glanced at Patrick to see if he was getting this peculiarly vicious musical comedy. His face looked smoothly indifferent.

Ellen was silent. Her color had risen. Daphne, in well-meaning confusion, squealed, "Ellen, you must see the Tchelichew Exhibition. It's quite nice. But not thrilling, of course, the way they were in Paris. But at least something. He's going to be the rage. You'll be sorry you didn't bring out the portrait he did of you in Paris, instead of your pink umbrella."

"But Ellen would rather have the pink umbrella," Louis Bland drawled.

Ellen said to us, *"The Pink Umbrella* is a picture."

Daphne chirped, "Of Sue and Dick on the beach, under a pink umbrella. Hank painted it, Pat."

Mary Kent blew smoke through her nose. "Hank seemed horribly entertained. Who is she, Ellen?"

"Mary, you shouldn't tease Ellen," Daphne cried. She opened her bag for a handkerchief. A little enamel box fell out and spilled a flock of deadly-looking white tablets on the rug. "Just pick up the box," Daphne said, as Patrick stooped to rescue the stuff. "Never mind. I'm always spilling, you must remember that. Oh, you should have seen us, running from Paris, clutching our jewels and furs and newest Alix models, except Ellen, who thought to bring a primus stove and baskets of food—"

"And that picture she loves, *The Pink Umbrella*," Louis said. Gently, like an adder.

"Ellen's food saved our lives," Daphne declared. *"Quel horreur!* I shall never forget it."

"For God's sake!" Louis flared out at Daphne. "Shut up, will you? Ellen, where's Dick? Where's Sue? Did you tell them to stay away because you thought I would be here?"

Ellen seemed unperturbed.

"No, I didn't. They should come soon, Louis."

Louis almost screamed. "You're lying, Ellen!"

I caught Patrick's eye, which agreed we should go. We said so nice to meet you, and so on and so sweet of you, to Ellen. Louis was again completely charming. He saw us out. I never knew if Mary Kent noticed our going or not. Clint knew because he was playing "Little Dogies" with one hand and *Tristan* with the other as Louis accompanied us to the drawing-room door. Downstairs Anna materialized out of the thick mauve gloom of the back hall, produced our garments, and let us out. Her manner suggested eviction.

"I suppose we really should have stayed on a while," Patrick said, taking my arm as we trotted down the steps. "Louis was winding up for a fit."

"I thought he had one."

"No. That was part of a prelude."

I said, "It was enough. What a bunch of dillies, dear!"

"Shush!" Patrick warned me. A girl standing with a boy a little way west of the house ran towards us and threw her arms about Patrick. "Sue!" He cried. He introduced us. "Meet the boyfriend, kids," Sue said. "Bill—Pat and—I guess this is Mrs. Pat. We've been prowling along here for a good twenty minutes hoping you'd come out of that dump, Pat. We knew Louis was there, because when he isn't Mother won't let Anna close the curtains. We want to avoid Louis, at all costs, that is, I do, but Bill insists that he ought to ask my parent formally for my hand. We're going to get married."

"Congratulations," we both said.

"Isn't he marvelous?" Susan raved. She kissed Bill. Bill blushed. We laughed, and asked the kids to come in for cocktails tomorrow—provided Bill was still here to come and Patrick still on hand to play host—and went on.

"Sweet kids," I said, near Park Avenue. They did something to me, made me feel glowing inside.

"Um-m. Just the right kind of guy for Sue, I should guess."

"What were those tablets Daphne spilled?"

"Saccharine."

"Oh. She need them?"

"She thinks they help her keep thin. She never seems to get any thinner. The idea seems fairly harmless."

"Oh." I felt relieved for some reason. "I was afraid they were something mysterious. Isn't Clint something, though? Did you notice his playing tunes to match the conversation?"

"That's his pet stunt. Clint's a cousin of Louis's, incidentally."

"What does he do? For a living, I mean?"

"Nothing. None of them do anything. Lilies is the word you want, isn't it? Not dillies. You know—of the field."

I laughed and squeezed Patrick's arm. "Did you notice the Tristan-and-Isolde business Clint produced whenever Louis said something? Pretty elegant, what? And do you like the Kent?"

"Not very much."

"She's wonderfully chic," I said.

"Chic? Nothing in the right places, in my opinion. She certainly took a lousy dig at Hank. Not a word of real truth in it, probably, either. Just plain malice."

"She took my green hat," I said. I told him again about Hortense and the hat. "She was barking at Hortense when I went in. I think Hortense wanted money. I guess rich people never do pay their bills."

The light changed. We crossed the Avenue. I could see that Patrick did not properly understand about the hat. I didn't try to make him. He understands practically everything but he has no real intuition when it comes to hats.

"Have you seen the pink umbrella picture they talked about?"

"Hanged if I know. I'll ask Ellen."

"Oh, Pat!" I objected. "Let's not see any more of them. Please."

"Okay. But you asked the kids to come for cocktails—"

"Right. But that's enough. I don't mean to be selfish, but we've got so little time, and, really, they're just too dillyish. The father hates the mother. The mother hates the father. The mother loves the kids too much. Mary Kent hates everybody. Clint and Daphne are nuts. And that housekeeper—Anna—is stark staring crazy."

"You're absolutely right," Patrick agreed. "Except for one little item. And that item is what makes most of the trouble."

"What's that, dear?"

"Louis Bland is wild about Ellen. She is the only thing on earth he loves almost as much as himself." Patrick looked grim. "I thought five years ago we'd wake up any morning and find he'd murdered her. And the nagging is still going on! Good God!" he said indignantly. "Why the hell doesn't Hank take better care of Ellen?"

CHAPTER SIX

We made another night of it and got back to the hotel super-wide-awake about twenty after three. Patrick sat right down to make some notes for a letter to Lulu Murphy and I sat at the dressing table in my slip, brushing my hair and wondering if life would be glamorous instead of plain interesting and sometimes exciting if instead of short and black, it were long and that bright metallic yellow like Mary Kent's, and asking myself why a face like a gargoyle would have whatever chic is, when the telephone rang. "I'll get it," Patrick said. He got it. "Hello?" he said. Then he said, "Sure thing. Come on up."

He cradled the receiver.

"That was Ellen," he said.

I put on my robe and looked for a lipstick. Patrick was as unconcerned as though it were perfectly normal for a lady to drop in at four or so A. M. Maybe it is in New York. But I couldn't help but feel, as I glanced around the room to see if it was in proper receiving order, that some special something must be bringing Ellen here.

We had an elegant room. A large corner room the hotel called a living-bed-room. One end was a sort of bay, with windows overlooking Fifth Avenue. Chairs and a sofa were grouped around a coffee table there making a place to sit, though I had hardly thought of doing any entertaining there. The bed, dressing table, chest, clothes closet, and bath were at the opposite side of the room.

Patrick went along the corridor to meet Ellen.

She came in wearing a long black velvet coat over the dress she'd worn at teatime. She was apologetic for what she called the intrusion. "I came because I was frightened about Dick," she said. She didn't seem exactly frightened. But she *wouldn't*, I thought. "I got it into my head he'd come here. He came home right after you left last night but went out again. You didn't run into him, by any chance?" Patrick shook his head and persuaded her to sit down. She seated herself on the edge of a blue-upholstered chair. I sat down on the sofa. Patrick pulled up another chair. "I shouldn't have come here like this. But Sue is out, too. Susan's not coming home, either, was a special worry. She has never stayed out this late." Ellen paused, as though holding back something, then said, "I was silly to have been so upset. I hope you don't mind my coming here too much? You see, I never have anyone to turn to. Hank can't help me ever—Louis would know about it. If I ask any of the others, Louis is likely to hear of it and that means more trouble for Dick. Dick is my problem child. Sue can take care of herself." Again, that slight hesitation. "But Dick can't. I go to almost any length sometimes to prevent Louis's jumping on Dick."

"Like not drawing the curtains?"

Ellen's eyes widened. "Did you know why I did that?"

Patrick grinned. "We saw Sue outside. She said she knew that Louis was there because the curtains were closed. I knew there must be some darn good reason for the way you bucked Anna."

"I don't like to. Believe me. I think she knows now why I don't want the curtains drawn. She's so obstinate of late. Anna's getting very difficult. We keep two other maids, a cook and housemaid, but Anna won't let either show herself upstairs when visitors come. I think Anna feels all visitors need watching. The other maids live out. Anna won't let them live in. It's not a very comfortable way of life for the children and me. But of course, it won't go on. We're leaving the house as soon as Louis is gone."

"You seem awfully sure he is going."

"Oh, yes. I've never been sure before, really. But he really can't stand it here. He's frantic to get away, otherwise I'm sure he never would have decided after all these years to marry Mrs. Kent." Ellen added quickly, "That's a good thing, Pat. It's a most suitable match. They'll get on. And Louis has to have someone. He can't bear to be alone, you know. He keeps a valet, not because he needs one the way he is living now, but because he wants somebody near. He's always been like that."

"Any specific reason?"

Ellen waited before answering. "No-o. But he isn't too well." She changed it. "That is, he thinks he isn't."

"How come he's not in the army?"

"Louis is now forty-six. Oh, he'll go to South America, Pat. I feel sure about that. Everything is arranged. But he can't take his man, and he won't go alone, so I'm sure they'll get married."

Patrick laughed.

"I shouldn't think Mary Kent would relish being married just to be somebody along."

Ellen looked serious.

"Mary has wanted Louis for a very long time. She likes him in spite of his disposition and all the rest. She caters to it, in fact. She knows that so long as he is entertained and fussed over he'll be what he calls happy." Her tone changed and she said briskly, "Listen, you poor people, now that I've taken the time really to think, I know I was silly to come here. I'll go along home. I expect the children are together. They may have returned while I've been here."

"Want to phone the house and ask?"

"Oh, we can't phone. There is only one in the house, in the downstairs hall just outside Anna's room. It was put there for her use when she was alone in the house. Louis hasn't allowed us an extension."

Patrick snorted.

"What a guy!"

Ellen said, "If there had been another phone, I would have called you instead of coming here. But being where it is, Anna would have overheard. The corner drugstore was closed—so I walked on over."

"Ellen, how long has Dick been drinking?"

Ellen's eyelids went down. "Not very long, only a few weeks, in fact. It's his father. Dick wants to join up. Louis is forcing him to go to college."

"Will you let him join up? When Louis goes?"

"He'll soon be seventeen. I won't stop him. I couldn't anyway—I have no say-so, Pat."

"We'll walk home with you," Patrick said. I got up and got my suit and sweater from the coat closet and left the bathroom door partly open while I dressed. I heard Patrick ask, "Were you at home all night, Ellen?"

Ellen said, "I had dinner with Hank Rawlings. After everyone left the house, I put on my things and went out to a public telephone and rang him up at his apartment, got him luckily, and we had dinner at a little place in the Village. Louis never goes near the Village, so it is pretty safe. I see Hank quite often, really. I was rather startled to hear that he was here today, though. Usually he lets me know—this was something urgent, some government thing."

She didn't say what time she had got home. Patrick didn't ask.

He said, "There must be hundreds of places Dick could go in this town, Ellen. If you have any idea where I should look, or if we can call up from here—"

"I don't know, Pat. He usually goes where Clint Moran is, at some time or other during an evening. Clint keeps an eye on him, in his fashion. I shouldn't have gone out last night. I blame myself. I knew how grim things had got between Dick and Louis."

"Stop it! That's what you always say, always have said. You went out and had a fine time. Swell. Now, where can we call Clint?"

Ellen shook her head.

"I've no idea. He's changed jobs."

"Has Clint a job?"

"He has no money left at all, Pat. Nothing. He makes a living playing here or there, in nightclubs and places. He's not too reliable, so he doesn't stay long in each place. Daphne would know where he is. She keeps an eye on Clint. But she would tell Mary Kent, and Mary would tell Louis I was looking for Clint, and it would all come back on Dick. Let's not do it. Forget it—I think I was pretty hysterical. If Dick isn't home when I get there—or doesn't come in—" Her voice trailed off.

"Where does Clint live?"

"He has a room in a rooming house, a pretty grim place, on Third Avenue near Forty-second. There's a phone in the house but no one would answer it at this time of night."

I had finished dressing. I emerged, Ellen and Patrick stood up. We left the room and the hotel. We didn't set eyes on a cab on the short walk to Ellen's house. We didn't even see a pedestrian, which is what the dim-out has done to New York. The up-and-down and cross streets were equally lifeless. The tops of the sky-scrapers disappeared in an eerie blend of moonlight and haze. East of Park Avenue, we overtook and passed a patrolman on his beat. He carried a flashlight and played it into the areaways below the old houses. He whistled, as he sauntered, "Moonlight Becomes You."

We overtook him and went ahead.

"Light in your house, Ellen," Patrick said.

One of the tall French windows in the drawing room, the middle one, stood open. Light blazed out.

Ellen said, "Dick must have come home. He's got the chandeliers turned on, I'm afraid. I've troubled you for nothing."

"We've loved the walk," I said.

We climbed the steps together. There was a key in the lock. Ellen turned the lock and without comment slipped the key into her bag. "Thank you, so much," she said. She acted as if she wanted to be rid of us suddenly—though Patrick never has agreed with me on that point. "I feel apologetic. Good night, and thank you again, both of you."

She stepped into the hall. I felt almost as if the door would be closed in our faces.

"Hey!" the policeman shouted. He had got to the bottom of the steps. "You the leddy of the house?" he asked me.

Ellen heard him, and did not close the door.

I thought, at once, of the areaway. The policeman had been flashing his light into the areaways. I glanced down, over the black iron railing with its urn-shaped ornamental finials. I saw the gray, sprawling, bat-shaped shadow lying against the paler gray of cement. It's Dick, I thought. Horribly. He has fallen from the window. He's dead.

CHAPTER SEVEN

At this moment I had another shock, a mild one, but significant. The light from the drawing room window fell clearly on the policeman's upturned, heart-shaped, brown-eyed face. He was the one who had eyed us on the corner of Park Avenue night before last, when Patrick had kissed me in the abandoned fashion of our wild-west, and then had got funny about it.

Ellen stepped out and stood with her hand on the knob of the partly opened door. She was absolutely calm. She no longer sounded anxious to be rid of us, either.

"You pipple live here?" inquired the policeman.

Ellen said, "I do, Officer. What is it?"

"That light, leddy." Ellen let out a tiny breath, as of relief. "Don't you relize it's against regulations you should leave a big bright winda open thataway? Enemy plane flies over. Bombs hospil. Your fault, see?"

"I'm so sorry. I'll go right in and turn it off."

But she made no move to go in. She waited.

The beetle-brown eyes softened. Even a policeman couldn't stay tough with Ellen.

"I don't make the regalations, leddy," he apologized.

"I know," Ellen said. Her tone was perfect. It hooked the policeman.

Ellen took a half-step into the hall. She paused. Patrick said, "Dim-out keep you pretty busy, Sergeant?"

"Patrolman," the policeman corrected him. "Yah. Drunks come over from Third Avenue. Bed down in these areas, see." *Drunks.* Ellen must have recoiled from the word. But it gave me a kind of relief. Maybe Dick was only drunk, maybe he hadn't fallen, just couldn't get up the steps, and had gone down instead and collapsed. I kept waiting for the policeman to go on. Then I would tell Pat about the figure on the cement. They wouldn't want the police mixed up in it. I could understand that.

Ellen was waiting for the same reason, perhaps. She had also seen the gray shadow, I thought. She was waiting for the policeman to go along.

"Have to check three, four times night," he offered. "Well, so long."

"So long," Patrick said. Neither Ellen nor I spoke.

The man strolled on, his lips puckering already to whistle. He even issued a couple of sweet notes. We three stood perfectly still, Ellen waiting as I waited, and Patrick waiting. We had all seen the shadow. We were each of us waiting, I thought at that time, till the man was out of the way, before speaking of it to one another. Ellen was astonishingly the calmest, even calmer than Patrick, whose heart, he said afterward, was pounding.

The man stopped whistling.

"Holy cow, here's one now," he growled. He played the flash from the other end of the area on a heap of gray flannel. "Woulda seen it before if hadn't stopped to talk," he said, accusingly.

Patrick gave me a little push.

"You go inside with Ellen," he said. Oh God, I thought. It's Dick all right. Ellen went on into the hall. She found the chain controlling the hall-light. The gloomy place swam out. Just before I closed the door I heard the policeman say, "Tell the leddies they should stay inside, buddy. It's a stiff."

So the worst was true.

Ellen hadn't heard that part. Or had she?

"Is there one in our area? Is that what it is?" she asked me, casually. She laid a finger on her mouth. "Oh dear, I hope they don't wake Anna. Do sit down, Jean. I'll slip upstairs and turn off those lights." Her head was tilted a little. Her elegant face looked serious but not unduly worried. I didn't understand her at all.

"Perhaps we should wait down here," I said.

She lifted her brows.

"All right. Take the chair. I'll lean against the post. They won't be long, I imagine."

There was only one chair, beside a mahogany table with a Chinese bronze vase on it. The table stood against the staircase between the newel post and the hall closet.

Patrick came in. When Ellen saw his face she looked afraid. She turned white and grasped the post for support. He saw it and said, "Hang onto yourself, Ellen. It's Anna."

"Oh, thank God!" Ellen said. She relaxed. Then backed up and sat down on the stairs. "I can't tell you! I've been stiff with fear. I've been saying over and over to myself 'It isn't Dick, I won't let it be Dick, I won't.' "

Her joy was almost painful. And it added to my general confusion.

"Ellen, Anna is dead."

"Dead?"

"She apparently fell from the window. She's got on a gray robe of some sort over her nightgown. The patrolman asked me to call the station house and report an accidental death."

Ellen jumped right up.

"We should call our doctor first," she declared. "Dr. Seward must come at once. I'll call him. There's no need to get mixed up with the police. Dr. Seward will give the death certificate and see that the body goes to a mortuary."

She went to the back of the hall, turned on another light, and started dialing a number evidently familiar.

Patrick lit a cigarette. He did not look at me and he said nothing.

I sat like a lump on the chair and wondered why Ellen was first so calm, then so excited, and finally so efficient. I wasn't calm myself, certainly; I was shocked, though I had never even heard of the woman till a few hours ago. I felt dashed that anyone so lately and so belligerently alive could be so dead. In my mind, I saw that quilted small-eyed face flaunting her victory over Ellen, saw her red hands pulling the weights which regulated the disputed curtains, and finally her deep reverent expression when she looked at Louis Bland.

Patrick spoke up. "She's dead all right. I'll call the police as soon as Ellen gets her doctor. That's all right. He should come, of course. She may have had a bad heart. She has a bruise on one temple, her head may have struck one of those ornaments on the railing. Jean, would you mind turning off those lights in the drawing room? Don't close the window or touch anything, just the lights. The patrolman is fussing about them. You might go up and see if Dick and Susan have come in. Ellen had better wait here in case the police want anything."

I knew he didn't want her fitting about the house and rousing their suspicion. But I said nothing.

I started up the stairs. Patrick said, "Don't tell the kids anything. If they're here, just say they're to get up and dress. If Dick can't, let him alone, till later."

On the second floor, the drawing room doors were both closed. No hint of the light blazing within escaped into the hall. I opened the forward door. The brilliance being flung into the dim-out was due to the refraction on the white ceiling of the combined light of two crystal chandeliers. I ran an eye quickly over the room, saw no one, saw nothing out of its place save, lying on a Persian rug before the open window, a picture—or rather a picture frame, because it lay face down. The fire had died. I snapped the light switch, accidentally turned on the lamps— the switches were side by side—found the switch for the ceiling lights, flicked both and the room was in darkness. I closed the door, and went onto the third floor. The hall up here was very dim. I couldn't find a switch, so I opened the first door I came to, leading into the front bedroom, and felt the wall to the left, found the toggle and flipped it, needing the light for guidance in the hall.

I looked into a plain chaste-looking white bedroom. The bedcovers were folded back for an occupant, and two pillows were plumped smoothly against the head. The bed hadn't been used this night.

The hall light operated by a chain. I found it, turned off the bedroom light, explored along the hall and found another bedroom. Two rosy lamps revealed a girl's room, more covers folded back, plump pillows, and no occupant.

I turned off the light. There was no other bedroom on this floor. I came back and climbed the stairs to the top floor.

Dick had a suite, a bedroom, bath and sitting room. All his rooms were furnished in a period many years past. There were pennants and framed college photographs of boys in tall collars on the walls. One glass case was full of technical-looking books. In the bedroom, the bed was ready, but unoccupied.

I went down to report. Ellen, still in her long velvet coat, was standing in the dark hall outside the drawing room door.

"There's no one upstairs, Ellen."

"I'm glad!" she said. "It's bad enough without the children being around. Oh, Patrick says we can wait in the drawing room, if we're careful to touch nothing." She opened the door. The room was still dark. She flicked a switch, the one which controlled the lamps, and said for me to sit down and be comfortable. "I'll be back at once," she said, and then added, "Dr. Seward came. I heard an ambulance, too."

She closed the door.

I sat down on the sofa where I had sat at teatime. The ashes had been removed from the grate. It looked very clean. The ashtrays were once again immaculate. A paperknife in a sheath of Florentine leather lay on the low table. It would belong there, I thought. It had been removed at teatime to make room for the silver tea tray. But ordinarily it would be there, on the table, because Anna would see to it that everything was always in its proper place.

The window was still open. I could hear voices in the area. "Yes, Doctor," a young man's voice would say solicitously. He was the ambulance doctor, from the police station. An older gruffer voice would answer. I heard this one say, "A bad temper all her life. Very likely she stepped onto the balcony, had a stroke, and fell, striking her head on one of those iron things." The young voice said, "How long dead, Doctor," The gruff voice said, "I'd say offhand under an hour. Body's still pretty warm, you notice, could be a little longer, of course." "Do you think a post-mortem is indicated, Doctor?" the young doctor asked then. The other doctor said, "I think an autopsy is always advisable in cases of sudden death. But offhand, I should say death was due to cerebral hemorrhage following a blow on the temple, from one of those iron knobs. Nasty things to hit your head on. An autopsy will show if I'm right—I'll perform it myself at the mortuary."

"Want the boys should take it where you said in the wagon, Doc?" Patrolman Goldberg inquired, matily. The older doctor said no, they would send for it, and Goldberg said, "Might as well we should send it, see. They got the basket. Against regalations you should keep it laying in the street, drawn a crowd, Doc." The doctor said the mortuary was open all night, but he'd step inside and telephone.

"Thank you, Doctor," the young ambulance doctor said.

Goldberg said, "Boys, take it away."

A hush accompanied the moving of the dead. Footsteps shuffled, voices went low. A motor whirred. The ambulance moved away gently.

My eyes roamed over the room the dead woman had loved so dearly that she had kept it looking brand new for what must have been forty years. They stopped short on the rug where I had seen the picture lying facedown beside the open window. The picture was gone.

CHAPTER EIGHT

Ellen entered and closed the door soundlessly and sat down facing me across the fireless fireplace. She still wore her long coat and carried her bag. It occurred to me later that perhaps she wanted to look as though she had not left this room after coming up from the lower hall.

Her straight black brows were drawn in one line.

"It's not like Sue to do this. I looked in her room again. It seems as if she must be here." She was explaining her going upstairs, I thought. She didn't mention the picture. She would assume that I had reached in and snapped off the lights without noticing the picture. "It's different with Dick. That was why I got so frightened. There—downstairs."

"Didn't you see it, too?" I asked. "Before the policeman discovered it?"

She spoke almost crisply.

"No, I did not. But you did, didn't you? I sensed something odd, in both of you. That's why I waited, there at the door."

Oh? Indeed! Very neat!

"Patrick must have seen it all the time, Ellen. He always sees everything. He can see in the dark like a cat. I think he saw it and talked to the policeman, thinking to distract him so that he would go on by. He wouldn't know it was Anna, though, and that she was dead."

Ellen turned her head slightly towards the open window.

"I wonder how long they'll be?"

"I think they've already taken her away."

"I'm glad. I've been afraid the children would come in, while—she was there. I wonder what they decided?"

"They called it an accident, I think. Dr. Seward said he would phone some mortuary, and then the police ambulance took the body there—I think."

Patrick came in, closed the door, and then stood thoroughly eyeing the room. He moved to the mantel and leaned his back against it and said, still looking the place up and down. "The police will be up in a minute, Ellen."

"But why?" Ellen spoke sharply. She said, in a more even tone, "It's no difference, but I thought Dr. Seward had taken care of things?"

"They have to ask questions. Matter of routine. Don't let it upset you. They called it an accident."

"Of course it was an accident!" Ellen snapped out. "What else could it be? Who said it wasn't?"

"No one, so far, Ellen. Watch your nerves." Patrick spoke very evenly. "By the way, wasn't there a key in the front door? When we arrived?"

Ellen started at the rug under her feet. "It was mine. I must have left it in the lock when I came home—I mean, earlier, from dinner. And then I went out again without noticing it. By the way, please don't say to anyone that I had dinner with Hank, will you not? We have to be so very careful."

Patrick said, "I don't see why it should come up, Ellen. But of course, we won't mention it. Does everyone have a key?"

"Yes. Of course."

"Does Louis?"

"Yes. Why are you asking me this, Pat?"

"I'm bothered about that key. The patrolman doesn't know about the key, Ellen. With the key in the door, any passerby could have got into the house. That might explain Anna's going out on the balcony. Anna may have thought she heard someone in the house and got up to investigate, and got herself pushed into the area."

Ellen made a gesture of impatience.

"She was always prowling, always imagining herself hearing things in the night, and getting into her gray flannel robe and tiptoeing about. She's frightened me terribly, countless times. What did Dr. Seward say, Pat?"

"He said she had a bad temper and could have had a stroke. They all thought she might have thought she'd heard some suspicious noise and had investigated and ended by falling into the area. None of them know about the key, Ellen." Patrick grinned and said lightly, "I suspect Goldberg takes anything he does very seriously. A mere patrolman who corrects you for addressing him as a sergeant is bound to be a very honest man. I hear them coming now."

He had better ears than mine. I didn't hear them till he said they were coming.

Then he saw something near the window. His eyes gleamed greenly for an instant and he made a swift step in that direction, then stepped back and resumed his careless stance against the mantel. Goldberg came in first.

The patrolman noted the silent hinges. He swung the door back and forth.

"Muss keep't erled?" he inquired.

"Anna was a wonderful housekeeper," Ellen replied.

"Accept my sympathy, ma'am. Too bad. Wot should she be doing on the balcony, though?"

"She went to bed very early and woke easily. She often got up and poked around the house. She was always imagining burglars."

Goldberg nodded. "Yah. Could be. Maybe there should be a drunk in the areaway. Maybe she chases him out and then had that stroke the way the doctor said. Could be." He took out his notebook. "Regalations, I should take names and addresses," he apologized.

He took Ellen's, then mine.

He eyed me suspiciously, cocking his heart-shaped face sidewise and squinting his beetle-brown eyes. "Ain't I seen you before somewheres, leddy?" I said I was only a visitor in New York. "Yah?" he said. He looked me over after he wrote down my name. When Patrick said I was his wife, his suspicion increased.

Dr. Seward surged in. He was a huge man, fat, with imperious gray eyes, bushy gray eyebrows, a bushy gray mustache to match, and a plump pursed mouth. He took Ellen's hand and held it, with a professional-seeming sympathy. Ellen introduced him to me. He gave me a nod.

His voice was plushy as an unguent. "A tragedy, Ellen. Anna was a real old-fashioned servant, entirely devoted to her work. They don't come like that any more. But at least her death was merciful. Chances are she never knew what happened. Maybe she's been spared some unhappy old age, one never knows, but my experience is that sudden death is merciful to its victims. I've called Louis, by the way. Told him about it."

Ellen seemed to shrink.

"He's not coming over now?"

"Oh, no. I told him where I'd sent the body and said there was nothing he could possibly do until morning."

The doctor produced a cigar, fished out a match, and took his time lighting it.

Patrick picked up the paper knife. He slipped it from its sheath. The blade was slim and darting as a stiletto. He put it back in the sheath and laid it down.

Goldberg was prowling about the room. A tall thin patrolman named Trill came in and said he had searched everywhere on the first floor and in the basement and that there appeared to have been no one around, certainly nobody was here now. Goldberg said, "Excuse me, leddy, but is it all right for us to go upstairs?"

"Yes, of course, Officer," Ellen said.

"You go, Trill," Goldberg said. "I'll stay here."

The thin tall policeman went out. Goldberg sidled about the room. He ventured his weight gingerly onto the balcony, peered over, and wrote down notes.

"Have you kept well, Ellen?" Dr. Seward asked.

Ellen smiled. "Yes, thank you, Doctor. Have you seen Louis lately? He's looking fine, don't you think?"

"Splendid. He came in for a checkup the other day. He's in fine shape—that is, for him. Delighted, of course, to be getting away. Mary's just the woman for him, Ellen."

They pattered along, small talk, smooth and easy. The doctor looked as though he made lots of money. His clothes cost plenty, and he certainly looked well-fed.

Patrick leaned against the mantel, all nonchalance.

Patrolman Goldberg discovered that the hinges of the French windows were also oiled. He swung them back and forth. He poked at the sill, tugged at the drapes, stared hard at the Persian rug. He wrote notes.

"Where are Sue and Dick?" Dr. Seward asked.

"I don't know. They're out together probably and didn't call me because there's only one phone, you know. It disturbs—disturbed—Anna."

"Ought to be some extensions, Ellen."

"Louis objected to the expense. Now there are priorities."

"I appreciate that. But there should have been an extension on every floor. Might have saved Anna's life somehow. You'd all be safer."

Patrolman Trill returned.

"There's nobody at all in the house, Ike," he said to Goldberg. "People was expected evidently, because there's three beds turned back as if waiting for people, but nobody has slept in two of them. The bed in the room over this is the one that has been slept in, the others ain't."

My eyes met Ellen's. Hers went coldly defiant before they moved away. Or did they?

"Whose room would that be, leddy?" Goldberg asked Ellen.

"Mine."

"Who else lives here?"

"My son and daughter. They haven't come home. It's most unusual, Officer. Frankly, it worries me."

"Kids is funny. Got some my own," Goldberg said. "Were you home all night, leddy?"

"You know I wasn't, Officer. You saw me arrive home. I got worried because my children hadn't come in and went to see our friends, the Abbotts, at their hotel. I thought my children might be with them, because they had turned up suddenly after we hadn't seen them for years—that is, Mr. Abbott was an old friend—and I thought the youngsters had gone with them. It was a silly idea, of course. But they were very kind, and walked back home with me."

"What time did you leave the house, leddy?"

"I think I was away about forty minutes."

"What time she come to the hotel, Mr. Abbott?"

"It was about three-thirty. It's a seven- to ten-minute walk, or less. Say seven minutes. That would mean that Mrs. Bland left this house at twenty-three minutes past three."

Goldberg was a little irked at Patrick's precision, but he wrote it down.

"You asleep when she called?"

"No. Mrs. Abbott and I had come in only a few minutes before Mrs. Bland rang up. We'd been to a nightclub, The Blue Angel—to be exact."

"*Mrs.* Abbott," murmured Patrolman Goldberg. It was just a murmur, that's all, very soft, and packing wallops of suspicion. "You're *Mrs.* Abbott?" he inquired of me.

"Of course," I said.

"Yah?" he replied. He coughed delicately.

"I must say," cut in Dr. Seward, "you are dragging this business out interminably, Officer. What's the point? We'd like to get back to our beds, you know."

"Sure, Doc, but you gotta ask questions. Routine. You didn't see the deceased before leaving the house, did you, ma'am?"

"No. And I hadn't heard her about, either."

"Mebbe she heard you go out and that should make her get up to have a look around, see?"

"Oh, dear!" Ellen said.

"You can't blame yourself that an accident should happen, leddy." The man looked at his notes. "Well, I guess that covers everything for now."

Patrolman Goldberg put his notebook in his pocket. Patrolman Trill rested one hand on the door knob.

Patrolman Goldberg made a last cruise about the room. Near the window his eyes glistened suddenly. He stooped and picked up something with his handkerchief and slipped it stealthily into a pocket.

He stood up. "Maybe you better all come back here at three o'clock this afternoon. Just in case. Might be there should be some more questions, see?"

Dr. Seward objected, but Goldberg was firm. When the policeman had gone, the doctor knocked a fat cigar ash into a tray and said, "Now that those fellows have left, there's something I've got to tell you, Ellen." He gave us a fishy stare. "In private," he said.

Ellen said, "You can speak before the Abbotts, Dr. Seward. We may need Mr. Abbott's advice. He's a detective."

The doctor gave Patrick a glance of refined distaste.

"Well, here goes, Ellen. Did you know that Louis was in this house tonight? A little before three o'clock, he thinks it was. He left his key in the front door, he thinks. I decided not to mention it, Ellen. No need of Louis's getting mixed up in a lot of red tape just when he's getting away. He'd better go while he's still got the chance. Getting harder and harder to travel."

Ellen gasped, "How did you know about his being here, Dr. Seward?"

"He told me, on the phone. When I called just now."

"Didn't the policeman hear you?"

"They hadn't come in from the areaway then. I called Louis to notify him of Anna's death, and to ask if she had any near relations who ought to be notified.

She hasn't. Louis told me about coming to the house. He didn't see her or anyone while here. Seems he went to the top floor, however. Looking for Dick, whom he specially wants to see, because he's leaving. He thinks he was in the house ten or fifteen minutes. Maybe longer. Sat down in this room and waited a while, he said." The doctor took an impressive draft on the cigar. "Louis got excited when I said Anna was dead. He asked if she was murdered. I said that was utter nonsense, the woman simply fell out the window and died, I told him, and I warned him that he'd better watch his step about what he said or he'd be detained in this country as a material witness to something that didn't actually happen. I mean murder." The doctor waved a pink hand. "It wasn't murder, of course. Incidentally, I'll go along and have a talk with Louis when I leave here. I didn't care to be too explicit on the phone."

Patrick said, "I beg your pardon, Dr. Seward, but did Bland come here alone?"

"Fortunately, no. Someone was with him. He didn't say whom."

Ellen said, "But, Doctor Seward, no one had any reason to harm Anna."

The doctor frowned hard.

"Louis has quite a bit of money, Ellen. All sorts of relatives you never heard of are likely to pop up, and sue. They always do. If anyone saw Louis come to the house—at three in the morning—well, there you are!"

"But—"

He lifted a hand.

"Ellen, I know what I'm talking about!" The doctor heaved himself out of the chair. "Mind what I say. No talking. Louis, and you too, Ellen, must see his lawyer first thing tomorrow morning." He allowed himself a look at Patrick. "As you doubtless know, policemen on patrol duty are all alike, a bunch of ignorant fellows on the make and all dying to discover a Park Avenue murder and get their names in the papers. But they usually take the word of the family physician."

Patrick's smile was not without malice. The doctor didn't notice. He headed monumentally towards the door.

"Will call myself a taxi, on the phone downstairs. To go to Louis's hotel. Ought to have an extension. Good night," he said.

He picked up his bag and opened the door.

The front door downstairs burst open. Light steps mounted the stairs. The doctor stepped back into the drawing room. He was frowning. More interference.

Susan dashed in, followed by her ruddy Ensign Reynolds.

My heart softened, they looked such kids, so healthy, but so vulnerable.

Susan stopped. She looked us over.

"Mother?" she cried. Then, "What goes on? First a policeman parked outside wanted to know our business here. Then—Dr. Seward, why are you here? Has something happened? Is it Dick? Oh, Mother—"

Doctor Seward clasped Susan's slim brown hand in his fat pink one. In his best bedside manner, he said, "Susan my dear, there has been an accident. Anna fell from the balcony yonder, and—"

"*Anna?*" Susan looked almost exalted. "Oh, Lord! I've been so frightened. I knew it was something serious, but I thought Dick was the one. I was so sure it was Dick."

She took the hand from Dr. Seward's and slipped it into Bill's. It was a lovely thing to see, her young, warm feeling for Bill.

"Anna was injured. Fatally," Dr. Seward said. His dulcet tones held a carefully tempered reproof.

"You mean, she's dead?"

"Yes, Sue. Painlessly, we hope—"

"Well, I hope not!" Susan said, defiantly. "She didn't mind hurting other people. I guess she was snooping, as usual, and leaned out too far. Was that it?"

"Susan!" Dr. Seward said.

Sue began to laugh hard. "The only thing wrong with the picture is that it wasn't Louis instead of Anna," she said.

"Susan!" Dr. Seward reiterated, shocked. "Do be careful. You're likely to let your family in for a murder investigation. Remember—the police."

"Sue didn't mean that," Ellen said. She rose and started towards Susan, who said, "Oh, yes, Sue did!" She wheeled and threw herself into Bill's arms. Bill closed them tight around her and gave all and sundry a dare-you-to-touch-her glare.

Dr. Seward gave Sue's shoulder a plushy pat. Then Ellen's. "You all need to take a sedative and go to bed," he said. He set down his bag on a chair and snapped open the catches.

"Can't we go now, Pat?" I asked.

"Sure," he said.

Ellen came with us to the front door.

"I can't thank you enough," she said. "It would have been too awful to have found it—all alone. And I want to apologize for fibbing about that key. It wasn't mine. I thought it was Dick's. I slipped it out. When the body turned out to be Anna—you must understand I didn't think Dick had anything to do with it, but Louis can be so terrible that I'm just automatically cautious, about everything—I decided not to mention the key. I didn't think you noticed it."

"Pat sees everything," I said.

Ellen closed the door. Patrick took my arm as we went down the steps.

Patrolman Trill was standing a short distance east of the house, under a small citified tree.

A sort of dawn was breaking over the city. The air felt silky and smelled of smoke and refuse.

I was so tired that I squeaked with delight when a taxi rolled up. It stopped in front of the house because, I thought at first, Patrick signaled it. The door opened. Dick Bland staggered out, boiled as an owl. "I'll take care of the fare," Patrick told the driver. "Wait in the cab, Jean. I'll hand Dick over to Bill Reynolds and be right back."

I looked at the meter. It said ninety cents.

Patrick was back in a couple of minutes. We drove on towards the Rexley. I had a shoulder and an arm to ease my weariness, but that didn't help my temper. I was sore about the whole thing. I blamed it all on Ellen Bland.

Then Patrick said, "Darned good thing Ellen wasn't alone in that house when it happened."

I rasped, "What makes you think she wasn't?"

"She was with us."

"You think so?"

"She wouldn't lie about a thing like that, or leave the woman lying there, like that, while she walked to the hotel and sat in our room, and then walked back. Slowly, without hurrying even. Ellen wouldn't do that."

"She lied about the key."

"That was merely discretion. She thought it was Dick's; she was afraid he had come in and gone out again when he didn't find her at home, and of course it would look very odd to the police, if he had. He certainly had a load on. She would think of that."

"She's going to lie to other people about being with Hank last night."

"My God! She'd better. You don't know Louis."

"Pat, I'm going to tell you something. I have to. I went upstairs to see if anybody was home, as you know, and I turned on Ellen's light in the process. Her bed hadn't been used. It was smooth as possible, the pillows plumped up, and the sheet turned back over the blankets the way a good maid fixes the beds at night just before she goes off duty for the day. Not a crease, not a wrinkle or a head print on the pillow. All the beds were the same. Then Patrolman Trill went up later and reported back that Ellen's bed had been slept in."

"Maybe you were mistaken, dear?"

"Pat! Listen to me. Ellen went up after I came down. I was there in the drawing room. She mussed her bed to make it look slept in. It's the only thing that could have happened, because Trill was the next to go up to that room."

I said, "Another thing. When I looked into the drawing room to turn off the chandeliers, as you asked me to, there was a picture, or at least a picture frame, lying in front of the open window. When I came down after looking around upstairs the picture was gone. Ellen must have been in the room in the meantime."

Patrick apparently thought nothing of it, because he said, "Did you notice Goldberg's picking up something from under the rug near the window?" I nodded. "I could kick myself for overlooking that—whatever it was." Then, "Young Sue was sure mad at Louis."

We were getting close to the hotel.

"Pat, did you notice how Goldberg looked at me? He thinks we aren't married."

"What-t?"

"He was the one on that corner the other night. When you kissed me, and then pulled that line about how you'd marry me if you could get rid of your wife. He must have believed it."

Patrick laughed.

"I don't think it's at all funny," I said.

Patrick howled. The driver, pulling up outside the Rexley, stared with disapproval at such a display of amusement. I walked quickly into the lobby, very annoyed. We had to wait for an elevator. Patrick continued to laugh, in a gurgling fashion which made me simply furious.

"Laugh," I said. "It's not you he's suspicious of. It's me. He didn't see your face that night. But he got a good look at me, and he remembered me tonight, and if you think it's pleasant to be suspected by a policeman you are quite mistaken." Patrick was still gurgling. "New York is the kind of place where everybody tries to act like the best people because nobody knows if they are or aren't." Patrick just laughed, that held-in lumpy laughter that drives you simply haywire, so I said, "A little something like that starts a person being suspicious and then anything else, almost anything, will pile up more suspicion. It spreads. You wouldn't laugh if Goldberg's evil thoughts about me led him into suspecting something evil about your precious Ellen, would you? Maybe he thinks she keeps peculiar company, meaning me?"

"Darling, you're so wonderful!"

"Laugh. You won't laugh if the suspicion started by your little joke leads into a murder investigation, Pat."

He went on laughing. He controlled it, but I could tell it was there. I maintained a haughty silence in the elevator and along the jointed corridor to our room, meaning to say my say when we got there. Inside the room I felt like crying, but Patrick said sweet things then and tucked me into bed tenderly, and then, though I meant to stay thoroughly mad all night, I couldn't because I blacked out two minutes after I hit the pillow.

CHAPTER NINE

I woke halfway and heard a little humming which was like bees. In my mind I saw Toby, our black Persian, and Pancho, our red dachshund, frolicking together the way they do in our tiny green San Francisco garden. Then I heard a hum accompanying the hum.

The second hum was "The Last Time I Saw Paris."

Patrick was humming as he shaved. The hum like bees was from his razor. "What are you thinking about, Pat?" I called, then.

The humming stopped.

"Paris."

"Paris in the spring?"

Patrick came to the door. He was in his blue pajama trousers without the jacket. He had dark hair on his chest and fine muscles in his arms and shoulders you'd never suspect because he looked so lean when dressed.

His face was half-shaved, which gave it a cockeyed look—very endearing.

"Not in the spring, darling. Paris in the morning. Any morning, when you're having your coffee outdoors along the sidewalk, under a striped awning. The sidewalk is dappled with the sunshine pouring through the flat leaves of plane trees. Everything smells wonderful. The streets are freshly washed. Taxis whiz by honking like mad and men in aprons are carrying huge trays of fresh-smelling bread and lots of short-legged, dark-haired girls dressed in black are bustling along to work. Everything is so alive. Everybody is insulting everybody else in the most animated fashion. Everybody is full of that special energy you have in Paris." He paused, to breathe, "It's the air. It's the sky. It's the French. It's Paris."

"I wish I could see it, dear."

"You will, darling. I'll take you there myself."

"I want to see it now. I feel jealous of Paris. I feel jealous of everybody who knows Paris."

"I wish I knew it better. It's got everything. It's even got a street called the Rue Madame. Nobody but the French would think to name a street that."

"Missus Street—well, it wouldn't do in English."

"We wouldn't do it if it did." Patrick sighed romantically and turned back to his shaving. "I guess if we had lived as long in Paris as those people have we'd be that way about it ourselves."

Oh, dear, I thought. Here we were, back with the Blands, and their circle. At the start of a fresh day. Anyhow, I thought, getting myself a cigarette, I'd be glad to have this country to come back to. If I were Louis Bland and Mary Kent and such. But I didn't say it. I didn't want to spoil Patrick's lovely mood by saying anything too frank about his old acquaintances, just then.

"How about arising, my love? I could eat a horse."

I arose without a word. When I woke first in a hotel I always had breakfast sent up. When Patrick was first, he hurried to shave so as to say he was already dressed and preferred to eat in a proper eating-place. He'd won today.

I took a shower, got into my black suit and a green blouse and was ready before he was. Twenty minutes later we were eating breakfast in the Alpine Grill, a paneled nooky room with a bar, which we preferred to the formal dining room.

We were talking about what to do after breakfast when Dick Bland came in, saw us, and ambled over. Patrick invited him to sit.

Dick sat, made an involuntary grimace of disgust when we suggested coffee, but accepted a pot of green tea. "Got a hell of a hangover," he apologized.

His good-looking, dark-eyed, downy young face looked it. It roused my compassion, it was so young to be ravaged like that, for that reason. His gray flannel suit and the little round hat didn't go with a drunk, either.

"I didn't think about your eating or anything, at this hour," he went on apologizing. "I owe you for a couple of taxi fares, Pat." He turned red. "I was just passing by and I thought if you were here, I'd square up." Patrick said to forget it. Dick insisted on paying. He knew how much, too. "Funny how you remember what you do when you're plastered. I remember everything. But I can't do anything about it. I saw you give that guy the five bucks. He was gypping me already but I even let him get away with that. No guts. That's me, when I drink."

Patrick said, cryptically, "You disappoint me, Dick."

The kid straightened up and gave Patrick an eye-to-eye glance.

"You see before you a reformed character. I've learned my lesson. What happened last night to Anna taught me something, Pat. It might have been Mother."

His voice broke slightly. Patrick said yes, it could have been.

The boy's grin was pallid. "You're a swell guy, Pat. I've been a jerk and you know it. In your place a lot of guys would be giving me hell. Mother's had trouble enough without my pulling the stuff I pull."

"Where were you last night, Dick?"

"Oh, at a dive. Several dives. Sorry to say. Louis is a lousy son of—oh, excuse me, Mrs. Abbott."

An apology for bad language, I thought, certainly made him very young, or me very old, one or the other.

The waiter brought Dick's tea, poured a cup, and retired to a polite distance. The kid stared at it without tasting it.

"If you want the truth about Anna, it is really Louis's fault, Pat. I don't know that you could say that Louis murdered Anna, but it's his fault that no one was at home, and if anybody had been there she might not be dead."

"That's an angle, Dick."

"You know what happened, don't you?"

"What?"

"It was right after you left last evening. At teatime. Sue came in, with Bill. Louis jumped on Bill and ordered him out of the house, and Sue jumped right back on Louis. Of course, it was her fault—the fight—though."

"How come?"

"Oh, the way she did it. I got home about that time too and the kids were in the hall downstairs talking about getting married. Bill thought they ought to talk it over with Mother and Louis first but Sue said no. Bill's stubborn, but he said okay, then, and started to walk out. Then Sue said all right, to come along up and they'd get it over with, so they went upstairs and opened the door and Sue says, very American, which drives Louis nuts too, 'Hi, folks, meet the guy I'm marrying. Folks, Bill.' It was a riot. Mary Kent was there and Daphne Garnett and Mother and Louis and Clint. Well, Clint right away starts a wedding march and already Louis was literally jumping up and down and screaming, you know how, and the louder he screamed, the louder Clint played, and of course Louis hates Clint like a snake, so—"

"Why?" Patrick eased in.

"Because Louis done him wrong. You always hate people you've done mean things to. You feel ashamed, see, only if you're Louis you justify yourself and scream and go on being meaner and meaner, the way he has to Clint. He's a good egg, Clint is, Pat."

"What did Louis do to Clint?"

"I don't know. Something to do with money."

He tasted the tea, made a face, so I pulled his cup over and fixed it with sugar and cream, cambric style. After that he drank it.

"Anyhow, finally, Louis yelled at Sue that she couldn't marry. Told her she had a disease."

"Disease?" Patrick asked.

"She's the healthiest-looking girl I ever saw," I said.

"Oh, sure. Nothing to it. It's just the sort of thing Louis does. He couldn't yell Sue into getting rid of Bill. Her lungs are better than Louis's. So he thought fast and said something that he thought would make Bill stand Sue up, see. He's just against Bill. He doesn't care how he gets rid of him."

"What happened then?" I asked.

"Oh, there was one of those awkward silences for about half a second during which I fondly hoped that Bill would thrash the hide off Louis, only he must have had scruples or something, because he didn't start anything, and then Mother said, 'Sue, you and Bill run along and have dinner somewhere!' I guess Sue was slightly stunned because she yanked Bill out of there pronto and meanwhile Louis jumped on Mother, and Clint jumped on Louis—Clint always takes Mother's part." (Whoops! Another one pro Ellen, I thought.) "Sue and Bill left. They tried to get married but had to wait, for some reason, and now Sue has thought it over and thinks maybe there is some family taint or something and is in a mood to hie her to a nunnery, if she can find one. It's a mess. Not unusual with the Blands, though."

"Drink your tea, dear," I urged him. Dick smiled a wispy smile and I felt like taking the long gangling kid on my lap and rocking him. I would hate to have been his mother. He was the kind that got into your heart and broke it. He had Louis's looks, plus fine white teeth, and that quality of rousing the mother in you which Louis could never have had to that extent. "There isn't a family taint, is there, Dick? It was just said in anger, wasn't it?"

"Of course. We said that. Or didn't we? Sue's all wound up, though. She's going to talk it over with Dr. Seward—That quack! Can you tie it? Out of the pan into the ashes. That's Sue. Listen, Pat, do you really think old Anna died a natural death?"

"An accident is hardly natural, Dick."

"You wouldn't be sidestepping me, would you, Pat?"

Patrick grinned. "Who would want her dead, Dick?"

"Anybody that really knew her, Pat." The kid was being very serious. "Listen, if Louis comes around here hinting at anything you tell him to go to hell, see. Mother treated Anna better than anyone else did, and all she got for it was more complaining and grumbling from Anna. Mother let that old woman get away with murder. Mother would always say that the house was really more Anna's than ours, said she loved the thing, and we didn't, and all the time Mother was treating her so super-decent, she was snooping round trying to get things on Mother to pass along to Louis. She called Mother a divorced woman—right to her face if Mother happened to oppose her in any way, which she would sometimes if it was something which concerned us kids. Mother always tries to stand between us and Louis. Mother even protected me when I was drunk, not because she approved but to keep it from getting to Louis. We had signals by which I would know if he was there and hide in the area or slip up the back stairs. To avoid him. Not that she approved of me, not at all, but she knows Louis doesn't play fair. Anna always loved to snoop at that window. Because for some reason you can hear even a whisper on the sidewalk in front, or at the front door, if you open that window a little and stand and listen just inside. That's why Anna kept the hinges oiled. She snooped once too often. I told Mother I was going to stand up this afternoon when the police came back to ask questions and tell the truth about Anna, but Mother says it isn't fair to say unpleasant things about the dead. The dead can't answer back, she says. Funny to be fair about Anna, though."

Patrick said, "You might make people imagine that perhaps she had something worth snooping for, too."

"Maybe you're right. I won't say anything I shouldn't. I promised Mother."

Dick picked up his teacup and drained it.

"What you think of my joining the Army, Pat?"

"It's an idea," Patrick said.

The boy took it for approval, and beamed.

He bounced up awkwardly, knocked against the table, apologized, and said, "Be seeing you, kids. Got to get along, was passing, and remembered the dough I owed you, so—" A stray wave of embarrassment left the sentence hanging. Dick abruptly scooped up his little hat, grinned, and departed.

"He's a pet," I said. "But I'd hate to be his mother. He gets at you so. He affects you so differently from Louis, yet they look terribly alike. Why?"

"The kid isn't vain, like his father. Also, he feels."

The things of the night came back. Ellen's call. The body in the areaway. The key in the lock. The bed that hadn't been slept in, then had. The picture by the window, then not. The doctor's guarding Louis Bland from inquiry. Ellen's mercurial behavior about the key. Suspicion burgeoning in Patrolman Goldberg. What had he found on the rug by the open window that made him ask us to come back to that room this afternoon? What had Louis done to Clint Moran? And what was this family taint?

"What do you think it is?" I quizzed Patrick, as we sat over our cigarettes.

"Nothing. Just as Dick said. Quick thinking for breaking up Sue's romance."

"What a heel!"

"You'll find out."

Then Hank Rawlings dropped in to see Patrick, and was directed to the Grill. I saw him coming and before I knew who he was I was drawn to him by the magnetism he undoubtedly had and was, I think, entirely unaware of. It would have spoiled it if he had been conscious of it, of course. He was thin, not very tall, a little stooped. He had sensitive hazel eyes in a thin face, straight brown hair, and a straight thin sensitive mouth. I never notice noses unless they are wrong for a face, and his wasn't. His voice was rather deeper than you'd expect, and though his walk was rather nervous, because he would want to get places faster than the legs could make it, I think, his rather blunt, craftsman's hand, holding a cigarette, was completely relaxed. I sat noticing these things while he and Patrick with a few matter-of-fact questions and answers, picked up from where they'd left off when they'd last seen each other five years ago. Then Hank left by the street exit to keep a luncheon appointment and we sat on for another five minutes at the table.

"Well, how do you like him?" Patrick asked.

"I think he's stunning. I don't know why exactly. Only two or three people in all my life—including you, dear—have got at me so instantly, like that. You know how cynical I am about people, though. What is it Hank's got?"

"I think it's plainly and simply that he is exactly as true as he seems."

I didn't say so, but Hank complicated the whole business. I made up my mind instantly that he was much too good for Ellen.

CHAPTER TEN

When we went back to the lobby, Louis Bland and Mary Kent were standing at the desk. Louis was asking the clerk something. Mary Kent just stood, but she made an art of it. They were a striking pair, Louis so dark, Mary Kent so fair, both so tall and so elegantly dressed. The clerk said something then and Louis wheeled, saw us, and beckoned Patrick imperiously with his cane. "There you are!" he announced, making it the more important with a frown. "Can you spare me a minute, Abbott." It wasn't a request. It was an order. There were no greetings. Patrick lifted an eyebrow, considered the time, said that a minute was about all he could spare, which was about the only answer an upstanding citizen could make to such a summons, and he and Louis sallied in the direction of a nook, leaving me with Mary Kent.

She chose to be friendly. She said, with a half smile, "We might as well sit down, hadn't we?" and we picked another nook, a kind of imitation alcove contrived with flower boxes in which pink hyacinths bloomed and dispelled a heavy fragrance quite different from Mary Kent's dry chic French perfume. We sat down in two easy chairs angling up to a low table. With that stealthy stealing in and out of fingers, now in black gloves, Mary Kent procured her cigarette, bringing out a flat gold case this time and offering me one. I accepted it, and a light. The aromatic Egyptian tobacco smoke soon mingled with the fragrance of the hyacinths.

She wore black, a black tailored suit superbly designed for her tall narrow-hipped, broad-shouldered figure, silver foxes, and a tiny black hat. Her only color was in her sapphire earrings. She always wore some of that blue to prevent her round surface-set eyes from looking washed out.

"Louis is here to see Pat professionally," she said then. Her inflection held a touch like dry humor.

I lifted eyebrows. Stealing her own technique, I did it as though they weighed tons and made lifting a chore.

It got me places, too. She said, in a very decent, rather anxious tone, "Louis thinks that servant Anna Forbes was murdered."

I managed, "Really?"

She spoke sincerely, to make me really comprehend the seriousness of things. "It's strictly *entre nous*, Mrs. Abbott. I shouldn't mention it, but of course Pat tells you everything?"

Like fish he does! But I smiled a wise smile, in the affirmative. It worked.

"You're not one, too, are you?" Mary Kent asked. Her distaste was polite but present. "I've heard of girls being. Here, of course. Not in France, naturally."

She meant a detective. I smiled condescendingly and said, "Oh—not *now*."

It got by. She thought I had been, but now wasn't.

"Now that you're married, you mean. I daresay Pat makes pots of money?" Sometimes he does and sometimes he doesn't, and he spends it like water regardless. But I hitched a shoulder, meaning yes-of-course. I was getting in deeper every minute. "America is the most astonishing place. The things women do *here*."

Mary Kent had lived so long abroad that her uncouth native land continually amazed and disgusted her. She forgot the immediate subject for a moment, and inhaled and exhaled disapproval through her chic tip-tilted nose.

Then she said in a businesslike voice, "Louis is making a mistake to fuss about this Anna Forbes thing, Mrs. Abbott, and I hope you will say so to Pat. I mean, sleeping dogs should be let lie. Don't you agree? The woman had no near relations so far as anyone knows, so nobody's likely to pop up and sue. So what, really, has Louis to gain from any sort of investigation? It will be a bother to start with, lead goodness knows where, and, whatever else, detain us in New York. Perhaps indefinitely. I simply can't bear it! In Paris a thing like this would get started and finished at once. But here the courts and all are too utterly incompetent and it would drag out no end and here we'd be, stuck in New York. Besides, what good could it possibly do? The woman is dead. You can't bring her back to life, you know. She was getting old and would have died soon in any case. But Louis does have such a conscience! It's his duty, he thinks."

That was a fresh slant on Louis. He had a conscience.

I slipped a glance at the two men standing talking at the other side of the busy room. They were about the same height. Patrick wore his blue suit and gray felt hat. Louis's black Homburg sat at a stylish angle. He wore a black Chesterfield overcoat. He was smoking a cigarette in the long black holder and talking at the same time and impatiently swinging the walking stick.

Mary Kent asked bluntly, "Mrs. Abbott, won't you please ask Pat not to take this case? He adores you, Mrs. Abbott. I noticed it at once. I'm sure he'll do anything you ask."

I was amused, inside. If Patrick chose to take the case he would take it, no matter what I said.

Then I remembered the Marines.

"Pat's joined up, Mrs. Kent. He won't have time to do any detecting for a while, I think."

She smiled. "Oh, of course. I remember now—we spoke of it at Ellen's. Louis forgot it, too."

She stubbed out her cigarette and said, in a quiet, serious and wholly attractive manner, "I wonder if Pat realizes that any investigation might make serious trouble for Ellen?" I put up my eyebrows. She went on. "I think Pat is very fond of Ellen. That's why I'm saying this. Ellen didn't kill the woman, Mrs. Abbott—Ellen is too even-tempered to commit a violent crime. But the police are said to be pretty crude sometimes and they are sure to suspect Ellen because she and Anna didn't get on. I'm not self-controlled, like Ellen. In her place I should have brained that woman long ago. The insults Ellen had to take, my dear! Anna spied on Ellen, and carried such tales, all of them lies, probably. Louis spoiled old Anna." Mary Kent looked disapproving. "He was awfully fond of her, really. He had a sort of little-boy devotion because she had been his nurse. He knew her faults as well as any-one, but he wouldn't do anything—scold her or anything, I mean. And now that she's dead he feels as if he must do something—everything—in case it was per-haps—murder." She sighed. "I've tried to dissuade him. But, frankly, I'm de-lighted that Patrick's not disengaged, or whatever you call it, because any kind of probing would make awful trouble for Ellen, and also inconvenience for our-selves. Detain us here, I mean. We don't know any other detectives personally, so Pat's refusal will probably decide Louis to let well enough alone." She glanced at the men. "I think he's doing it now."

Patrick was saying something Louis didn't like, anyway.

Louis had a scowl on his handsome face.

Mary Kent asked bluntly, "What do you think of Ellen, Mrs. Abbott?"

"I think she's most attractive," I declared.

"Isn't she? And so clever. I do admire her, enormously." She took out a ciga-rette and lit it. "Have you met Hank Rawlings?" I managed to look very blank. "He's a very nice person, really. I shouldn't have said what I did last night about the picture—*The Pink Umbrella.*"

Louis Bland, approaching, cut in. "Abbott agrees with you, Mary." His voice was angry and he looked ruffled because Patrick hadn't fallen in with his plans. "It seems the Abbotts were with Ellen when the body was found. Ellen was away from the house, and with the Abbotts, when Anna was killed, which gives her what is called an alibi, I believe it's called."

Mary Kent rose, and said, with patent relief, "How splendid, Louis! I'm glad." She smiled at me. "I've been talking a dime a dozen, I'm afraid, out of sheer terror that Pat would think Louis ought to do something."

Patrick's face was a tanned mask.

Louis frowned, and inhaled.

"Abbott thinks the death could easily have been accidental—just as Dr. Seward says. He thinks Anna may have heard a noise in the street, or even in the house, and imagined it a burglar or something, and so went upstairs and, finding no one in the drawing room, opened the window to look outside and then tripped on the sill, or perhaps had a stroke—which was Seward's idea."

"I'm sure that's just what happened, Louis, dear."

They looked at each other. He liked her. Her approval gave him a sort of strength.

"Well, I expect you're both right. Better let well enough alone," he said.

"Oh, yes, Louis. I'm so glad!"

Louis thanked Patrick for listening and we exchanged brief ideas about the war and we asked about the weather, which we ourselves hadn't experienced since around 5 P. M. They reported it good. Louis lit a fresh cigarette from his stub and fitted it into the holder. They said good-bye then, and went.

"How did you and Mary Kent get on?" Patrick asked.

"All right. She was very decent, Pat. By the way she referred again to *The Pink Umbrella.* There was a picture, you know—on the rug beside the open window." Patrick didn't seem to take what I would call real interest. "You know, somehow, I think Mary Kent thinks Ellen did it—killed Anna—but at the same time she doesn't want her accused. Why?"

"Didn't she tell you?"

"Well, she did say that an inquiry of any kind might detain them here."

Patrick grinned wryly. "Charming couple," he said. "Too bad if they're incon-venienced." His eyes narrowed. "Maybe they both know more than they're tell-ing. Neither of them is entirely above suspicion—if you ask me. But of course there is the matter of motive. Why would either of them want Anna Forbes dead?"

Patrick said, "Of course, it would be very much to Mary Kent's interest to have Ellen entirely out of the picture. At the same time she might not want her charged

with the murder. That would hold them here, as material witnesses, and perhaps
cost them their trip to South America entirely before they were finished with it.
Also, very likely, Mary knows in her heart why Louis wants to make trouble for
Ellen."

"Why does he?" I asked.

"Because—this is just a theory, Jeanie—he wants, after she is accused, to use
his money and influence to clear her. He knows she's not guilty. Then, maybe, she
would have a change of heart and marry him again—or so he thinks."

"Mary Kent would sense that, being in love with him," I said, "and try to keep
him from starting anything which would turn out badly for herself."

"Um-m. Here's another notion. Maybe Mary Kent does know something about
Ellen, or, more likely about one of the kids, which she can use to make Ellen toe
the line. If one of the kids is involved and Mary Kent knows it, all she would have
to say would be 'frog' and Ellen would jump, pronto."

I frowned.

"The kids? But the kids weren't at the house when Anna was killed?"

Patrick spoke softly. "How do we know?"

"I can't even imagine such a thing," I said. "Neither Sue nor Dick would kill
anyone, Pat."

"Probably you're right. But Sue seems very impulsive and Dick—"

I put in, "You mean, the way he drinks? The poor kid. Now if it were Ellen that
was dead instead of Anna we could probably say straight off that Mary Kent did it
and then go along and enjoy ourselves, but—"

"But it's Anna who is dead, dear."

I said, "What would happen to Mary Kent if Louis's scheme—your theory, I
mean—worked? If he got Ellen back?"

"He'd probably offer her money—"

"But surely she has money? Look at her clothes!"

"Well, he'd probably tell her to go fry an egg or something. Only he won't have
to. He'll never get Ellen back, so—"

"Listen, darling, he likes Mary Kent."

"You mean, he likes her approval."

"Okay. You win. Just why, though, did he pick on you to investigate Ellen?"

Patrick lit a cigarette. "He thinks I'm fond of Ellen. He thinks he could count
on my not going too far. Well, anyhow, you'll have to admit it's an interesting
setup, chum. Ex-husband wants ex-wife suspected so he can play Galahad. Ex-
husband's betrothed wants . . . what?"

"You'll have to answer that, darling. I don't understand these people. I do think,
though, that Louis could have saved everybody a lot of headaches by not divorc-
ing Ellen in the first place."

"Louis likes to give the people he's fond of headaches."

"Funny kind of fondness."

"Happens every day."

I groaned. "People are too complicated for me, Pat. Let's spend the rest of the day at the zoo."

Patrick grinned. "Let's spend it somewhere else than here," he said. "Let's go."

"Where?"

"Anywhere but here."

We started towards the door.

"Will Louis go to another detective, Pat?"

"I warned him if he did I'd sick the police on him," Patrick said. "He didn't know, till I mentioned it, that Dr. Seward had told us about his having been in the house last night, approximately at the time Anna must have been killed. I suggested that he himself might know more than he was telling. I even hinted that I suspected he'd pushed Anna off the balcony, which seemed to make him take serious thought. Walk faster, darling. Scram!"

We scrammed, and a small mouse-shaped man scrammed in our wake. It was the first time, but not the last, that we were followed.

CHAPTER ELEVEN

The officer who questioned us that afternoon was a police-detective lieutenant named Jeffrey Dorn. He had not only a pretty name but also a face like an angel, a round face with round sky-blue eyes, thick wavy blond hair, a short innocent-looking nose, and a little mouth with a full underlip and the sweetest expression—till he smiled. The smile was plump and snug. He kept his lips pressed together and let it curve up neatly into one of the most poisonous little crescents it was ever my bad fortune to behold. He wore a suit of gray English tweed, a blue shirt, and dark brown polished shoes. The handkerchief in his coat pocket was very white and very neat. There was plenty of the right blue in his necktie. A careful dresser, an artful investigator, the possessor of a very cold heart,—Lieutenant Jeffrey Dorn of the Homicide Bureau of the Police of the City of New York.

The drawing room furniture had been shifted in a way which would have stricken the woman we were here to talk about, the sofas pushed together to make a row with their backs to the fireplace and other chairs drawn up in a loose arc—an arrangement intended to keep all faces facing Lieutenant Dorn.

First, Patrolman Isaac Goldberg told his story. The patrolman looked very tidy, in a clean, pressed uniform, black socks, and black shoes. His black shining hair was parted in the middle. His heart-shaped face and beetle-brown eyes were super-solemn.

"I was patroln my reglur beat, see," he said. His voice suggested crackling eggshells. "A patrolmn has to be alert, see. He frequently examines all doors, windas, areaways, gates—"

Lieutenant Dorn said, "That's all right, Goldberg. Get on with your story."

The patrolman winced. "Yez'r. Anyways, that winda there, the mittle one, was opn, see, and the lights on. And then I should turn the flash in the areaway and see the stiff—the corpse lay'n on the face, dead as a rock, see."

"You mean, life was extinct?"

"And how." The patrolman coughed, neatly. "Yez'r."

"Were you alone when you found the body?"

"No'zr. The leddy of the house, anodder leddy and a gem just then come up. The gem being a dick asks that he should phone the station house—"

"You found the body. Then what, please?"

Patrolman Goldberg looked neatly pained. "I was telling you, Lootnant. Afta making sure it should be dead, I ast the gem that he should phone the station house. I stayed by the stiff, see, that's strickly regulations, it's apt they should draw a crowd, so—"

Dorn showed symptoms of impatience at having the Manual of Rules and Regulations of the New York Police Department quoted at him. So often and with such zeal.

"Yes?"

"Well, the wagon got here in a jiff—"

"What's a jiff, man? And you sent for an ambulance, didn't you? Be accurate!"

Patrolman Goldberg reddened and consulted his notebook.

"The gem—ah, Mr. Abbott there—he said he reckanized the dame and he should call the family doc—doctor—but it don't seem right by me that should be all, so I says he should also phone the doctor from the station house too, just in case should it be according to regalations, see. Okay, he says, so—" Goldberg eyed his notebook meticulously—"four minutes afta we called, the wagon—amlance—rolled up with the city doc—doctor. Also Dr. Maxton Seward, the family doctor, got there about the same time. Botha them examined the corpse and pronounced it strickly dead, and as it is against regalations you should let them lay on the street on account they collect crowds—"

"Yes, yes! Did anything suggest to you that the woman's death might *not* have been accidental?"

Patrolman Goldberg hesitated visibly. Then he lied. He lied with a give away gulp. "No'zr." He lied badly, but once in it, he finished up. "No'zr. It looked just like it should be a accident to me, which is what botha doctors said. Yez'r. I figgered they was right and that was what it should be, see. Accident, see."

Patrolman Trill was nervous under questioning. He had come along in the ambulance from the station house to assist Patrolman Goldberg and had stayed and searched the house, finding no traces of any intruders, and nothing to arouse suspicion of any kind that Anna Forbes had died in any way other than the doctors had agreed on.

The young ambulance surgeon reported that, with Dr. Seward's permission, he had assisted at an autopsy this morning. I slipped a little glance at Patrick, wondering if it was usual for a New York Police doctor to ask a doctor in private practice to assist with a post mortem. The autopsy had confirmed their diagnosis on the scene of the death—that death had been due to cerebral hemorrhage following a cerebral accident caused by a sharp blow on the left temporal region of the cranium.

Dr. Seward testified plushily that he had known and attended Anna Forbes for perhaps twenty-five years. He stated that while her health was good, for her age, sixty-two, she had lately shown a tendency to high blood pressure. He was positive that she had suffered a cerebral accident—a stroke—while on the balcony and had fallen to her instant death. He was unprepared to give an opinion on whether she would have lived had she not fallen from the balcony. Offhand, the chances were, she might have, with perhaps a partial paralysis.

The doctor gave his evidence like a man who expects everyone to believe every word and give up all thought, instantly, of even thinking anything different.

Lieutenant Dorn listened with a round angelic face.

Dick Bland was next. He fidgeted and stammered and blushed. He admitted having been plastered. "I got home after it was all over, drunk as a skunk," he said, attempting a sort of bravado while blushing like mad. He had last seen the deceased about eight o'clock the night before. She was in his room about that time, turning back his bed. "She always did that job," he said. "She liked to do all the jobs which were sort of keeping an eye on us, I guess."

The lieutenant watched him uncritically.

"Do you remember everything you do when you're drunk?" he asked.

Dick blushed with acute embarrassment. "Yes, I do. But I'm on the wagon from now on. Things like this teach you a lesson."

"How's that?" the lieutenant asked with feline softness.

"It could happen to your mother or sister and you wouldn't be there to call a doctor or something!"

"I see."

Chills crawled up my spine. The soft way Dorn treated Dick made me anxious.

Susan Bland was not embarrassed. She stood straight and very fresh and pretty, and looked directly into the detective's eyes as she answered his questions. No, she had not been at home. She was with a friend. They had gone dancing, and to a 1 A. M. movie, a double feature which lasted hours and hours.

Lieutenant Dorn liked Susan Bland. He did not prod her, and when she volunteered that Anna Forbes probably fell out the window in one of her rages he merely listened politely and then asked, "Did she often have rages?"

"Oh, every day. Several times a day," Susan said. "She was practically never entirely under control. She had one yesterday because Mother wanted to invite people to dinner, so Mother called it off. Anna didn't have to help with or serve the dinner in any way when we did dare to have guests, but she always griped. She griped and she groused all the time. We had a dreadful time keeping a cook and housemaid, because Anna interfered with everything. She thought she owned this house. Mother let her get away with it, but it certainly got on my nerves."

The lieutenant smiled with his angelic eyes only. Susan didn't look as though she had a nerve, that was why. She looked fresh and sweet as an energetic pink.

The cook and housemaid both said that Anna was hard to deal with. They lived out. They had left the house shortly after eight o'clock last evening and didn't return till seven this morning, at which time they learned that Anna was dead.

I was the next. Patrolman Goldberg gave me a suspicious squint when I said I was Mrs. Patrick Abbott and I wondered if it wouldn't be a good idea to carry my marriage certificate in that little leather case in my bag which held my driver's license and ration cards, but Lieutenant Dorn treated me with unsuspicious politeness. I told how I happened to be at the house when the body was found. Patrick confirmed the story and said he had called the station house at Patrolman Goldberg's request.

"You also called Dr. Seward, didn't you, Mr. Abbott?"

"No, I did not."

"Who did call him?" Dorn asked, the feline back in his voice.

Dr. Seward spoke up from the room's largest and most comfortable chair. "Mrs. Bland called me. Naturally, she would."

"Ah," said Lieutenant Dorn. He certainly could put plenty in an *ah*. "That's all, Mr. Abbott. Thanks very much."

Louis Bland behaved admirably. He stated that Anna Forbes had been in the employ of his family for forty-four years. Yes, she was touch and go, but a very loyal servant. He had seen her last about half-past seven last night. He had dropped in at the house with some friends and Anna had let them out when they left. Yes, she had been temperish, it was quite usual, but she was so good and so conscientious that the family overlooked it. He was smooth as wax. You'd think there was never a ripple of discord in his life.

"She would have no reason for suicide, Mr. Bland?"

"Suicide? What an idea! And why throw herself from the balcony? It isn't far enough above the ground to guarantee certain death, you know."

"Quite."

Ellen was last. She looked pale and her eyes were circled, but she was perfectly composed, as apparently always. She spoke about her worry because her children were staying out so late and how, on an impulse, she had got up and dressed shortly after three in the morning and had come to our hotel, had come up to our room a few minutes, and how we had very considerately, in her words, walked home with her.

"Do you make a practice of calling on your friends at three in the morning, Mrs. Bland?" Lieutenant Dorn inquired.

Ellen declined to take offense at his sarcasm.

"Oh, no, indeed. I never did such a thing before in my life."

"The coincidence—your paying a social visit at that hour and the maid's falling to her death while you were out—was rather extraordinary, Mrs. Bland."

"Yes, it was," Ellen replied.

"No doubt, you think it providential that you were not alone in the house when the accident occurred?"

"Indeed I do not!" Ellen said, indignantly. "If I had been there to get the doctor at once we might have saved her life."

"Not a chance, Ellen," Dr. Seward proclaimed. "The blow killed her instantly, in my opinion."

Lieutenant Dorn looked at the doctor, who grunted, "Sorry!" in a way which said he wasn't sorry in the least.

"There appears to have been a good deal of coincidence in this business," Dorn said. "Mrs. Bland pays a call on her friends, at three-thirty in the morning. Coincidentally, the woman has fallen out the window while Mrs. Bland was away, and, coincidentally, our good Patrolman Goldberg was just then passing by, so that you all coincidentally discovered the body together. Very neat. Very neat indeed." He paused to let it sink in and then cracked out a sharp question, "What were your personal feelings for the deceased, Mrs. Bland?"

"She was a splendid woman. Entirely trustworthy and good. She was of course like a member of the family from having been with us so long."

"Did you like her, or didn't you?"

"I admired and trusted her."

"You don't mention her bad disposition, Mrs. Bland?"

"I don't like to, because, really, she was such a good woman at heart. I think we irritated her unbearably. She had got so used to living alone in the house, with no one at all to interfere with and upset her. She wasn't young, you know."

"Mrs. Bland, did you know Anna Forbes was dead when you telephoned Dr. Seward?"

"Yes, of course. Mr. Abbott came in to the house and said it was Anna and that she was dead, so I called the doctor because I knew he must sign a death certificate. It was the first thing I thought of."

"Just why would you think of that, I wonder?"

Ellen said, "Possibly because I am a trained nurse."

"Ah?" said Lieutenant Dorn. He added, "Ah!"

He put the tip of his thumb into his mouth and gnawed it thoughtfully, and then he said, "That's all. You may go. It looks like a simple case of death by misadventure, just as our doctors agreed. Thank you all for coming."

The lieutenant was the first to go.

"The City of New York must like to throw its money around," Dr. Seward complained loudly. "They might as well take the family doctor's word for things like this, save everybody time and trouble. When are you leaving for South America, Louis?"

"At once after the funeral."

"Flying?"

"From Miami on."

"I envy you, my boy. Wish I could get away myself."

"Let's get out of here," I whispered to Patrick. We said good-bye to Ellen and the kids and exited. "Well, I guess everything's under control," I said, on the street, "so we can go on enjoying ourselves till the Marines get you. Louis behaved all right, didn't he?" Patrick nodded. He was strangely quiet. "Ellen was swell. Didn't you love the way she snapped right back when that lieutenant asked her if it wasn't lucky that she wasn't alone in the house when it happened?"

"Well, that's Ellen for you, Jean."

"Did you know she was a nurse?"

"I think so. I don't remember."

"What do you think of that Lieutenant Dorn?"

"I think he bears watching."

"Anyhow Goldberg didn't pull a fast one—I mean produce whatever it was he found beside the window."

"God, Jeanie, I wish he had! Dorn wouldn't allow it, of course."

"Oh," I said. "Why?"

"I'd like to know."

We walked on a while.

"Nothing was said about Louis's coming to the house at 2 or 3 A. M., either."

"No."

"Pat—how do you feel—I mean, think? Was Anna murdered?"

He took out a cigarette and lit it very very slowly.

"I wish I really believed she wasn't."

I thought and thought.

"That Dorn is one real dilly," I said, then.

CHAPTER TWELVE

A black felt beret, even when French, means nothing when your heart is set on a green hat. I wasn't even wearing the new beret, but, the day being fine, my skull-cap of shining yellow feathers. Anyhow, when we got to Madison Avenue, I piloted Patrick left past one after another of those delicious little shops and presently we arrived outside Chez Hortense. A love of a green bonnet was perched on one of the pegs. But it smacked somehow of the harem. And also it was the wrong green, one that my emeralds, real and synthetic, would simply make shambles of. I walked on beside Patrick. Anyhow, were I to go in, I should lose him. I wouldn't dare try to get him into a hat shop. If I went in alone he would take himself off to an art show or a police station or even back to sympathize with Ellen, so I said nix on hats to myself for the moment.

We turned west again on Fifty-third Street. There was a Shanty opposite and Patrick proposed coffee.

We hung up on high stools at the counter. The girl had just handed us our coffee when, in the mirror, in a booth opposite and well along the narrow room, I saw Hank Rawlings and a perfectly luscious brunette.

I nudged Patrick before I saw that he had seen them and it had caused a brooding look to settle in his long blue eyes.

"I love her looks," I said. Patrick said nothing. "She must be the one. *Appétisante* is certainly the word." He kept silent. "I'm old-fashioned, Pat. I think if you want a man you ought to grab him before some other woman gets her hooks in. Ellen kept him dangling too long."

"Dangling isn't the word," Patrick said, with coolness.

"Maybe it's dilly," I said. Very cool. "I wouldn't know, my angel, but I do know that if I caught you dallying with a girl who looked like that one, I'd do something. She's lush."

Patrick put his ration of sugar, also mine, in his coffee and stirred it slowly, watching his hand holding the spoon, as if that were necessary.

"There's a French film with Jean Gabin in it at a theater on Third Avenue," he said.

I was watching the girl—Hank had his back slightly towards us, so that I could see only his profile. She had great midnight-black eyes, a white skin, and her crimson lips revealed beautiful teeth. She was really lovely, in a soft-fleshed, love-to-touch way.

"There's only one reason why a man would like a girl like that, Pat."

"Damn good reason."

"Don't be trite, dear."

"You asked for it. You made a very snap judgment, didn't you?"

"But the way she looks at him!"

"How does *he* look at her?"

"I can't see through the back of his head, de-ar."

"Then give the guy a break. Also the girl. She may have a Boston soul in a deep South shape. Happens. About this Gabin picture, it's an old one, I think, but said to be swell. Let's see it tonight, shall we?"

"Oh. Well, all right, only I'd like to skate on that lovely pond in Rockefeller Center. It would be fun to skate when the air is warm and nice."

"We can do both. We'll have dinner at a French *bistro* I've heard about, also on Third Avenue, then see the picture, then go skate. You can drink at the café by the rink. The more I drink the better I skate."

I said all right. The French affairs both preceded the skating, you notice, but

Patrick would soon go away with the Marines and if I didn't give in now I would be sorry then, so I didn't argue. I sipped my black coffee and had another look at the girl. Hank was watching her, in his intent fashion, and talking. I imagined his sensitive hazel eyes, how they would make anything he was telling her or saying seem important, because that was how he had looked at Patrick, and at me.

Suddenly Hank glanced around, saw us, excused himself and came over. We shook hands. "I've been trying to reach you on the phone, Pat." I looked at the girl. She was watching Hank. Her face looked rather envious. My, she's crazy about him, I thought. "I've got to get back to Washington on a six-o'clock train, want to give you my address there, in case you get down—also mine here, when I get up here, which is all too seldom." He took out a card and a pencil.

Patrick asked him abruptly, "Hank—you know what happened, don't you?"

Oddly, Hank's face went white.

"That housekeeper at Ellen's. Her name was Anna Forbes. She's dead."

"My God, you gave me a turn," Hank said. "I must be jumpy, Pat. Overwork." He wrote out the addresses, gave Patrick the card, and took out a cigarette and lit it. His fingers were trembling. "Too bad," he said, then.

"Hank, did you take Ellen home last night?"

Hank's eyes veiled. "Ellen?"

"You don't have to pretend with me, Hank. Ellen told us she was with you. And I'm not just horning in. I want to tip you off that the police have got evidence of some kind that makes them think Anna Forbes was murdered. I'm concerned for Ellen."

"But why?" Hank asked.

"Aren't you?"

"Why should I be, Pat?"

Patrick said coldly, "I guess it was just an idea."

I said, "The police think Ellen's mixed up in it."

"That's absurd," Hank said.

"Sure," Patrick said crisply. "But they can be very unpleasant, Hank."

Hank inhaled slowly. "No, I didn't take Ellen home. She wouldn't let me. She never will. I—ah—listen, can't we talk this over somewhere? I haven't time now. Are you at the Rexley? Could I see you there about five-thirty?"

"Sure," Patrick said. He sounded brittle.

Hank smiled his shy smile at me, nodded at Patrick, and hurried back to the girl. Hurried is the word.

I thought, "He doesn't want to lose any time with her."

Patrick didn't say a word during the five- or six-minute walk to the Rexley. I thought he was sunk. The murder was haunting him and he wasn't quite clear about Hank and Ellen.

Otherwise I enjoyed the walk. The day was sweet from spring. A lot of wonderfully dressed women were about, walking well the way so many New York women seem to, and dressed in spring pastels—turquoise, blue, yellow and warm pink. Florists' windows were gay with the so sweetly gay spring flowers. The buildings stood massively deep-blue in the late light and the sky, what could be seen of it between the skyscrapers, was pale green. I kept thinking about Hank Rawlings and Ellen Bland. Now that I had seen him I felt differently about their romance, only that wasn't the word for it, because the word romance sounds too trivial for Hank and Ellen. I don't mind saying now that to begin with I had thought it ridiculous. They seemed too old to be romantic, or, rather, old enough to do some-thing about it. They didn't look over thirty, either of them. But they were. I had felt detached, at first. Now I didn't, and it was because I had fallen so hard for Hank. Oh, not in a romantic way, naturally—not when I was so nuts about Pat—but because he had character and great charm and sweetness and kindness, and you knew it, straightaway. But I couldn't figure out where the girl came in. That girl was nuts about Hank, if appearances meant anything. I thought of her very white skin and black eyes and her soft-looking, dusky hair. Probably she had the enticing body that goes with that kind of face. But that wouldn't make Ellen push Anna Forbes off a balcony, would it? Or would it? Or what?

As we entered the hotel a ruddy boy in a Navy blue uniform came striding to meet us. "Bill?" we both said.

"I've got to see you, Mr. Abbott!" Bill blurted. "It's about Sue. Sue's crazy. I can't even talk to her. What ought I to do, Mr. Abbott?"

There were people about. Patrick shushed Bill and headed for the Alpine Grill. This was also peopled, but we got our favorite table in the corner. Bill refused a drink. He said he was on his way somewhere official where a previous drink would not be appreciated. I suspected he didn't drink anyhow. He took a coke, when pressed. I remembered then that I had asked them for cocktails this evening. Bill didn't know if Susan had forgotten it, or not. He frankly wasn't interested.

"Sue's kicked me out, Mr. Abbott. She doesn't want to see me again. That's why I'm here. She admires you and also Mrs. Abbott. I thought maybe you could talk some sense into her head."

Patrick offered the boy a cigarette. He refused it.

"Sue's had a shock," Patrick said.

"You mean, because that old woman's dead? Sue's not shocked about that. She's glad. That's not like Sue, either. I mean, it seems hard. She's not hard. She likes to talk as if she is, but she's not. But I'm no doormat. I've got no great wealth, like they have, but she can't knock me around, Mr. Abbott."

"Bill, I meant it. She's had a shock. I didn't say the shock was from Anna's death."

"I don't want theories," Bill said, frowning. "I want to get something done, Mr. Abbott. But you're right about one thing. It isn't what happened to the old woman that is making trouble for me and Sue. It's what Mr. Bland said to her last night. Sue and her father had a fight. It happened right after we saw you out in front of their house last night. We had decided we'd get married and Sue said there wasn't any use waiting till her father left town because even though it was only a few days maybe I'd have to leave before he did—you see, Mr. Abbott, in the Merchant Marine you never know. Sue doesn't think her mother ought to keep things from her father the way she does. To keep her father from yelling around the way he does. She said we'd got to tell him we were going to get married. It was okay by me. I don't know the guy very well and what I had seen I didn't like, but if there was going to be any trouble for Sue I wanted to be around when she broke the news, see, though she wanted to do the talking herself, not have me to do it because—and it's the truth—she's the only one of them that can talk back hard enough to make him listen." Bill paused and stared at the glass the waiter set in front of him. "Well, we went in. That woman that's dead was in the downstairs hall, as usual. She gave me a sour look which I guess she thinks, or thought, made an impression—if I hadn't known Mr. Bland was against me from himself, Mr. Abbott, I'd've known it from that woman because, in my opinion, she thought and acted exactly the way he gave orders for her to. Well, Sue and I went upstairs to the living room and there was a whole crowd. I guessed that would stop Sue for the moment but she said, yelled it almost, because of the piano, 'Hello, everybody. Glad you're all here to meet the guy I'm marrying tomorrow.' " Bill grinned with pride. "You know how Sue talks."

I smiled, with sympathy and all.

Patrick asked, "What happened then, Bill?"

"Nothing. For about half a minute. Then the one at the piano, his name is Clint something, played a wedding march, then Sue's mother stood up and came towards us, and when she got close she said, 'Come upstairs, both of you,' and went on out and meanwhile Sue's father started screaming."

"Screaming?" I asked.

"Sure he screamed. No other word for it. He jumped up and stamped his feet and started yapping about what could and couldn't happen. I guess he thinks maybe I'm not good enough for Sue. I never said I was—who would be?—but it's not for Mr. Bland to decide, in my opinion. Well, he kept yapping and the one at the piano played louder and louder. Mr. Bland didn't come near us, didn't try to lay hands on Sue or anything, or I guess I would have forgotten myself and kicked his slats in. Listen, he doesn't like to touch people, Mr. Abbott."

"You've noticed that?" Patrick asked. His eyes looked appreciative.

Bill nodded. The waiter came back and brought Patrick Scotch and me the Dubonnet cocktail I'd asked for, having heard Dubonnet was now hard to get. He went away.

"It didn't last long. I told him to pipe down and took Sue by one arm and marched her downstairs, not up—I forgot all about her mother just then for some reason. Mr. Bland followed us. That maid was in the downstairs hall. She buzzed along into her room, which is behind the dining room on that floor, but once when

I was facing that way I saw her listening at the crack. Mr. Bland told us in a very suddenly quiet voice that Sue couldn't marry because of some family disease."

I wondered if Dick had overheard this. Perhaps Sue had told him.

"Sue laughed in his face. She said everybody knew he was insane, and she would do her best to live down the family taint of insanity, then she gave him a tongue lashing till I honestly got to feeling sorry for Mr. Bland. Finally we walked out. But later on Sue started worrying. She thought maybe he had told the truth. Sue's so honest. We kept going places till there wasn't any place left to go and then went back to their house and got there after the police had just left. You remember." Bill frowned hard. "Then, some time, Sue went to see that Dr. Seward. He must be a crook. He wouldn't say one thing or another." Bill heaved his big shoulders. "So Sue gave me the air."

"Is there any special hurry about getting married, Bill?"

"There's a war on!" Bill snorted. "And I'm in the Merchant Marine! On the Russian—" He broke off. You didn't talk, in the Merchant Marine.

Patrick patted Bill's shoulder. "Of course. Just keep the chin up, kid. That family's a little keyed up. The rest of us may have to help them do their thinking for a while. Take it easy."

"Sue loves you and you love Sue, and that is really what will count, Bill," I said.

Bill looked doubtful in general. But subsided.

"Mr. Abbott, who do you think killed that woman?"

"Do you think she was murdered, Bill?" Patrick's voice had a touch of Dorn's felinity.

"Sue thinks she was murdered. She accused her father of it. Then she said it was temper, that she had no proof—I can't figure out just why, but I think that is one reason Sue is standing me up now. She knows something. Do you think maybe Mrs. Bland had something to do with it?"

"Certainly not!" Patrick snapped.

"Well, I wouldn't blame her if she had, and neither would anybody else who had been around there much. I don't see the sense in her having had to stand for what she stood from that old woman, and I said so to Sue, but they were used to it, they didn't think about it like other people do, not even Sue, though she talked about it the most. Dick's goofy but okay. He agreed with Sue about the old girl. They used to sit and talk about ways to bump her off—all in fun, see. My mother would have kicked that woman out the back door the first time she talked impudent like that, but Mrs. Bland—well, they're different. I don't like it either. I don't think it's American, somehow."

"The Blands lived abroad a long time. They may have picked up some un-American habits—such as thinking they have to be waited on, and putting up with a good deal of punishment to have it."

Bill nodded solemnly. Then he said, "Have you any idea what the so-called family taint is, Mr. Abbott?"

"I never heard of it till today, Bill."

"You know them pretty well, don't you?"

"Not that well," Patrick said.

"Then there is something?"

"Frankly, I don't know."

After Bill had gone Patrick proposed calling Ellen to ask if they were or weren't coming over for a drink. I insisted on going upstairs first. I wanted to get a bath. I had nerves, but it was nothing a good bath couldn't fix. I thought if I stood under a needle shower going full blast for about twenty minutes I might forget all about the Bland family.

"All right. I'll call Ellen from the room," Patrick said.

I sensed right then that something would interfere with that bath, and, sure enough, as we turned into our corridor, we saw Lieutenant Dorn leaning against our door and smoking a cigar. He smiled at us cheerfully. He was waiting to ask us a few questions, he said, as Patrick unlocked the door. "If you will be so kind as to ask me in," he said then. He was already in when he said it.

CHAPTER THIRTEEN

The room itself smelled of cigar smoke. Patrick opened a window. I crossed to the dressing table and, sensing that it had been disturbed, pulled open a drawer. Everything was stirred up. I glanced at the men, who were about to get settled in the bay, and said, "I think Sergeant Goldberg has been here. Probably looking for our marriage license, dear."

Lieutenant Dorn said, apologetically, "I'm afraid it was I, Mrs. Abbott."

"Why should you go through our things?" I asked indignantly.

"I'm so sorry, Mrs. Abbott. Matter of routine."

"No doubt you have a search warrant?" Patrick asked, amiably.

"But of course, Mr. Abbott." He produced it. "Naturally, I intended to tell you I'd been in here before you came upstairs, particularly after Mr. Abbott discerned the stale odor of cigar smoke and opened the window."

Patrick said, "My wife no doubt noticed it first. She has a very splendid sense of smell."

"Indeed?" The baby-blue eyes rested on me across the room. "May we sit down, Mrs. Abbott?"

"Of course. Though I'm rather surprised you bother to ask."

"Don't be too hard on him, darling," Patrick said. "It's just his job. I think he's pretty good at it myself."

They sat down. I picked up the evening paper which we had got on the way up and sat down edgewise on the bed. Dorn was saying, "Naturally, I had every intention of saying I had been in the room before you came upstairs. I made no attempt to cover up the fact that I've gone through your things, Mr. Abbott. I did think, however, you would give me more time. When our man downstairs warned me—"

"A mousy man in a raincoat," Patrick stated.

"Right. It's all a matter of routine, Mr. Abbott."

"I understand."

Dorn had taken the blue easy chair. Patrick sprawled on the sofa.

"Well, as I was saying, I had made only the most superficial search when he rang up saying you were on your way upstairs."

"Did you find anything incriminating, Lieutenant?"

"I must admit, frankly, that I didn't."

I sat pretending to read the paper, turning the pages now and then. I could have taken the bath. But I didn't want to miss this, in case it turned out to be interesting. Dorn talked smoothly. Lucky to have had a trained operative, meaning Patrick, on this Anna Forbes business from the start, he said. Very sly, I thought. I turned a page, making it rustle, not too little, I hoped, and still not too much, and listened. The guy intrigued me. He was a rogue, but rogues made swell dicks. Patrick was full of tricks himself when on a case. Dorn's snooping in our belongings was right up Pat's street. When detecting, I mean. Only, like as not Patrick would chance it without a warrant, if it suited him to do so. When detecting, Patrick detected everything and everybody he suspected connected with the crime, and with a shocking disregard for the niceties he observed scrupulously in his personal life.

"I want to talk to you about the Bland family, Mr. Abbott."

"Talk away, Lieutenant."

"I'm a little puzzled about how they stand. Mrs. Bland is divorced from Mr. Bland, I believe?"

"Yes."

"Yet, according to the two maids, whom I've interviewed personally just a few minutes ago, he spends a good deal of time about the house and interferes considerably and constantly in every way he can."

Patrick nodded.

"Why does she permit it? She seems like a woman with quite a will of her own?"

"She has endured it for years, for the children's sake."

Unbelief clouded the sky-blue eyes.

"Really, Mr. Abbott! If the servants' stories are true she has put up with a great deal more than makes sense. Why?"

"You'll have to ask her," Patrick said. He lit a cigarette, slowly, his head down a little and his eyes angling shrewdly at Dorn. "I think I can explain why she put up with it in Paris, however. She had no money—"

"But she has, Mr. Abbott."

Patrick thought fast. "Compared with him—if you will permit me to finish, Lieutenant. He got the legal custody of the children. She's a very conscientious mother and she was in a foreign country. The children lived with her. He permitted that. He provided for them, very well, though—mind you, this is hearsay, but I understand she's had no personal allowance from Bland since the divorce, only money for the kids. In this country, I am quite sure she would have managed differently. In Paris, it was a different story. To get work and therefore independence, she would have had to come home, and to get custody of the children under a set of such complicated circumstances would have been well-nigh impossible. Seen Bland in action yet, Lieutenant?"

"He behaved most gallantly at the house this afternoon, Mr. Abbott."

"Louis's company manners are okay, when he keeps remembering to use them. And he remembers, when good manners are useful."

Dorn asked, "How has all that affected the children?"

"I don't think it has hurt the girl too much. The boy was younger and more impressionable. If you want to get psycho, Lieutenant, you could probably deduce that the boy's taking to drink at sixteen is probably due to his being crazy about his mother, but also much affected by his father. He really doesn't know yet just how he feels about his father. He lets him bother him. Too much. The girl's different. She knows what she wants to do, and does it. She's less complex than the boy. But why talk to me, Lieutenant? Go and get acquainted with the Blands."

"Thank you," Dorn said. In general.

He took something from his pocket, an envelope, and holding it open, allowed Patrick to peep.

"This was found under the edge of the rug by the window, where Anna Forbes fell."

Patrick looked owlish. "Yeah?"

"It contains a deadly poison, Mr. Abbott."

Patrick said, "You didn't mention that the autopsy disclosed poison in the body, Lieutenant?"

Dorn chuckled and returned the mysterious envelope to his pocket.

"No. She wasn't poisoned, Mr. Abbott. She died from the blow on her head. A cerebral accident, just as Dr. Seward said. From the outside of her head, not inside the brain."

Patrick's eyes narrowed.

"Goldberg was pretty slick. You ought to promote him."

Dorn merely smiled.

"You knew before today that Mrs. Bland was once a trained nurse, didn't you, Mr. Abbott?"

"I seem to remember it. Vaguely."

Dorn patted his pocket. "The average person wouldn't know much about using one of these things."

"No?"

Dorn looked shrewd. "You don't ask what poison it is, Mr. Abbott?"

"What difference, if it wasn't used?"

"It happens to be a very interesting poison, Mr. Abbott. If Anna Forbes knew what it was and then had that thing brandished before her face, she might back out the window in sheer terror. Just an idea, you understand." Patrick looked polite. "What do you know about the relations of Mrs. Ellen Bland and a man named Hank Rawlings, Mr. Abbott?"

"Not a damn thing!" Patrick barked.

Dorn was delighted, at the rise. He talked on, supersmooth. "Mrs. Bland was with Rawlings, last night. They arrived together in a cab outside Rawlings's apartment about one-thirty in the morning. Rawlings got out and Mrs. Bland drove on in the cab. When the cab got near Fifth Avenue, Mrs. Bland asked the driver to take her around the Park, which he did, dropping her later on the corner of Fifty-sixth and Fifth. It was then around two o'clock, the driver said. He was fairly sure of this, he said. Perhaps I'd better explain that the doorman at Rawlings's place described Mrs. Bland. There's no question that it was she. Her hair is rather striking. The doorman happened to know the cabdriver, so her movements, up to the time she dismissed the cab, were easy to trace. The driver reported that she seemed very disturbed about something. He had the impression that she and Rawlings quarreled. I can understand her not caring to have Rawlings drop her at her home, considering the activities of the housekeeper, but why, after she was alone, did she get out at Fifty-sixth and Fifth Avenue? And where did she go then? She didn't go home, or if she did, she didn't remain long. She wasn't at home between twenty minutes past two and twenty-five minutes of three." Patrick lifted his eyebrows. "Mr. Louis Bland dropped in at the house at twenty after two. He was accompanied by a Miss Garnett and a Mrs. Mary Kent. Mr. Bland and Mrs. Kent came voluntarily to the police with this information, which is most important, because Anna Forbes was alive when they were at the house."

"How do you know that, Lieutenant?"

"They heard her snoring from the hall as they left the house. Mrs. Kent made a little joke about it, and they laughed over it."

Patrick asked, "They didn't look in, see that it was Anna snoring, and that it was ordinary snoring, not something else? Apoplexy, perhaps?"

"We assume that it was ordinary snoring. The window wasn't open or the lights on when they were there. If they had been, they would have looked into the area and found the woman. No, she was in her bed. She was snoring. If it had been apoplexy she would not have left her bed."

"Perhaps not."

"Mr. Bland left his key in the lock when he went into the house, forgot to take it when he left, though Mrs. Bland didn't mention it this afternoon when we questioned her."

"You didn't ask her anything about a key."

"No," Dorn said cheerfully. "No, I didn't. And I didn't ask Mr. Bland too many questions about his having been in the house in the small hours of the night. I had my reasons. The questioning this afternoon was not exactly a formal inquest. No one is yet accused of murdering Anna Forbes."

Patrick smiled. "You just wanted to get acquainted, didn't you? When you really examine them, you take them one at a time."

"Right!" Dorn said.

Patrick asked, "Well, don't you think that was a strange time of night for Bland and his lady friends to be flitting around Mrs. Bland's house?"

"The house is Bland's, Mr. Abbott. Besides, they keep late hours, people like that. They all went from there directly to their hotels and stayed there, were in their rooms, therefore, when the woman was killed—by accident or what you will."

"Can they prove it?"

"Bland keeps a man. He says Bland came in at three forty-five and stayed in. Mrs. Kent and Miss Garnett live at the Hotel Dijon. No one saw them go out of the hotel after they came in at three-forty; but three people—an elevator boy, a night janitor and a cleaning woman,—saw them come in. Both hotels are on East Fifty-third and about five or six minutes' walk from the Bland house. They walked."

Patrick said, "If Bland left his key in the door, anybody could have walked into the house and hidden, in a closet or a basement, and murdered Anna Forbes later when she got up and started prowling."

"Right."

"Mrs. Bland wouldn't seem to have much privacy, Lieutenant?"

Dorn shrugged. "I don't really care about that—at the moment. What I want to know is where Mrs. Bland was from the time she paid off the cab at Fifty-sixth and Fifth Avenue at approximately two in the morning, until she showed up at your hotel at three-thirty? She didn't go back to Rawlings's apartment hotel. The doorman was on the job all the time. Rawlings didn't go out. It was a fairly disagreeable night to be out. Hazy. She certainly wouldn't have walked the streets for an hour and a half, or wouldn't be likely to. Mind you, it wasn't raining. She could have rambled around by herself for an hour and a half at that hour and in that queer light, but would she?"

"Have you asked her?"

Dorn smiled the smile. "In due time, Mr. Abbott. Tell me this, didn't Mrs. Bland really come to you for advice, because when she got home she found Anna Forbes lying dead in the areaway?"

Patrick laughed aloud.

"I thought you implied a minute ago that she brandished that—hum—you-know-what—at Anna Forbes, who pronto backed off the balcony?"

Dorn smiled.

He kept silent.

Patrick said, "No, Lieutenant Dorn. Mrs. Bland came to me because she was worried about her brats. Just as she said."

Dorn knocked off an ash. "It was merely an idea," he said.

"Bland didn't ask you to investigate Mrs. Bland, did he, Lieutenant?"

The blue eyes flickered.

"No-o. He said his wife was a wonderful woman, absolutely above suspicion. He said he suspected no one, but hoped we would do everything to apprehend the murderer—if there is one—in justice to the dead woman."

"I see."

Dorn considered. "I wonder if Bland knows as much about his former wife as he thinks he does? She's rather a puzzle for me, Mr. Abbott. Eating her cake and having it, too—perhaps?"

Patrick's slow glance raked the detective. "She's had no cake, Lieutenant. I hope it won't hurt your feelings, but Louis Bland tried to hire me before he came to you. He wanted me to give Mrs. Bland a good scare."

Dorn smiled. "He told us he came to you."

"But he didn't tell you why exactly?"

"No. We guessed it. Revenge. He's got it in for her, for some reason, maybe because the kids like her better than him. Happens all the time. We know that. I hope you don't think I'm favoring Bland personally, Mr. Abbott?"

"Of course not, Lieutenant." Patrick sounded like the smooth one now.

"It would look a lot better, however, if Mrs. Bland and the Forbes woman hadn't been on such bad terms. Also, Rawlings was the corespondent in the divorce case. In Paris, several years ago. It all adds up to something pretty queer. Another thing—why did Anna Forbes, or whoever did it, leave that light blazing? If she was eavesdropping on the balcony would that light have been on behind her? Hardly. It's a funny case, Mr. Abbott." Dorn ground out the cigar and carefully deposited the butt on the tray. "When the cool ones do go haywire they're the worst," he concluded.

"Mrs. Bland didn't kill Anna Forbes, Lieutenant."

"Then who did?" The detective's voice was icily precise.

"I'd like to know that myself," Patrick said. "For Mrs. Bland's sake, specially. If Anna *was* murdered. You have not yet convinced me that she was."

Dorn stood up to go.

"There's another thing, Mr. Abbott. It's just gossip, but it's interesting. It seems that Mrs. Bland is still crazy about this man Rawlings, and that only last night she learned he was stepping out with another woman. Maybe that's why they quarreled."

"Bland was very thorough."

"We didn't get that item from Bland." Dorn didn't say where he did get it. He moved towards the door. "Thanks for the talk, Mr. Abbott. Good-bye, Mrs. Abbott." I said good-bye. Patrick said good-bye. They shook hands cordially. Patrick let him out the door.

Patrick came over and threw himself on the bed. "My God," he groaned.

I said, "Ellen ought not to lie."

"Maybe she didn't."

"I'm afraid she did, Pat. She wasn't entirely truthful with you about last night. Dorn's got something there."

"If she lied about it, she did it because of the kids, or for Hank, or something. She'd have a good reason."

"Well, she should have told us the whole truth. You, I mean. Just in case. You should know the truth, Pat."

"She wouldn't think of that. She would be thinking of Hank, or the kids, or somebody."

"Why didn't you tell him about Ellen thinking the key left in the door might be Dick's?"

Patrick scowled. "Let him do his own sleuthing!"

"Mary Kent must have tipped the police off about Hank and the lush brunette."

"Why not Daphne? Or Clint?"

"Listen, what did Dorn have in the envelope?"

Patrick grinned, showing his fine white teeth in his tanned face. "Wasn't that cute? It's a hypodermic syringe. My, oh my. I'll bet he lets everybody peep. But I would like to know what poison's in it. Just for fun."

"He pined for you to ask him," I said.

"Seriously, I'd like to know why Anna Forbes really did go up to the drawing room, Jeanie," Patrick said.

I said, "Maybe she went up to empty the ashtrays. You know how fussy she was. Isn't it holding back material evidence not to tell Dorn everything, darling?"

"I wouldn't know."

"Well, anyhow, I'm going to get my bath." I got up and skinned off my sweater.

The telephone rang.

CHAPTER FOURTEEN

I put on my sweater.

"Hello," Patrick said into the phone. "Oh, hello, Hank."

He sat down on the bed as if expecting a long talk.

I waited.

"You're downstairs? Well, come on up— Oh— Sure I will— Yes, I certainly do understand her position— Okay, fine— So long."

To me, "That was Hank. He stopped in to see me about something and then found he hadn't time to stay. Didn't know it was so late and has to catch a six o'clock train to Washington. Asked me to keep a watchful eye on Ellen."

I smiled sweetly and took my bath, making the shower cold and rough to eradicate general irritation aggravated by acute distaste for Ellen.

We walked to the *bistro*. The evening was warmish. All the color and gaiety of the afternoon had perished. The air was drowsy, murky, and made you sad. In a haze which seemed denser than it was noises were exaggerated. Pedestrians appeared and vanished quickly and mysteriously. You had an odd feeling that each one might be somehow evil, and your back felt creepy for seconds after each was past.

Smells abounded, not all of them pleasant by any means, especially as we got near Third Avenue.

Our plans had been changed because Dorn had stayed talking so long. We were eating first now, and seeing the French picture afterward.

The *bistro* had gingham curtains and tablecloths, and charged high prices. Patrick was disgusted because there was a cocktail bar in the place where, in Paris, Madame La Patronne would be sitting in a cashier's box. Never having been in Paris, I thought the place was swell. The food was delicious. We drank Chablis, which I thought was wonderful, and for dessert had strawberries and cream, but they were not, alas—according to Patrick—wild strawberries with the thick sweet-sour cream in little brown jars served with them in France. The clientele seemed to be the American-French sort, like Daphne Garnett and Mary Kent. There was a lot of dyed hair, much lipstick, and lovely clothes. The women made eyes at Patrick. Possibly because their own men were inclined to present a dapper, faded appearance.

The movie turned out to be a manhunt, pretty terrific, with a sad ending, and gave me a headache. It depressed me utterly. I felt limp as a rag when Gabin was finally slaughtered and we emerged into the smelly murk.

I couldn't imagine going skating now, on that gay beautiful pond, and neither could Patrick. We started walking slowly back to the hotel.

We turned up Lexington and then west on Fifty-fifth Street.

There were lights in the drawing room at Ellen Bland's. The curtains were drawn, but not so perfectly as Anna had closed them, so light seeped out. Another light showed from Ellen's room, and another from Dick's.

We met Patrolman Goldberg a few doors along.

"Hello, Goldberg," Patrick said.

"Evening, Mr. Abbott." He looked at me and said stiffly, "Evening."

"How goes everything?"

"Okay." The patrolman looked gloomy. "Of course, when you ask the homicide squad they should think a thing over they hog it, Mr. Abbott. They think they know everything. They see that you yourself should go right on doing the woik, though."

"Mr. Goldberg," I asked, "why is it you think we aren't properly married?"

Patrolman Goldberg blushed, "I know you are," he mumbled.

"Did you check on us, Goldberg?" Patrick asked.

"I took the precaution of wiring Frisco for the information. In my opinion it was not a very nice joke, Mr. Abbott."

"I apologize," Patrick said.

"If he didn't I'd do it for him, Mr. Goldberg."

"Aw, it's okay," the patrolman said. He smiled as if he had a load off his mind, but the detail added another item to my depression. Think of being checked on by the police!

We told him good night and walked on, and, near the corner of Madison and Fifty-fifth, stopped in a drugstore for coffee. We had been there only a couple of minutes when Daphne Garnett and Clint Moran came in. Daphne was swaddled in minks and had another bouquet-style hat. Clint wore the suit he'd worn yesterday. One more day hadn't made it any cleaner. Daphne, squealing hellos, hopped onto the stool next Patrick's. Clint acknowledged us with one glance from his opaque greenish eyes and sat down beside me. I said something about always running into people and Daphne said the people they knew all lived in this neighborhood and had the same hangouts. "We practically live on the streets," she said. Being hotel-dwellers, she meant. "Pat, I've been wanting to talk to you. A man came to see me. A detective. *C'est incroyable, mon cher!* He asked me if I knew how to use a hypodermic syringe. Imagine! I said certainly not. He asked the most silly questions, and then he said the questions didn't amount to anything, that he was from the police and just checking up on something. He went to Mary Kent the same way, I mean asked the same things. Louis carries one sometimes—I mean a hypodermic—but I didn't tell the police. Louis doesn't think anyone knows he does, though. I don't think it's any of their business. *Quel horreur*—having the police nosing into everything! It's this New Deal, my dear. It wouldn't happen in France!" She set the exquisite little box with the saccharine on the counter and took off an overtight glove to drop a tablet into her coffee cup. "I was hoping I could talk to you this evening, Pat, drop in at your hotel or something, but I'm keeping my eye on Clint. He's got a new job and maybe it will turn out to be a good one. In a restaurant. He plays at the dinner hour and pretty soon now he has to go back for the supper club show. Isn't it dreadful about poor old Anna? It might have been us walking in and finding her, like that. We were over there only an hour or so before." Daphne sighed.

Patrick asked solemnly, "Are you psychic, Daphne?"

"Me?" Daphne was delighted. "Well. Quite."

"Then how do you think it happened?"

"You mean, to Anna? Why, she had a stroke. The doctor said so. She had such a temper, you know, and therefore she had the stroke." Daphne remembered to be psychic. "But—but somehow I've known that something tragic would happen in that house."

"I think it was a simple fall, Daphne. I am sure she slipped on the rug, caught her toe on the sill, and pitched over the balcony railing."

Daphne played with the pretty enamel box. "I wonder. Of course, we'll never know. Probably she was spying. Ellen was out somewhere last night. After what Mary said about Hank and that woman—at teatime—oh, she was a gorgeous creature, Pat, but very sexy—I never would have mentioned seeing them to Ellen, never—but in Ellen's place I think I would have gone right out to find out what Hank was up to, and maybe she did, and maybe he brought her back to the house and Anna happened to hear them outside, got up, looked out, and fell over."

Daphne sighed again and said that after all old Anna had so little in her life.

"I'm terribly fond of Ellen, Pat, and no one can say I'm not really her best friend, but I can't say I really understand her." Daphne considered, for half a second. "She was never quite one of us, Pat, if you know what I mean. She's too serious, or something. There was always something odd about her, different, you know." When Patrick got off to himself and boiled it down he certainly wouldn't congratulate himself on the residue. "Ellen was poor when Louis married her, Pat, but in Paris, all the French, I mean the exclusive French, treated Ellen as though she were better than the rest of us. It drove Mary Kent wild. Well, I didn't like it myself, either."

"I can understand that, Daphne."

"Oh, my dear! You don't half know!"

Clint sat sipping his coffee, taking no part in the talk and seemingly no interest in anything or anybody.

"How long have you known Mary Kent, Daphne?"

"Oh, all our lives. She's younger than I am, she's even younger than Ellen, a little, but we grew up in the same set, went to school together and all. We're really old New York families, you know—all but Ellen."

"Who was Kent?"

"A man with a lot of money. Oil. He died five years after they married and left it to Mary. She always wanted Louis, you know. Ellen cut her out. Ellen was Dr. Seward's special nurse. She came to the Blands to nurse Louis's mother through something or other and Louis went wild over her and married her. Made everybody mad, even Dr. Seward."

"Did Louis's parents object?"

"His mother. Not his father. But whatever Louis did was always all right with his people, in the end. For some reason they were kind of glad to have him marry a nurse, too. I'm devoted to Louis, of course. Louis has been frightfully mean to Clint—not that it's any of my business. Life is complex, *n'est-ce pas?*"

Patrick said it was. Daphne sighed a galaxy of small sighs. "Mary almost perished when Louis married Ellen. She took Kent on the rebound, he was three times her age, but she got millions when he died. She's clever with money. I lost thousands in German munitions, and so would Louis have done if he could have laid hands on his capital—his father tied it up some way—but not Mary—no, she's too smart."

"How does she invest her money?"

"My dear, you never know. She's terribly closemouthed."

"I can see you know a lot about people, Daphne?"

Daphne dimpled with pleasure.

"But definitely, Pat."

"Do you understand Louis?"

"Louis is simple as a child. So long as he has everything he wants, he's perfectly sweet."

"I believe you're right there, Daphne."

Daphne glowed. "But of course. That's why I sympathize with Ellen so. She isn't really a gold-digger, never was. She adored Louis to start. But she couldn't stand his fussing so—he does make a lot of trouble—strictly *entre nous*. Really, Mary Kent is the better woman for Louis because she doesn't mind what he does. She likes him the way he is, and Ellen couldn't stand him when she really found him out." Maybe I had underrated Daphne. I began to take closer notice. "But I do wish he and Mary would get married and get away from here. You said I was psychic. I am. And I know there is going to be terrible trouble there unless those people get married and get out—*tout de suite*. Clint, darling, we've got to get going. Listen, Pat, I'm going to tell you something. Maybe it's nothing, but it worried me so. Last night when we were at the house Louis went upstairs. Mary and I sat in the drawing room all the time we were there. When he came down he had that picture, that *Pink Umbrella* picture that Hank Rawlings painted of the children, years and years ago. He said he was going to take it away with him. Said he wanted it himself. Mary Kent made him leave it. Louis left it on the coffee table near the fireplace. It's all so sort of childish. Ellen is mad about that picture, simply mad, and Louis resents it."

"I think you're right."

"Yes," Daphne agreed, "but she ought to get rid of it. It makes a lot of hard feelings. And for what? Ellen will never marry Hank, now." Daphne digressed and said, "We must be going. Poor dear Clint has to pay for his living now, he hasn't a sou except what he earns, and he had every right, once, to be quite as well off as Louis. You know all about it, of course?" Patrick managed to look just right to keep her on the subject. "Clint's mother and Louis's inherited alike, and they both let Louis's father invest their money and everything went fine till Clint's mother died and then, suddenly, for some reason, Clint had nothing. So the Blands looked out for him—and why not? They sent him to Yale, with Louis, and he practically lived in that house, in vacations, and Mr. Bland arranged for him to have an allowance and all. Louis wasn't strong, or so they thought, so Mr. Bland made a will letting Clint inherit, in case Louis should die—the old man's conscience must have troubled him, *n'est-ce pas?* If Louis got married and had children, they would inherit. There is still some sort of fund for Clint, though, but Louis has to die before he gets it, so meanwhile Clint manages as best he can. Poor dear, he's not a very good manager." Daphne fiddled with her little box. "Still, he's happier when he has something to do, and I think he drinks less, so here I am on his trail tonight seeing that he gets to his new job on time and all. It's a sweet place. It's called La Fleur Verte." My mind translated, "The Green Flower." "It will make a hit, I think. Drink can be pretty awful, Pat. It runs in that family. Poor Dick!"

Clint got up and went out. His exit was so sudden that he was out of the store before Daphne could collect her wits and rush after him.

We left after a few minutes and walked slowly back to the hotel.

I said, as Patrick and I walked towards the hotel, "If Daphne knew Louis always carries a hypodermic, everybody knows it. Maybe he's a dope fiend?"

"I think not."

"Maybe he killed Anna himself and wants to pin it on Ellen? And he left the hypo on purpose to make people suspect her, since she's a nurse."

"A little farfetched."

"If Louis were the dead one, we could blame Clint. Isn't he something, though."

"Um-m."

There was only one message in our box. It said, "Mr. Henry Rawlings telephoned at 12:02. Asks you call Murray Hill 7-9132. Urgent."

It was now twelve-five by the hotel clock.

I waited near the desk while Patrick went to a booth and asked for the number. The mousy man was nowhere in sight. I forgot him for hours at a time, then he would materialize, suddenly.

Patrick returned.

"No answer," he said. "How about a nightcap in the Grill?"

We had our favorite corner table. There were a few people about, contented-looking people.

A machine somewhere played the eternally sweet and fresh *Show Boat* music. Patrick ordered Scotch. I tried their Cuba Libre.

"This place is a dilly," I said.

"*Gemütlich* is the word, even though German," Patrick corrected me. "Funny about Hank. I wonder if he missed his train—or changed his mind. Wonder where he called from?"

"Maybe it's his own telephone number," I said.

Patrick asked for a directory and looked up the Rawlingses. Hank's telephone wasn't listed.

We had our drinks. Patrick had a telephone brought and tried three times again to get the number on the slip. He called Information and asked whose number it was. A macabre female voice informed him that they couldn't give out that information.

CHAPTER FIFTEEN

I woke first next morning and got to the telephone and ordered breakfast sent up. Patrick groaned and eyed me balefully with one eye open and one closed, then poked his head under his pillow. I closed the window. The weather had changed for the worse. Rain fell. On the sidewalks far below people were peripatetic umbrellas. I shivered and was glad for the warm elegance of the living-bedroom even though we couldn't afford it.

I opened the hall door, picked up the paper, threw it at Patrick, then kissed him, then took a shower. Breakfast arrived. We had it in the bay.

Three quarters of an hour later, breakfast was finished and the things taken away and Patrick was sprawled in his pajamas on the sofa reading the newspaper while I sat in bed fixing my nails.

I selected a polish dark enough to not look Christmasy with my emeralds and said,

"Let's do something common for a change. Visit Grant's Tomb, or something."

"Um-m."

"Have you ever been in Grant's Tomb?"

"Nu'm."

"Know anybody who has?"

"Nuh."

"Then that isn't common enough." I removed the polish and tried another of the four shades in my kit. I wanted something dark, but not so dark as the shade Mary Kent had been wearing yesterday. I couldn't ever understand that color's being fashionable. But, on her, it had chic. So help me, she was smart! It was a gift. "It's no day to do the Empire State, dear. Because it's raining. How about Chinatown—no, that would never do for us San Franciscans—Are you listening, Pat?"

"Heard every word."

"I'm just having fun, darling. I don't care what we do and I'll do anything, only I hope it won't be anything French."

Patrick made no answer.

"It isn't that I don't like the French. Only—here somehow—things trying to be French when they're not French makes me sad. I keep thinking about the real French. I feel like crying and this is supposed to be a vacation."

Patrick got up and stalked over and sat down beside me and hooked an arm across my mouth so I couldn't talk and went on reading. I could feel his heart beating. Slow and steady, just as it should.

I wriggled free—as free as I cared to be, which was only enough to talk—and said, "Why don't we stay here all day? We could hang a sign on the door saying don't disturb and tell the desk not to put through any calls and have all our food sent up. It's raining. It's lovely to stay in a lovely nice-smelling room in the rain."

Patrick dropped the paper on the bed and reached for the phone book.

I picked up the paper.

It opened to page three. I saw first thing a photo of the girl we'd seen yesterday with Hank.

I read the item.

RAWLINGS SECRETARY FOUND DEAD

Mrs. Laura Gilbert, 24, private secretary of Henry James Rawlings, of Rawlings, Mayhart and Rawlings, chemical engineers with offices in the Shandon Building, was found early this morning, dead, in an apartment which she occupied on East 40th Street. The body was discovered by Miss Sarah Dow, a defense worker, who occupies the apartment across the hall. Miss Dow, coming home shortly before one o'clock, noticed that the door of Mrs. Gilbert's apartment stood open, rang the bell, got no answer, and stepped inside. She turned on the lights and saw the body lying on a sofa in the small living room. Some money in Mrs. Gilbert's bag and her rings were not disturbed. Police are investigating.

"I was going to show it to you," Patrick said, from the directory. "By the way, Laura Gilbert's telephone number is Murray Hill 7-9132."

"That's the number Hank asked you to call, Pat? How odd! So he didn't leave for Washington, after all?"

Patrick slammed down the book.

"Good God! The damn fool! Why didn't he? If Hank really wants to look after Ellen—"

I said, coldly, "If I may say so, I have seldom seen anyone who really needs so little looking-after as Ellen."

"You don't know a damn thing about it!"

"Is that so! All right. Maybe I don't. But I know a little about women and Ellen is perfectly competent to look after herself if ever I saw a competent woman. Yet every man we meet is breaking his neck to look after Ellen. Dick looks after Ellen. Louis clamors to. Hank asks you to, though he doesn't seem to do too good a job of it himself. Patrolman Goldberg, even, wanted to protect and solace Ellen."

Patrick lit a cigarette and proposed my piping down.

"I'll not pipe down. You're the worst of the lot. Because you're the most intelligent. Yet every minute, since we've run into Ellen, you've been mentally looking after her. I won't have it, hear? And I am not letting you get mixed up in this mess any further. Hear?"

His eyes were green, and very narrow.

"I'll get mixed up when I damn please."

He meant it. I tried reasoning. "I'm sorry, Pat. But I have really been very patient about your screwy Paris-American friends. Haven't I? I haven't said a word, or only one or two anyhow, but I am going to say some now. I don't like them. That means all of them. I don't like Ellen. Everything's her fault. She's got no guts, she wouldn't be in the spot she's in, with Louis fluttering around like a hen, and Hank cheating—"

"What makes you think he cheats?"

"You saw the girl."

"You're nuts!"

"Well, she's dead, dear. She's murdered. You know what everyone will say, don't you? That Ellen did it."

"More reason for her friends to stand by."

"Stand by? But what about our vacation? Oh, Pat, you can't do anything. They're middle-aged, and—"

"Middle-aged?" Patrick snorted.

"They're almost forty."

Patrick gave me a long straight look. "In France, people aren't considered interesting till they're getting on towards forty."

"France!" I blazed. "I want to see New York. This is my very first trip to New York, and all I see and hear is France and the French, and it makes me very unhappy. And now we've got murder. Corpses all over the place!"

Patrick silently picked up the paper and went back to the sofa.

The telephone rang. I threw myself full length across the bed and grabbed the phone first.

"Hello," I said, very nice.

"Long distance," said a hollow voice. "Calling Mr. Patrick Abbott."

"I'll take it," I said. I gave Patrick a sugary smile. He lit a cigarette. His eyes were still slits.

"Sorry. Personal call for Mr. Abbott," the voice said.

I handed it over, got up, and started to dress. I'd get out of here quick, and not let him know where I was all day. He could do a little worrying about me, for a change. He needed disciplining. I fastened my bra, stepped into my step-ins, and slipped on my slip. I'd be out of this room in about three minutes.

Patrick said, "Hank?—well, hello— Damn glad to hear it— Yes, saw that in the paper— Oh— How about making it lunch?— Two o'clock's fine— Here? Swell— So long."

I sat down to put on my stockings.

Patrick cradled the receiver, walked towards me with his eyes fixed on mine, laid down his cigarette, picked me up, sat down on the bed, and held me firmly on his knees and eyed me hard.

"I love you, darling," he said. I fastened my supporters, with indifference. "But you're an awful fool. I've got to start beating you regularly. It's the only way."

"But, darling—"

He cut in.

"What are you doing today, Jeanie?"

I reconsidered. "Well, that depends on you—"

"Oh. It does, does it? You aren't a free agent?"

"I never said I was."

"Then why do you expect Ellen Bland to be one?"

"But—"

Patrick kissed me. I braced myself hard against weakening.

"Let me tell you what I really know about Ellen. I haven't before. She grew up in a poverty-stricken home. Her father was a lawyer, in a small town, and a good one, but he drank himself out of any business. Her mother died when Ellen was fifteen, and right away her father married again, so Ellen left what they called home and came to New York and went to a hospital, told them she was eighteen and was accepted and took her nurse's training. When she was really eighteen she was finished and on her own." She had even lied about that, I thought. She couldn't get away with it now. Nurses had to be certified. "She fell in love with Louis Bland. Really in love. She wouldn't have married him otherwise. He has charm. The money didn't matter, except she had never had any before. She never quite believed it would keep on coming effortlessly, like that, though. The marriage didn't work, simply because Louis is a liar and a cheat. As well as being a fuss-budget. He has always fooled round with other women, always—it flatters his vanity—but Ellen had notions about a home and kids. She hadn't had any happy childhood herself and she meant that hers should have. Besides, she knew that Louis, even when unfaithful, loved her as much as he had ever loved anyone, or could ever love anyone, with his shallow vain nature. She would stick it out, she decided, till the children were old enough for college, then she would leave him. Now, to go back a bit—I asked you what you were doing today, dear. You said it depended on me.

"Well, Ellen asked herself when she finally lost hope in Louis, what she would do for the next six or seven years, decided it depended on her children, and settled down to put in her time interestingly and progressively until they were grown. She was one of very few of the Americans I knew in Paris who weren't just playing around. She made something of her opportunity. She learned the language, really learned it, and got acquainted with the French. Then along came Hank and presently Ellen fell in love—you know that part. They waited."

"But, darling—five years—six, maybe—"

"They didn't expect that. Ellen thought Louis would marry. He needs women. Men despise him, but women pet and mother him. Then there was Mary Kent, hanging round waiting to take possession of Louis. Ellen felt sure Louis would marry her at once."

"Well, he hasn't."

"Nope. Time has gone by."

"What will happen?"

"Things are happening. Two people are dead."

"But—can't you see? Only Ellen, of them all, would want them dead—those two people—"

"Ellen didn't do it, Jeanie."

"Then who did?"

Patrick's face looked furrowed.

He didn't answer.

"Maybe it was Louis," I said. "He seems so unstable. Maybe he went completely haywire."

Patrick said, "I have always thought that could happen to Louis, and for that reason I've always been afraid, for Ellen. But she isn't afraid. I daresay she knows him better than anyone, though. . . ."

He left it in the air.

"Are Hank and Ellen lovers?" I asked.

"I don't know," Patrick snapped, "and I don't care. That's their business. You ought to know the way I think on that subject by this time, Jean."

"Six years is a long time to wait."

"I'd've waited ten for the woman I wanted, darling."

"Lucky woman."

"Very lucky, though she sometimes forgets it." Patrick said. He kissed me again. "Too bad she's dumb. Now you get dressed and I'll shave in about two shakes and we'll get going. There's things to do."

"Hank got his train, didn't he, dear?"

"Fortunately."

"But who called you last night? And left Laura Gilbert's number?"

"Whoever murdered her, I suspect."

"Hank will have an alibi—if he was on a train?"

"That was why I said *fortunately*."

CHAPTER SIXTEEN

The telephone rang again as we were leaving the room. Patrick ducked back to get it. "That was Louis Bland," he reported, as he joined me along the corridor. "He's downstairs. Again he thinks he needs the services of a detective, meaning me, I believe." I dropped a glove, accidentally, turned to pick it up and saw a short dark man in a brown suit step quickly back behind the angle of the wall where the corridor leading to our room joined the one we were in. There were two such angles between our corner room and the elevators.

"We're being shadowed again, Pat."

"The man in the raincoat?"

"A different one. In a brown suit."

"It must be wonderful to be married to a detective, darling. When he's not frisking other people's joints other detectives are frisking his."

"I don't mind," I said. I didn't. Everything was fine now. I was glad I wasn't having to spend the day alone, mad. I'd tried that a few times since we'd been married, and frankly, it was dull. Also painful. And you felt such a fool afterwards.

Louis Bland stood up from one of the chairs facing the elevators. He was dressed formally in a black overcoat and black Homburg, a white muffler and dark gray gloves. He looked like Esquire.

He was also pale. The darkness of his hair and mustache made contrast with his pallor.

"Good morning," he said, unsmilingly. We said good morning. There was no hand shaking.

"Is there some place where we can talk?"

The pseudo-alcove where I had sat with Mary Kent yesterday morning was not occupied. As we sat down the man in the brown suit left an elevator, and found himself a chair not far away. I signaled Patrick with my eyes that he was the one. He looked brighter, I decided, than the one in the raincoat.

"I've just come from Anna's funeral," Louis said. That explained his clothes. "We had it at ten o'clock, because Mary and I expected to get away this afternoon. At this minute I am supposed to be with my lawyers, winding up my affairs." Louis waved his cigarette-holder. "As I was leaving my hotel, Mary called me about this Gilbert affair. I'm afraid that's going to be pretty nasty for Ellen, Pat?"

It was Pat today. Patrick lifted a polite eyebrow, more or less over things in general, and waited.

"You knew it, of course? It was in the papers. The tabloids used a lot of pictures. The woman was virtually—undressed." Louis's expression evinced distaste. "Most unpleasant, really."

"What's it got to do with you, Bland?"

"For God's sake, Pat! She was the woman we saw with Rawlings. I can't have Ellen's name hauled into this affair. I want you to persuade Ellen to go away, go out West, or to Mexico or South America, anywhere till this thing blows over. She'll listen to you, Pat. We've always liked you. I can't have Ellen and my children dragged into this filthy scandal."

"I don't see why they would be, Bland."

"You must be a fool!"

"I've often suspected I am."

Louis sunk his yellowish teeth in his underlip. "It's the kind of thing that kind of newspaper plays to the limit, Pat. You can't be too careful. Then, there's Clint."

"Clint?"

"Clint sells gossip. He doesn't talk much, but he never misses a thing. He hates me passionately. If he can do anything to harm me and at the same time get paid for it—"

"I thought it was Ellen you were worrying about?"

"Certainly it's Ellen. And the children. Don't you understand? The woman was naked—or practically so. You know what they'll make of that. Something very nasty, to say the least. And Clint will tell them all that old gossip from Paris—"

"Which you were responsible for, Bland."

Louis said, "I made a mistake. I shouldn't have done it. I admit it, now."

"Rather late, isn't it?"

Louis frowned. "Listen, we're wasting time. I'm asking you to go to Ellen and have her go to Clint and offer him anything—I'll pay—to keep his mouth shut."

"I'm under the impression that Clint is rather fond of Ellen, Bland. I don't believe he'd do anything to hurt Ellen."

"Clint will do anything to get money."

Patrick took another tack.

"When was this woman killed?"

Louis shuddered. "How would I know?"

"I assumed you were informed. You see, there's no reason why Rawlings should be tied up with it in any way whatever, aside from the fact that she's an employee. Hank wasn't in New York last night. He left about six o'clock for Washington, so, unless she was murdered before six—"

"Well, maybe she was?"

Patrick made no reply.

Louis began to plead. "I didn't say he did it, Pat. And I'm not asking you to go and talk with Ellen because I think Hank killed her. But you have probably had a lot of experience with murder and that sort of thing. Also, Ellen will listen to you. She likes you. I simply want to get her away—for her own sake—she's indiscreet—she may get herself involved." His voice beseeched. "I don't care what it costs, Pat. You must warn her. She must talk to Clint. We can buy Clint off ourselves. It's urgent. Such papers grab at stories like this, makes people forget the war. You can name your own price. I implore you, for Ellen's sake, Pat."

Patrick stood up and said, dryly, "Ellen ought to enjoy your taking such pains about her reputation at this late date, Bland. I'll talk with Ellen. I don't want your money."

He took my arm. We left Louis and went to the desk. Louis looked after us, appeared about to consider trailing us, then left the hotel.

There were ten or twelve letters, mostly business, none from the Marine Corps, but one from my cousin Peg, who lives in our home town of Elm Hill, Illinois. While I was reading it, Patrick picked up a couple of packets of cigarettes and a couple of tabloid newspapers, joined me, and suggested we have a drink. "That's what idleness will do to you, drinking in the morning," I said. We sat down at our pet table. I ordered coffee.

"Two coffees," Patrick said. He handed me one of the newspapers. They both had the same picture on the front, a photograph of Laura Gilbert in a semi-reclining position on a sofa. Her face was turned away half-hidden as it rested against the curve of one arm. The other arm hung gracefully, the fingers curved just a little. Her white robe had fallen open a little, disclosing the long line of a lovely leg from the thigh to the ankle. She might have been posed alive for the photograph.

"I'd hardly call that naked," I said.

"If I were allowed to mention Paris and the French," Patrick said, "I might remark that in *that* place *those* people would consider the photograph a thing of beauty, not depravity. As a detective I admire its novelty. Death seldom leaves the victim so gracefully posed."

"I feel badly that I spoke unkindly of her, Pat."

"You should. A girl can be made for love just the same as for hammering a typewriter. According to the French. Besides, she may have been just a good secretary."

The headlines in both papers said Beautiful Secretary Murdered. The copy, though slightly aflame, told no more than we had read in the conservative paper upstairs.

Our coffee had just been served when Mary Kent walked in. She came directly to our table. She wore blue, and the mink jacket. Patrick seated her and asked her to have something to drink. She declined.

"Louis phoned me that he had seen you here. I was just leaving my hotel and I decided to drop by and add my plea to his." She smiled rather wistfully. "I suppose you think it's queer that I want to help Ellen. Well, I don't. If Ellen is dragged into this awful business, it's her own fault. I don't want Louis to worry, that's all."

"But why come to me? His lawyers ought to know what to do," Patrick said.

Mary Kent's fingers stole after her cigarette.

"Maybe. Maybe not. They're the poky kind that deal only with money. Listen to me, Pat, you're clever, you can think of something—and at least you can talk to Ellen, she adores you, and so does Hank. You're the one. You could do more than any lawyer or doctor or anybody else. Talk to them both. Persuade them to get married at once and go away. Ellen could go to Washington."

Patrick just sat, as if waiting for her to go on.

Mary Kent set her small definite chin.

"You don't know Clint Moran. He hates Louis like poison. He thinks he should have some of Louis's money. It has something to do with their parents. He thinks Louis's father practically stole his mother's money, which is nonsense, of course, but Clint makes his living now partly by selling little bits to the tabloids and he's not going to pass this up. If he does, it will be because he's intending to blackmail Louis instead."

"Maybe he's sold his story already," Patrick said.

"Maybe he doesn't know about it yet. There's a chance. Clint never gets up before two or three in the afternoon. Then there's Daphne. She's not above picking up a little spare cash herself."

Patrick said, "If Hank and Ellen would get married, Louis would marry you, wouldn't he?"

Her round eyes flickered dangerously. "One other thing. Louis is too frantic over this business, too unnecessarily so. He's likely to make it worse himself, talking. The whole thing's too utterly mad really. If Ellen had married Hank years ago everything would have been all right for everybody." She bit her lips. "If you want me to up Louis's fee—whatever he offered—"

"You and Louis always think in terms of money, Mary. I don't want a fee and I am not going to mind Ellen and Hank's affairs just to accommodate you and Louis."

"You're being unkind, Pat."

"I'm sorry, Mary," Patrick said. "By the way, what is wrong with Louis's health?"

"Wrong?" She was about to pretend ignorance, then she thought better of it and said, with a deprecatory gesture, "Why, it's nerves, mostly, from worry and one thing or another. I don't think you realize what a trial this awful business has been for Louis. He always puts his worst foot forward, really. Louis has never been too well, I think—that was how Ellen got him to start with—by being a nurse."

Patrick said, "It isn't his heart, is it, Mary?"

"I mustn't talk about it, Pat. There's no reason—but I've promised."

"That's reason enough," Patrick said.

Mary Kent smiled appreciatively, and then stubbed out her cigarette and said,

"Now, to get back to Ellen. If we could persuade her to marry Hank it would really make everything right."

Patrick's frown stopped her.

He got up and left us. Mary Kent said, "I do hope Pat will talk with Ellen, Jean. But I don't want him to do it for nothing."

"Neither do I," I admitted frankly. "But I don't know anything I could do to prevent it. If he wanted to, I mean."

"But he will try to reason with her?"

"Honestly, I don't know."

Mary Kent said, "That's a lovely emerald."

"Thank you," I said.

"I can't wear emeralds. They're too awful, with my coloring. I do adore them, too."

We went on making that kind of talk till Patrick came back.

"I rang up Ellen. We'll go right over, Jean."

Mary Kent said, "That's sweet of you, Pat. I knew you'd do it. After all, it's for her sake as well as mine. If you change your mind you can name your own price, Pat."

Patrick made no answer. He had treated her rudely and for that reason I felt rather guilty, but I knew it was because he hates getting mixed up in people's troubles, in spite of always being mixed up in them. We parted with her at the entrance of the hotel. She took one cab and we another, which left our current shadow, the man in brown, standing cabless in the rain. Everything dripped from the rain. The dampness made the cab smell like fish. New York was a seaport, I remembered. I wondered if I would get to see the sea.

"We've lost our sleuth," I said.

"The way these New York police waste money. They've probably got a tail on everybody remotely connected with Anna Forbes."

"What about Laura Gilbert? Are you worried, I mean?"

"There may be no reason to connect the two murders, Jean. Provided Louis doesn't give the police the idea."

"We'll have to tell Dorn that they need only to have you watched, dear. Everything clears through the Abbotts at the Hotel Rexley."

Patrick grinned at me slantwise.

"By the way, Jean, what did we do last night?"

"Why?"

"Go ahead. Tell me."

"We had dinner at a French restaurant, saw a French picture, had coffee in a drugstore, and went back to the hotel."

"At what time?"

"Twelve-five."

"Then what?"

"Well, first you had a message saying to call Hank Rawlings."

"Just forget that part, for the moment."

"Don't you want the police to know?"

"They'll know. I want to do any talking that we do, that's all. Listen, Hank isn't mixed up in this . . . you know that, don't you?"

A youngish woman in a blue uniform opened the door. Ellen was waiting for us in the drawing room.

CHAPTER SEVENTEEN

Already the old-fashioned drawing room looked less drawing-roomish. There was a jolly sort of fire. A great jar of red tulips stood on the ebony piano. There were magazines on the coffee table and the paper knife in its Florentine sheath was lying carelessly on the mantel. There were ashes in the ashtrays. A little of such amiable carelessness changed the whole room—for the better, I thought.

Ellen was alone. She sat on the sofa with her back to the window knitting on a navy sweater for the Red Cross. She sat very straight with her elegant head bent only a little over a task she could look at or not, as she chose.

We sat down on the other sofa.

"You've been on my mind all morning," Ellen said, in that wonderful voice. "I've been dying to call you, Pat, but I hadn't the nerve, after what I got you into the other night. But I'm terribly worried over Sue."

"Sue?" Patrick barked.

Ellen stopped knitting. "Didn't Dick call you, Pat?"

"I did the calling. Dick answered. I asked to come, and Dick said to come on over."

Ellen resumed her knitting. She was smiling.

"I thought Dick had called you and then told me that you did the calling because he knew I was reluctant to ask you to help us again. Dick does things like that. He is a very sweet person."

"What about Sue?"

"She's gone away. She left in the night. She left a note saying we were to let her alone, and that she wasn't marrying Bill Reynolds or anybody else and would get in touch with us when she was ready. Said she wanted to think."

"Sue has a job, you said. Phoned there?"

Ellen nodded her dark head.

"Dick called her office. She's there."

"Oh, I hope she and Bill haven't quarreled?" I said.

Ellen said, "I'm afraid they have, and I'm sorry. I should like them to marry. I thought they would. Sue usually does what she likes and her father eventually gives in. This time he seems to have made an impression."

"She worrying about the family taint?" Patrick asked.

Ellen dropped her knitting. "Who told you about that, Pat? Not that there's anything in it. It's absurd. Susan is as healthy as a cabbage."

Patrick lit a cigarette and said, "If she thought Louis was fooling, why didn't she go to Dr. Seward?"

Ellen's eyes were inscrutable.

"She did. He was quite unnecessarily vague, in my opinion. He's afraid he'll make Louis mad. After all, Louis is his best patient, in this family, so he's taking no chances. Louis makes fabulous doctor bills. When Sue saw Dr. Seward, he hemmed and hawed and told her she was too young to marry anyway and to wait, which is what Louis has told him to tell her, of course. I talked to her afterwards—but she's so upset." Ellen went on knitting. "She'll be all right. Sue gets over things quickly. She has such good sense."

"After all, a bad heart needn't be hereditary," Patrick commented. Ellen gave Patrick a puzzled look. "Digitalis is rather a dangerous drug, however."

Ellen stopped knitting.

"Digitalis? Who said anything about that?"

"I thought Louis carried a hypo filled with digitalis? For emergency use?"

Ellen's eyelids dropped. "Oh," she said. "That." She went on knitting.

She began talking lightly. "Louis isn't so ill as he imagines he is, and he never was, but you can't argue him out of his obsession, Pat. I tried, goodness knows. But I hate having him impose his phobias on the children. Anyhow, if you see Sue, and it's not too much trouble, give her a good sensible talking-to. She'll take it, from you."

"Okay," Patrick said. "Tell me more about Louis, Ellen."

"There isn't any more. It's mostly in his mind. If Louis were really as ill as he thinks he would have burst some blood vessels in his tantrums and died of it long ago."

Patrick gave Ellen a thoughtful glance and was silent for a moment. "I think we can forget Sue temporarily, Ellen," he said then. "I want to talk about that murder last night." Ellen looked up, but knitted. "Hank's secretary." Ellen's hands faltered, then knitted on. "You knew about it, of course?"

"Yes. Hank called me, from Washington. He's so disturbed."

"He shouldn't have done that, Ellen."

"You mean, because of Louis? My dear, Anna is no longer here to carry tales. Hank or anyone else can telephone me any time they like."

"Who's your new maid?"

"She's temporary. The regular housemaid couldn't come today, so—"

"So the police provided you with one?"

"The police?"

"Your regular maid is probably under orders to stay at home. This one may be a detective. Ellen—but just forget all that for a minute, will you, and tell me what you did after leaving Hank at his place the other night? The night we found Anna Forbes dead."

Ellen said nothing for a moment, then she said stubbornly, "I didn't tell you I left Hank at his place, Pat?"

"No. You didn't. You gave me the impression, perhaps unintentionally, that you came home after having dinner with Hank, went to bed, and got up at three-thirty when the kids hadn't come in, and came over to see if we knew anything about them. As a matter of fact you dropped Hank from a taxi at his place at one-thirty, then you took a ride in the park by yourself, because you were worrying about something. You got out at the corner of Fifty-sixth and Fifth Avenue at about 2 A. M. Then what?"

Ellen had flushed an angry pink, but she knitted right on. "Why don't you tell me, Pat? You seem very well informed."

Patrick said, "See here, Ellen, I got that information from the police. They have gone to a good deal of trouble to find out what we've all been doing lately. They think you know more than you're telling about Anna Forbes's murder."

"She couldn't have been murdered," Ellen said indignantly. "Who would do it? Why? I'll never believe that. Never."

Her knitting lay now on her lap.

"The police believe she was murdered, Ellen. Remember that. And they found a hypodermic on the rug which, though she wasn't poisoned, they think the murderer dropped. You were once a trained nurse. The police didn't show you the hypo, did they, Ellen?" She shook her head. The information obviously surprised her. Or did it? "They think you'd be the only one in the family likely to know how to use a hypodermic."

"That's silly. Anyone can do it, Pat."

"Sure. But usually anyone doesn't. What did you do from two o'clock till three-thirty, Ellen?"

Ellen's face was pensive.

"Do you think I killed her, Pat?"

"You know I don't, Ellen."

Ellen bit at her lip. Then she spoke resolutely and fully.

"All right. I was upset. That night, Hank and I quarreled. We never had, before. We met for dinner, as I told you, and after we had dinner we went to a nightclub, a quiet little place in the village. Hank was tired. Hank said a few angry things and I said a few. I wanted to get married, you see, when I got back two years ago. I didn't tell you that. Hank was for it—but I wanted to keep it secret, because of Dick, and Hank wouldn't do that, then he went to Washington and when we meet—when we do meet—we always discuss the thing, but this time we both got angry. Also, Mary Kent had got under my skin with the things she said about that girl. I felt jealous. Hank said it was nonsense, that she trots around everywhere he does when he's here, because they have to get so much done in such short time, and they were working with somebody in an office near the Stork Club and when they got finished he bought the girl a drink. I think I was pretty small, really, about the whole thing. But I couldn't admit it then, and afterwards I took the ride in the Park alone to get it out of my system. I dismissed the cab at Fifty-sixth and Fifth simply because I hadn't money enough in my purse to drive on to our house and still give the man a tip."

Patrick grinned and Ellen laughed and said, "I walked along Fifty-sixth, saw Reuben's, went in and telephoned Hank. To apologize. Clint Moran was in there, at the bar. He bought me a cup of coffee. He offered to take me home but he couldn't have walked half a block, in his condition, so I finally went on by myself. When I got to the house, I went directly up to my room, then looked in on the kids. They were both out, and I got anxious, and came to you."

"What time was that?"

"A little after three. I came right to you. I must have stayed an hour at Reuben's."

"Was there a key in the door when you got to the house?"

"Yes. There was. I think that key was my own key, Pat. I've thought about it a lot. I think I left it in the door myself."

"Don't you know?"

"I always have several. Dick loses them places."

"Then what happened to Louis's key?"

"He could have been mistaken. He's got three keys himself. I know that key business seems queer to you, Pat, and also the fact that I went up and fixed my bed so that the police would think I had been in it, would seem odd, to you, but it was because I didn't want to have to do any talking about my having stayed out like that. Even Clint doesn't know I had just left Hank. How did you know, Pat?"

Patrick said, "A doorman. A taxicab driver. A police detective. There is always someone. You and Hank had better get married pronto, if you're going to, and cut out this foolishness. Just at the moment, however, you'd better keep away from Hank. Somebody wants badly to get Hank accused of his secretary's murder."

Ellen took the information without a ripple.

"But Hank had nothing to do with it?"

"Of course not. He was on a train when it happened."

Ellen sat, very still, her eyebrows in a line.

"The lights weren't on, or the window open, when you got home that night?"

"Oh, no. I would have looked in the drawing room, in that case. I would have turned them out."

"Ellen, may I see *The Pink Umbrella?*"

Ellen's face was a mask for a moment, then she said, "Why, of course. But it's not here just now. I sent it out to a framer."

"Wha-t?"

"For heaven's sake, Pat? Don't look at me like that. One corner of the frame was sprung a little. It had had a fall, I think. I found it on the floor by the window there, when we came from the Rexley and—found Anna."

"Does it have a heavy frame?"

"Very heavy. It must have had quite a fall. It's a handmade wooden frame. The corners were mortised. The man who made it was a fine cabinetmaker in Paris."

"How big is it?"

"Oh—about eighteen inches by maybe twenty-four—in all. It's a small picture really."

Someone tapped.

Dick came in. His skin looked fresh and his great eyes velvety dark. He shook hands with us, kissed his mother, then brought an ottoman which he straddled, his long legs drawn up so that his knees were near his chin.

"This dump isn't bad now, is it, Pat?" he inquired. "Quite human, in fact."

"Dick!" Ellen said.

"I'm new generation, Mums. We say what we think. She's dead and I'm glad of it. Listen, Pat, before you go, I wish you would come up to my digs a minute. I want to show you something."

"You mustn't bother Pat, Dick," Ellen demurred, quickly. But Pat wanted to go. Ellen tried again to prevent it, but he went along upstairs with Dick.

"What a darling boy Dick is, Ellen!" I said.

Her eyes glowed. "Yes. He's a wonderful boy. Dick's going through a phase. He'll be all right. I shall never regret any little sacrifice I've made for Dick." She looked nervous again, clasping and unclasping her hands. "Pat's got me worried," she said then. "Oh, I shall be so glad when Louis and those people he goes about with no longer come to our house. It won't be this house, either. They're a lawless, shiftless crowd, all of them. They make constant confusion and unhappiness. I am fond of Clint. What he is, he can't help, but he isn't malicious, like those others."

"He isn't?" I asked, remembering the piano-playing.

"I should qualify that a little. Clint never forgets or forgives an injury, and he thinks Louis did him wrong. As a matter of fact, Clint is himself much to blame for his own troubles. He ran through with his money and, like the others, he sank a lot in German munitions—it's astonishing how many silly people did that, they were so sure this country would never get into war, and that Germany would win quickly in Europe. I frankly don't know what will become of poor Clint."

I hazarded a question on my own. "Ellen, are you worried about Hank? Because of this Gilbert murder?"

"Of course not. Why?"

"We saw them yesterday. Having coffee." I told her where. She said yes, that was near the office where they had been having conferences with somebody. I said, "I saw her face. I thought she looked as if she were in love with Hank. Patrick hooted, but—oh, I shouldn't tell you this, Ellen?"

"But why not? It's a pity, that's all. To love somebody—and not be loved—"

She must be awfully sure of him. I was sorry I had mentioned it. Patrick and Dick returned.

Patrick didn't sit down, so I stood up, to go. Ellen rose. Patrick asked, "Where were you last night? Both of you? All night? Just in case it is something I should know."

"I was in my room from dusk till dawn," Dick said. "Hitting the pillow hard, fella."

Ellen said, smiling, "I spent the evening in this room. I had a fire and read till about eleven. I read in bed, later. I heard Susan go downstairs when she left the house. It was then half-past eleven. I didn't realize that she left the house, however. I didn't hear the front door open or close. My window was closed, because of the haze—it was thick last night and odorous."

"It stank," Dick put in.

"I didn't know that Sue had left us till the new maid this morning brought up the note she left on the newel post, saying she had gone and not to try to find her, that she would come back when she was ready."

"You kept the note?"

"No, I burned it. I never keep anything, Pat."

"Except *The Pink Umbrella*."

Ellen's smile was wan. "Yes. That. Now, what else? Well, Dick went to sleep with his light on. I went upstairs about one, or perhaps it was a little before, and turned it out. He was sleeping like a baby. It didn't occur to me to look in on Sue. Her door was dark. I supposed she was in bed, asleep, but of course, she was gone then."

"Did you see Hank at all yesterday, Ellen?"

"No."

"Did you talk to him?"

Ellen hesitated. "Yes, I did. I called him at his office, along in the afternoon, quite late—a little after five. He said he'd been away from the office for a couple of hours and had stopped in to pick up a briefcase, and that he was catching a train which left about six."

The new maid tapped, and admitted Daphne Garnett.

"Why, hello-a!" she squealed. She kissed Ellen. "What fun you're all here. I'm giving a party tonight at Clint's new place, where he's playing, you know. Now don't say it's no time for a party, Ellen, it's just ourselves, and dinner, in a cozy little French place, nothing that isn't all right to go to even though you have just had a funeral in the family, only she isn't in the family, of course."

Daphne rattled on.

The new maid was hanging about, emptying ashtrays, keeping her ears wide open. We accepted the invitation as vaguely as it was given and left Daphne rattling. Dick ran down to let us out the door. By that time, the new maid was hovering in the lower hall.

CHAPTER EIGHTEEN

The rain was still falling. It came down straight and thick and gray and drearily unending. We were lucky and picked up a cruising taxi. I saw the mousy man then, standing a little way east of the Bland house. Our man in brown had his coat collar up and his hat-brim down and stood bracing himself against the rain a little way west. I felt sorry for them. What a job! When we passed, the one in brown tried frantically to get another cab. We drove on, leaving him dashing around.

"What did Dick want, Pat?"

Patrick grinned.

"He wanted me to keep an eye on his mother. Said he had something to show me—which was a ruse to get me alone, that's all."

I said, with the old acid I had vowed to abandon, "You Ellen-protectors ought to form a club." Patrick made no reply. I said, "I'm sorry. She's just as worried about Dick as he is about her, I guess. Maybe they've got one of those complexes."

"If Dick comes out okay she will think it's all been worth it, chum."

"I suppose so. She spoke about Clint. She likes Clint."

"Ellen is kind."

"Yes, I suppose she is. I think Clint's a dilly, but I didn't say so. I'd like to see that *Pink Umbrella*."

"And I. Dumb of me not to think of that before this."

The red stopped us at Madison. "Ellen never tells quite all the truth, Pat."

"She does when it's necessary. After all, people who tell every little thing are tiresome."

"That key business, Pat."

"Um-m."

"She didn't fall for your sly delving after the family taint?"

"She's covering up for the kids. Also, in a way, for Louis. If she made a promise, hating him wouldn't alter it—not with Ellen."

"It's all very silly, really."

"Very." Patrick gave me a look. "I take it you refer to the taint?"

I said I did. The taxi moved on in the rain.

"The ones I am really concerned about are Sue and Bill. I don't want them broken up. I guess I'm being romantic but I hate to have kids like that all worried and all by their parents' troubles. Why don't you go see Dr. Seward, Pat? He might fix things."

"Maybe I will."

"Won't he have to tell the police?"

"Maybe. If they ask. Maybe, it isn't important, darling. Skip it, for the moment."

"It's the kind of thing that haunts you, but I'll try."

We got stopped again at Fifth Avenue. I put my head on Pat's shoulder and said that traffic lights were wonderful since it was about the only chance you had in peace and quiet when abroad with your boyfriend in New York. He kissed me. I remembered where we were, and looked out. A lot of people, under umbrellas, were staring at us from the sidewalk. I giggled and said I hoped Patrolman Goldberg wasn't in the crowd.

There was a traffic jam somewhere and we went on sitting there for five minutes, in the rain.

"I was glad of a chance to see Dick's rooms, Jean. They are Louis's rooms really. Old Anna never changed a thing. Dick came back from France with nothing, so he hadn't any stuff of his own to put in there either. There's a lot of medical books. Louis Bland is hardly the type who would take an interest in medicine with the idea of being useful to mankind. I assume he was always agitated about his health. He kept scrapbooks, of any printed items about himself. Some of the clippings were starred with red ink. One of these was a little piece about his going to the hospital to have a tooth extracted."

"The hospital, for a tooth?"

"He loves hospitals. He went once for a scraped kneecap, and once when he cut himself on a test-tube in a lab. There was a photo of Louis having a blood transfusion once—it bristled with nurses. There were circles of red ink around that one."

"He liked nurses, then?"

"Maybe. But who doesn't? That's not it. Any of his injuries may have been serious, though. You can die from a pinprick, of course."

It was one-thirty when we got to the hotel. Hank wasn't due until two.

Mary Kent was waiting just inside the main lobby. She hurried towards us.

"You talked with Ellen?" she asked. "What happened?"

"I didn't ask you to wait, did I, Mary?" Patrick said.

It made her angry. "I didn't wait! I came back. I've heard something. I am still debating if I should tell you. I don't want to make trouble for Hank." We didn't sit down. We stood, while she talked. "I don't care for Hank. Studious men bore me. But I don't want to do him any harm, and this might, but I must tell it to you. I must."

Patrick glanced at his watch. She took notice of it and spoke faster, and in a lowered tone. "Hank and that Gilbert woman had dinner at Schraffts' last night, Pat."

Patrick cocked an eyebrow.

"Sounds like an innocent place for a rendezvous, Mary."

"It wasn't a rendezvous. I don't know—but I didn't say that. It's not the place that matters, but the time. You said Hank left for Washington at six o'clock. He didn't. They were seen eating dinner together at Schraffts' at a quarter past eight."

"There are lots of Schraffts', aren't there?" Patrick said.

"It was the one on Forty-second, near Lexington."

"Who saw them?" Patrick asked.

"I can't tell you."

"Then it's no good. Anyway, it was probably somebody else."

"It wasn't anybody else. It was Hank and that woman."

Patrick took my arm. "If that's all, Mary—"

She put her hand on his sleeve. "All right, if I must tell you, I will, but you must promise me never to tell. Daphne Garnett saw them. She knows Hank by sight and she remembered the girl from the Stork Club. Of course, Hank didn't have anything to do with her murder, but why did he tell you he was on a train when he was here all the time?"

Patrick said coldly, "Just why are you telling me this, Mary?"

"You know why. Put yourself in Ellen's place, if you can. At least your wife can, and she will know how Ellen must have felt if Hank had told her he was leaving town on a six o'clock train and then was with this woman instead. I would certainly ask for some kind of showdown myself. Any woman would. I would go to the woman. Any woman would."

Patrick appeared to think about it.

"If it were a tête-à-tête, why would they go to Schraffts'?"

"Why not? Nobody they'd know goes to that one at night. It's a busy place at noon and anybody is likely to be there, but at night, no one—no one Hank is likely to know—would likely be there. It's a good place at night for people who don't want to be seen."

"Yet Daphne was there?"

"She was trying to find Clint Moran. She went to his rooming-house, which is just off Forty-second on Third Avenue, and she walked back towards Lexington trying to get a cab—you know how scarce they are—and she got hungry and went into Schraffts'. It was too unbelievably lucky that she saw them. It always seems to happen when people are trying not to be seen."

Patrick said, "We saw Daphne last night. She didn't mention seeing Hank."

"I know about that. She was taken up just then getting Clint to a new job. She didn't succeed, either. He stepped out of the taxi when they stopped for a red light somewhere and vanished. Daphne was frantic. She went to the restaurant and talked them into giving him another chance—tonight—but I must say I don't know why she bothers. I'll run along. I thought, after what we had said, I ought to tell you, Pat."

"Thank you," Patrick said.

We went into the Grill. It seemed cozy and warm after the rain. We had barely got seated when the man in the brown suit came in and sat down at a table on the other side of the bar.

Patrick had Scotch. I tried their daiquiri.

"So now Hank's lying," I said.

"What makes you think that?"

"Didn't he tell you he was on a train?"

"He said he was catching one. He didn't say on the phone this morning that he didn't catch the six o'clock. Maybe he didn't. We'll soon know."

"How?"

"He'll be here. I'll ask. Mary Kent might be lying, instead. Or Daphne might have been wrong, it may have been other people."

"No one else looks like Hank. And any woman would remember that girl, darling."

"Mary certainly goes out of her way to make trouble for Ellen," Patrick said.

I said, "Pat, you're getting set in your ways, specially in your way of thinking. You've made up your mind in advance that neither Ellen nor Hank could commit a murder and you can't budge. A good detective should have a fluid sort of mind, which would flow hither and thither and not settle on anything special until everything and everybody has been thoroughly investigated. Don't laugh. You're prejudiced for your friends though, and you know it."

Hank came in from the lobby, saw us, waved, and hurried over, walking too fast, as usual.

I slid a look at our sleuth. He was signaling with his eyes at someone out of sight behind a pillar, around which shelves held beer steins. I leaned back in my chair to see if I could see the other one. I got a partial glimpse of the angelic face of Lieutenant Jeffrey Dorn.

Hank looked haggard enough to have done a dozen murders. His face looked thinner, from concern, and gray, and his eyes twice as large. He sat down and asked for Scotch and then got right into his story, except that it began with his having a wire at his Washington Hotel when he'd got there this morning telling him of the murder of his secretary. "I blame myself," he declared. "I think I know why she was murdered."

Patrick made him order lunch before he would let him talk. A good many of the luncheon patrons had left the room, but Dorn remained, more or less invisible in his corner beyond the beer-steins, and the one in brown was taking his time over his meal.

"That's why I wanted to see you, Pat. I was afraid Louis's diseased brain would try to make something out of Mrs. Gilbert's murder. I'll tell you why in a minute. But I must tell you first what I think really happened. I think somebody went to Mrs. Gilbert's apartment to bully her into telling what she knew about that job we were on last night and it ended in her death."

Patrick interrupted him.

"Wait a minute, Hank. Why didn't you take the six o'clock train?"

"Because of what I've just been telling you. A job."

Patrick frowned. "You'd better begin—begin where we left off last night. You called our room. You said you were catching a train."

"And so I was. I was on my way then, had only to pick up my bag at my apartment." The waiter brought the food, steaks from the grill, French-fried potatoes, new peas, and hot rolls. He served, and went away. "I'll tell you why I came here last night, which is why I got the idea that Louis might also start meddling. The police were nosing around my place yesterday asking questions of the doorman and he got scared that he had said too much and he told me he had told them about Ellen's being at my place in the cab when we came up from the Village night before last. It seemed funny that they were asking questions about Ellen. I thought that it had to do with that Anna Forbes affair and thought maybe Louis had started it. You know Louis. I thought it wouldn't go any further, but Louis Bland is likely to do anything, so that's why I asked you to look after Ellen. So much for that."

Hank was warming up, his eyes intense. "I did intend to take that train. I was using the B. & O., they've got bus stations all over town, as you may know, which carry passengers to the railroad terminal in Jersey City. I usually take the bus from the Rockefeller Center station. I took a cab from here, picked up my bag at my place, and went on to the station. There was a message for me there, saying to call the office. I just had time to ring up. Mrs. Gilbert was still at the office. She said some material we had been waiting for had just come in by special messen-

ger and wanted to know if she should send it on to Washington. There are several
trains to Washington during the evening, so I said I'd come back to the office, see
what had to be done, and take the eight o'clock train. There's another bus station,
the main one, on Forty-second near Lexington. I took my bag there, left it in the
checkroom, and went to my office, in the Shandon Building on Pershing Square.
Mrs. Gilbert was still there. I was glad I had come back. The material required
immediate action, so we got right at it. Mrs. Gilbert's a good egg, will do anything, doesn't mind overtime, or anything else—I should say *was* and *didn't*, I
guess—so, excepting the half-hour we took out for dinner, we worked straight
through till eleven-thirty. Then I took a cab to the P.O. at Thirty-fourth and Eighth—
there are nearer ones but we were sure that one would be open—sent the stuff off,
drove back, dropped Mrs. G., and got the midnight train."

"You dropped Mrs. Gilbert? Where?"

"At her apartment. She went with me to the post office. Took down a couple of
letters en route."

"Did you take her into her apartment?"

"Nope. I didn't even get out of the cab."

"Did you see anybody suspicious, or anything?"

"Nothing. It didn't occur to me to see the girl into her house. It's a walk-up. I
was so tired I couldn't have been polite if I had thought of it."

"Eat your lunch, Hank," I said.

He gave me a surprised glance, as if he had forgotten I was there, and picked up
his knife and fork. A little time went by. Dorn was still in the room, and so was the
other one. Hank bolted his food.

Patrick said, "You went on in the same cab to the station, then?" Hank nodded.
"How much time did you have before your bus left?"

"I had exactly ten minutes. It was five minutes to twelve when I paid off the
taxi and walked into the station. The bus leaves at twelve-five. I got my bag from
the checkroom and went directly out to the bus. Do you know the arrangements
there? The busses come in at the back of the station which is on Forty-first Street.
But the waiting room is on Forty-second Street."

"Then you had nine or ten minutes to wait before your bus went out. Sit in the
bus all the time?"

"No, I didn't. After I got settled, I decided to ring up my brother and tell him
about the job we'd just got done. I came back to the waiting room and dialed his
apartment but got no answer. So I went back again to the bus."

"What time did you call your brother?"

"I don't know exactly. About midnight, I should guess."

"You didn't phone me here, did you, Hank?"

"You? Of course not. Why?"

Patrick let it go. "See anybody you knew around the station or anywhere last
night?"

"Not a soul. Oh, I know some of the railroad people to say hello to. Why?"

"Did you register your letters at the post office?"

"Yes. Why all the questions?"

"I want to have it all straight, just in case. Mrs. Gilbert go into the post office with you?"

"No. She waited in the cab."

"Where is her apartment?"

"I don't know the number. It's on Fortieth Street, just east of Park."

"Listen, Hank, what's Mrs. Gilbert's phone number?"

"God, how should I know? Why?"

"Let him alone till he finishes eating, Pat," I said. "He looks half-starved."

"Go ahead and eat, Hank," Patrick said. He took out an envelope and wrote something down. When Hank had stowed away his lunch to my satisfaction and we had ordered our dessert and coffee, Patrick showed Hank what he had written. I could see it, too. It was, "Mr. Henry Rawlings called and wants you to call him at Murray Hill 7-9132. Urgent."

Hank looked entirely blank.

Patrick said, "That's her number. That call came in here last night at two minutes past twelve, while you were still in the bus station, Hank. I think Mrs. Gilbert was dead then." Hank turned pale. "She was wearing a robe of some kind when she was murdered. There were pictures—you may have seen them?—taken after she was dead. Say you dropped her at ten minutes to twelve—is that about right?" Hank nodded. "She went to her apartment, got into the robe, and then admitted the murderer—unless he was there when she got there, which she didn't know, or unless he or she was a friend, an intimate friend, so that she would go right ahead and get out of her clothes and into that robe. What do you know about her, Hank?"

"Nothing. And that's the truth. She's worked for us about a year. I understood she was divorced."

"Was she in love with you, Hank?"

"Good Cod, no! She was just a sweet, motherly—"

"Motherly?" I exclaimed.

"Sure she was. She was always doing nice things for people in the office, little thoughtful things." Hank's fingers worked together. "She rather overdid it, I think. That made her a good employee—she'd work herself to a bone if you asked her to. Listen, how did we get into all this? I told you what I thought happened, and if you think it's a case for the FBI—"

"If it is, they'll know it by this time, Hank."

"What time did that woman find her—the one across the hall? I saw that in the papers."

"I don't know exactly. I think I'm going to learn very soon, however. We are practically surrounded with policemen at this minute. They'll know about the phone call last night, and about your calling here this morning, and about your calling Ellen from Washington." Hank's brows went together. "Ellen told me about that. We've just been there. Ellen is not unduly alarmed for you, Hank, but I must say I'm delighted about your alibi. I got rather a scare a few minutes ago when I heard you didn't take the six o'clock train."

"Scare? You don't think I—"

"No, but other people might."

"I'm going straight to the police."

"You haven't far to go," Patrick said.

"Clint!" I exclaimed suddenly, a few minutes later. Hank had left us.

"What about Clint?" Patrick asked.

"I just remembered how he played the Love-Death motif from *Tristan* whenever Louis talked—there at Ellen's. What did it mean?"

"For God's sake!" Patrick answered, completely exasperated.

CHAPTER NINETEEN

"What would it mean?" Patrick asked, presently. I said maybe it portended something, the way the motif did in the opera, creeping in and creepily foreshadowing tragedy and death for the lovers. Patrick said I was romantic. Of course, he said, teasingly however, if it were Louis or Mary Kent who was dead, instead of Anna Forbes and Laura Gilbert, there might be something in it. I said anyhow Clint was a dilly and would bear watching. Patrick flinched. He asked what dilly meant and I said I hoped it didn't mean anything because in that case you could use it to mean anything, and he said he thought I had something there only maybe a lot of people wouldn't appreciate it. Thus our talk was light, but covering up anything but lightness, because Patrick was deeply alarmed for Hank and Ellen.

"Neither of them know how to look out for themselves," he said.

The man in the brown suit still sat in the Grill when we left but Lieutenant Dorn had vanished, having gone out, I supposed, by the exit from the restaurant directly into the street.

In the elevator on our way up to our room, I was still thinking about Clint Moran. "I feel sorry for him, Pat. You know who. He's a queer guy, but having no money, and running around with that crowd with all their money and idleness—well, that's sad." Patrick said that what I was saying didn't mean I knew who was guilty of what, and I said, of course not, but it did make me sorry for him. I asked how old he was and Patrick said he guessed around forty and since that seems a very sad age to me, I got consequently sadder. In the corridor leading away from the elevators, I said, "Anyhow, Clint might know something. He must hear a lot more than most people, with such sensitive ears. Why don't we talk to him?"

"We could try," Patrick said. I could see he wasn't taking it very seriously though. "If you can dig anything out of Clint, Jeanie, you're the first, and if you do get something and can figure out what you've got, it could be, quite possibly, a clue."

He was poking fun at me. I let it ride, but said, "Anyhow, I do feel sorry for him." I was certain of that at least.

The corridor branched and we turned right and saw, standing near our door, Lieutenant Jeffrey Dorn. The police-detective wore another gray suit, a blue shirt, and another necktie with plenty of blue in it. His blond hair looked crisply wavy as he took off his gray felt hat.

His smile was plump and venomous.

"Good afternoon," he said. We said hello. "Thought you would come up," Dorn said. "Saw you in the Grill. Bad place to talk—too many people. May I come in?" He was already in. Patrick had unlocked the door and Dorn had entered on my heels, talking. He went through the motions, however, asked if he might sit down, meanwhile sitting, and if he might smoke, having already bitten off the tip of his cigar and accepted Patrick's light. Dorn chose the dark-blue chair he had sat in yesterday. Patrick again sprawled on the sofa. I went to the dressing table, after dropping my hat and jacket, and hoping it annoyed Dorn to see women brush their hair, I brushed my hair. He paid no notice.

"Got the idea somehow that you might know something about the secretary-murder, Mr. Abbott."

"Only what I saw in the papers, Lieutenant."

"Rawlings wouldn't have mentioned it, of course?"

"Naturally he mentioned it. That's why he's here. He plans to go straight to the police."

"But he came to you first, Mr. Abbott?"

"Yes," Patrick said. "But you could have stopped him."

Dorn waited a moment, then said, "I suppose he told you what he did last night?"

Patrick lit a cigarette, his long, narrow eyes lifted slantwise to Dorn's. "Sure."

"You don't have to tell us, Mr. Abbott. We know."

"Naturally. You would."

Lieutenant Dorn leaned back in his chair. "We didn't have a tail on Rawlings, as it happened, because we didn't connect him with the first murder—the Anna Forbes murder."

"Why should you?" Patrick asked, casually.

Dorn smiled. "We don't. Directly. And we didn't anticipate the Gilbert woman's murder, either. We were very short-sighted, I'm afraid."

Patrick smoked in silence.

Dorn said, "Seems that Rawlings has been seeing quite a lot of his secretary. Perhaps that could account for Mrs. Bland's being so worried, when she took that ride by herself in the park the other night?"

Patrick merely listened.

Dorn said, "Perhaps Rawlings promised her he wouldn't see the woman, then slipped up. Or maybe he told Mrs. Bland he was leaving town on the six o'clock train and then she found out he didn't go, and that he got a message from some woman when he got to the bus station which made him change his mind, go back to his office, where his secretary—she must have loved her work—was waiting for him. He left New York at five minutes past midnight, not at six o'clock. Maybe Mrs. Bland couldn't take it. So—exit one beautiful secretary."

Patrick lifted an eyebrow.

Dorn paused, and getting no answer, went on.

"Rawlings is well-known by the employees at both bus stations. One station is near where he lives. The other is near his office. He uses both, in going and coming from Washington. The night men on the elevators at the Shandon Building know him. They saw him arrive and leave. We talked with the cleaning woman who did his office."

"Did they do any work?" Patrick inquired very politely.

Dorn's sky-blue eyes glinted. "The cleaning woman thinks they worked, so do the elevator men, and the cabdriver who drove them to the post office says that Rawlings carried a large manila envelope which he must have posted because he took it in but didn't come back with it. The girl took shorthand notes during the ride. The driver watched her in his mirror. The waitress who served them at Schraffts' says they talked business. I think we can say that they worked. But a jealous woman would not appreciate that so much as we do, Mr. Abbott."

"Whom do you refer to, Lieutenant?"

"Mrs. Bland."

Patrick thought that over, and said, "I don't believe she's the jealous type."

I brushed hard. I was the type. Patrick had made it sound like a lower order.

"Rawlings could have murdered the woman himself," Dorn said then. I stopped brushing.

"In the cab?" Patrick asked. Again superpolite.

"Oh, no. Nothing happened in the cab. She took notes in a notebook. Rawlings dropped her at her apartment house on the way back from the post-office to the Forty-second Street station. He didn't even get out of the cab, so we can assume that he wasn't too anxious to please the lady—though, from other sources, we know she was very anxious to please him. We believe that he let her out of the taxi at approximately ten minutes to twelve. Maybe a minute earlier. The driver went on to Lexington, turned left, then left again and let Rawlings out on the opposite side of Forty-second Street from the station. It was then exactly seven minutes before midnight. The driver looked, because he stops work at midnight and he wondered if he had time to pick up another fare. Rawlings crossed in front of his cab directly to the station. He went in, picked up his bag at the checkroom, and went directly to the bus. We checked all this. It was then five or six minutes till midnight—at the time he got into the bus. He had ten or eleven minutes to spare, before the bus left the station. Everything being just right, Rawlings could have left the bus, used the back exit of the station, walked the short block to Mrs. Gilbert's place, gone in, killed her, got back to the station and departed on the same bus."

Patrick listened intently. Dorn laid an ash on the tray, took a couple of puffs on the cigar, and continued.

"The situation was ideal for Rawlings to do exactly that. The back of the station wouldn't have many people in it until about time for the bus to leave. Passengers prefer to wait in the brighter, more comfortable, waiting room. The street just back of the station is not one favored by pedestrians. It is dark and rather gloomy. The dim-out makes it, indeed, rather obscure. There was a thick haze, almost a fog, at midnight last night, very deep in that part of the city, because the smoke from the great buildings gathers in the deep narrow streets. There is no doorman in the building where Mrs. Gilbert lived. No one saw her come home. Possibly no one saw Rawlings leave the station, hurry along through the murk, enter the building, do the deed, leave, and return to the bus." Dorn paused, a little dramatically before saying, "He made a telephone call."

I was frightened. I sat very stiffly, forgetting to brush.

"You checked that, of course?" Patrick asked.

"We were fortunate," Dorn said, "in being able to do so, indirectly. He called your hotel, Mr. Abbott. The clerk made a note of it. He called at exactly twelve-two, which had given him five or six minutes, enough if he worked fast, to commit the crime. You were out. He left a message, told you to call Murray Hill 7-9132, Mrs. Gilbert's telephone number."

Patrick laughed.

"That's a wonderful yarn, Lieutenant. Too bad it doesn't make sense."

"Why doesn't it?"

"Well, to begin at your ending, why should he call my hotel and leave her phone number?"

"Conscience, perhaps?"

Patrick squared his chin. "You're barking up the wrong tree, Dorn. Rawlings didn't do it."

Dorn puffed a puff. Then he laughed.

"No. We don't think he did," he admitted.

I relaxed. Then stiffened. Now what?

"You wasted a lot of breath, Lieutenant," Patrick said.

"Yes. Just wanted to see if you would swallow it, Mr. Abbott. Mind you, he could have done it. The possibilities are fascinating, for that reason. But he didn't. He did make a telephone call, but he didn't make that one. The operator who took down the message that was left here thinks the speaker was a woman, says it was one of those low voices you can't be sure if it's a man or woman on the phone. Rawlings however has a very deep voice. He could probably disguise it, but we are *not* inclined to suspect, not as yet anyway, that he killed Mrs. Gilbert. Who did phone you, Mr. Abbott?"

"I wish I knew."

"And why did the person phone you? Why not the police?"

"I'm sure I don't know. Why call anybody?"

"Because the murderer wanted the body found and Rawlings suspected," Dorn said.

"I suppose you think you know who it was?"

The detective's smile was slow and very sure.

"It could be only one person. Mrs. Ellen Bland."

Patrick kept quiet, getting himself another cigarette, taking his time lighting it. I had stopped brushing my hair. I just listened, sitting at the dressing table.

Patrick asked, "How was it done, Lieutenant Dorn?"

"Don't you know?"

"Only what I read in the papers. They didn't tell."

"Oh. She was killed by a hard blow on the back of the head, in the medulla oblongata region. Saw a lot of that kind of thing in the last war." That made him older than he looked. "Paralyzes the entire body. If the blow is hard enough, it usually means instant death. We believe the victim entered the apartment, took off her street clothes at once—stepped out of them, it happens, for they were lying on the floor of her bedroom—put on a dressing gown, and then came back into the living room to answer the door. We believe the murderer was in the house when Mrs. Gilbert got there, Abbott. Waiting for her. But not in the apartment. Mrs. Gilbert wasn't frightened. I should say she was not much surprised. She sat down to talk to the visitor, on the sofa. The visitor made some excuse, perhaps to get a match or an ash tray from the table behind Mrs. Gilbert, got up and bashed in the back of her head when she wasn't looking. She never knew what happened. She couldn't have been frightened or she would have turned her head to see what the visitor wanted on the table. There would then have been a struggle. There was none."

"Mrs. Bland doesn't smoke."

"Another excuse would do as well. It makes no difference. Whatever it was, Mrs. Gilbert did not turn her head. There was no struggle."

"What served as the weapon?"

"A heavy bronze bookend, which had a flat thick base supporting a solid bronze elephant. An ideal object for the purpose. The murderer wore gloves. The hall door didn't catch as she went out, which was why Miss Howe, the neighbor, looked in. Miss Howe saw the door open and the light on and called to Mrs. Gilbert, then entered and found the corpse."

"What sort of woman is this Miss Howe?"

"Her looks would stop a clock," Dorn said.

"Maybe she did it?" Patrick said. "What do you know about Mrs. Gilbert's private life? She was divorced, for one thing. She may have had enemies. I think you are jumping to conclusions—"

"No," Dorn cut in. He slipped his hand into a pocket and removed it with a fat envelope, which he held out so that Patrick could peep. "There was this," he said. Patrick looked impressed. "It's the same kind and size. It is filled with the same poison." He waited. He said then, "But once again an autopsy discovered no poison in the body, Abbott. It's the work of a fiend. No normal woman—if a woman who does murder can be called normal—"

Patrick spoke out, with a sudden hard twist of jaw. "See here, Dorn! This has gone on long enough. Mrs. Bland didn't do it. See?"

Dorn smiled superciliously as he dropped the envelope in a pocket.

"No kidding!" Patrick warned.

Dorn rubbed out his cigar. The odor filled the room.

After a couple of minutes he went away. The murders were not again mentioned.

CHAPTER TWENTY

I said then, "It was another hypo, wasn't it? What's in them, dear?"

Patrick groaned. "Damn if I know." He threw himself on the bed and rested his feet on the headboard. He smoked gloomily.

"Why didn't you ask him?"

"That's what he wanted."

"Well—why not?"

I felt impatient.

"I don't suppose that poison is important, but—"

"Sure it's important!"

I didn't like the way he said it. I felt irked. So I offered another opinion. "Louis Bland dropped those hypos, of course. He carried them, it would seem. He did both murders—very likely."

Patrick scowled. "And left a trail of hypos? Why?"

I knew why Patrick was touchy. Dorn had got under his skin. That long yarn about Hank had been a strain for Patrick. I knew that. But I was tired of the whole business, so I said, knowing perfectly well it would get a rise, "I wish you'd drop it, Pat. All of it. Let's leave town. That dilly of a Dorn—"

Patrick said touchily, "Lay off that word!"

"Oh," I said. "Censoring my words now, are you?"

"There are plenty of words that mean something, dear."

I was angry. I said, "I'm just as tired of the word 'Ellen.' "

Patrick just looked at the ceiling. The silence then was too brittle to fool with, so I went into the bath and scrubbed my teeth and did a lot of bitter thinking, but

I hadn't quite decided how to put these thoughts into swift telling talk when the telephone rang. Patrick sat up and took the call. It was over almost instantly, then he got up and reached for his hat, "That was Dorn. He wants to see me downstairs. You got plenty of money, dear?"

"Plenty!" I snapped.

Patrick took out forty dollars and laid it on the bed. "You need a hat," he said, and walked out.

I flew at the money, stuffed it into my bag, grabbed my jacket and the French felt beret and dashed after him.

He wasn't by the elevators. It was an eternity before one came and another before I got to the lobby. Patrick wasn't there.

I looked all around. I hurried into the street. He was gone.

As a last resort I peeped into the Grill. He was sitting at the table behind the shelves of beer steins, talking to Dorn. I eased over, said hello, and sat down. Patrick was polite. Dorn, for an instant, looked annoyed.

They were drinking beer. I decided on a martini, a drink which is inclined to make me impetuous.

"The wood was in her hair," Dorn said then. He loathed having me here, but he couldn't think just what to do about it. "Please understand, Mrs. Abbott, that anything I say is confidential." His smile this time was a knife. "Tiny particles were found under the microscope around the bruise on the temple. Our expert on wood says it's a kind that doesn't grow in this country, and I doubt if we would have spotted the source of the particles so soon if Mrs. Bland hadn't sent the picture to a framer." He was talking about *The Pink Umbrella.* "We've known all along that Anna Forbes wasn't killed by hitting her head accidentally on one of those knobs on the railing—that is, we've known it since we held the autopsy— but we went easy on that score. Our surgeon was careful not to confide his own suspicions to Dr. Seward, even. Consequently, Mrs. Bland did not suspect that we would be watching, and sent out the picture to be repaired. We've appropriated it, of course. That's what killed Anna Forbes. A picture. The blow must have been struck with considerable force. Goldberg said the picture wasn't in the living room when he went upstairs after the body was taken away. Trill didn't remember seeing it anywhere, and he searched the bedrooms, and Trill's quite an observant man. What became of the picture after it was used to murder Anna Forbes?"

Patrick's reply was a question. "Isn't that new housemaid on the Force, Lieutenant?"

Dorn smiled. "You are very quick to notice things yourself, Mr. Abbott. Perhaps you can tell me about the picture?"

"I've never seen the picture, Lieutenant. And, incidentally, Mrs. Bland knows she's being watched. If she knew the picture was the murder weapon she is certainly too intelligent to risk attracting your notice by sending it to be mended now."

Dorn let that go by.

"I suppose you know nothing about the picture, Abbott?"

"A little."

"You know that Rawlings painted it?"

"Yes. Mrs. Bland would have cherished it no matter who painted it. It's a picture of her kids."

"See here—*what* is she to him?"

I waited for Patrick to explode.

He didn't explode.

"I'm afraid I can't answer that, Lieutenant." He was being very careful. "See here, you've probably got plenty of help on this job, Dorn. Didn't anybody see Mrs. Bland leave the house last night? And follow? She could hardly do murder fifteen or sixteen blocks from her home without getting there somehow."

Dorn groaned. "She was seen coming back. No one saw her go out, unfortunately."

Ellen had told us she didn't leave the house last night. No, she'd said she stayed in *all evening*.

Dorn said, "The traffic out of that house along about half-past eleven last night got to be a little too fast for my men. We had two watching the place. Along about half-past eleven the daughter came out carrying a small suitcase. She walked over to Park Avenue to get a cab. She couldn't get one at once, so she walked north a couple of blocks and finally picked one up near Fifty-seventh. Our man tailed her to a woman's hotel on West Fifty-seventh Street. She went in and registered—she's staying there now. Meanwhile the boy left the house. He must have guessed he was being followed, because he ducked around corners too fast for our man. There was a sort of fog, and the cab shortage. Our man went back to the house and about ten minutes after he got back there he saw Mrs. Bland *go into the house*." Dorn's blue eyes assumed a gimlet quality. "She tell you about that, Mr. Abbott?"

"Nope."

"You saw Mrs. Bland this morning?"

"Yes. She mentioned sending out the picture. I don't think she would have mentioned it had she thought the picture was under suspicion."

I looked into my martini. It tasted cool and clean, going down.

How they all lied! All the Blands lied.

Dorn noted the time. "I'm going to push along and have a little talk with that Miss Sarah Howe, the woman who found the body. Want to come with me, Mr. Abbott?"

He pointedly left me out.

Patrick's acceptance did the same. "Thanks. I'd like to. I've got nothing to do at the moment. My wife is on her way to buy a hat."

I let them go with only a very small smile. There wasn't much else I could do. I finished my drink quickly and left the Grill by the street door. A taxi came by. I beckoned it and asked the man to drive west on Fifty-seventh Street. The rain had turned into a Scotch mist. It chilled the body and the heart and made the taxicab crawl. When we stopped for the first red light I slid the window back and asked the driver if he knew of a hotel for women on West Fifty-seventh. He nodded and set me down ten minutes later at a huge structure which seemed too big to be a hotel. I walked through a long slender lobby and at the desk at the back asked if Susan Bland was registered here. She was, but she was out, so I walked back to a divan facing a long row of busy elevators and sat down to wait.

CHAPTER TWENTY-ONE

About ten minutes later, Susan walked in. She wore a camel's-hair coat, a little round brown felt, and low-heeled brown shoes. Her brown hair flowed away from the pink healthy face which still looked as though Sue hadn't a trouble in the world.

"Why, hello!" she greeted me cordially. Then she got suspicious. "How did you know I was here?" she demanded. She stood flat on her low heels and eyed me.

"I was just passing by—" I lied glibly.

It didn't work. Sue knew better, and said so.

"I'll own up," I said. "I heard a policeman tell Patrick you were here and I thought I would come along and see for myself."

"A policeman?"

"They're watching us all."

"For gosh sakes, why?"

"They think Anna Forbes was murdered."

"How perfectly silly!" Susan said. "Where's Pat?"

"He went off to look at—to see a woman, some woman the police detective was going to talk to. On account of the other murder."

Sue took no apparent interest in the second murder. And very little in the first. You could see that if she thought it was silly to say Anna was murdered, that made it silly.

There was a soda fountain off the lobby. I invited her to have a drink. We went in and sat down at a table. Susan ordered a double-chocolate malt and I, regretfully thinking what those delicious things do to you when you are twenty-seven, asked for coffee, couldn't have it, and settled for a coke.

"Have you seen Bill?" Susan asked with a perceptible step-up in vitality that she tried to conceal. I didn't reply. She said, "I was just wondering. Not that it makes any difference. We can never marry. I told him so. Bill can't get it into his head that I mean it."

I said, "If it is what your father said—"

"Well, it is."

"We were at your house awhile this morning, Sue. Your mother seems to think—"

"I don't care what she thinks," said Sue.

I was getting rather bored with Sue.

"She seems to trust you a lot," I said. "She thinks you have such good judgment. She said if you wanted to go away and think out your own problems it was the thing for you to do. Not many mothers have that much sense."

Susan said, "Mother's a cool one, all right." Then she anchored her face with the straw to the malt. She was a hard little number, I decided. She was so freshly pretty that I had overrated her. "I sometimes think Mother would get places faster if she wasn't such a wonderful thinker-outer," she said then. "Look at me! I am the result of Mother's thinking-out, am I not? Or am I? If she was so darn good at thinking things out why did she marry Louis and have me and Dick? We're a fine pair of sprouts. Well, aren't we?"

"What's wrong with you?" I asked.

"Nobody tells *me*, exactly. It's easy to tell what's wrong with Dick though. He's a drunk."

"Oh, no, he isn't," I said. Here I was on the other side now, batting for a Bland. "Not any more."

"You don't cure yourself that fast, baby. I suppose the family taint works one way with me and another with Dick. He's weak. That's an effect. I'm tainted. But anyhow I haven't a weak will."

"You're weak as water," I said. "You're behaving like a spoiled infant, and you know it. You're already ashamed of yourself. And if there was really anything wrong with you your doctor would tell you so,—that is, if he is any kind of a doctor."

"We've found him satisfactory," Susan said coldly.

"I wouldn't know. Also, your mother would tell you the truth." (And now I was batting for Ellen, who didn't tell the truth.)

"You tire me," Susan said. "Did Mother send you here, or didn't she?"

"She didn't." I considered, and said, "I came here because all the goings-on in your family have got Pat in a spot. I'm bored with it. We come here for a holiday and because nobody in your family, except your mother, can behave like a grown-up, our own good times are spoiled. Everywhere we go, we are followed by sleuths. I shouldn't wonder if one isn't listening to us right now. They think Pat knows more than he does know about the murders."

Susan Bland didn't stop sucking on her chocolate malt.

"Don't act dumb, Sue. You know about Anna Forbes. And didn't you see the papers? Don't you know about Mrs. Gilbert's death?"

"Who's she?"

"Hank Rawlings's secretary."

"Really," Susan said. She picked up her spoon and went after the ice cream in the depths of the malt. "Well, what's that got to do with me? I've got plenty to worry about, Jean, without going out of my way to fret over the murder of some-body I never heard of. After what I've been going through—"

"Rot!" I said.

Susan flamed. "Listen, I've had a horrible life, all my life! How would you like to grow up in a foreign country? Specially if you were American? None of the French kids could understand why an American lived in France. They all thought America was a kind of fairyland, a wonderful place, and they thought there was something awfully wrong with us, or we wouldn't be living and going to school in their country. Oh, they were patriotic and all, but they seemed to think we were outcasts or something never to come home. That was what I was up against in France. That and wearing a black sateen smock and black stockings, and having sisters for teachers. It was just like the dark ages, for a person like me. But I wasn't consulted! Oh, no! Having got me there, Louis and Mother proceeded to keep me there whether it was what I wanted or not. A fine thing to do to kids, if you ask me, which of course, you don't. I'm never consulted. I don't count."

"Well, you can't blame your mother—"

"Why not? She could have married Louis again any time and he would have eaten out of her hand. We could have come back here long ago then. But would she? No."

I said, "You're a hard girl, Sue."

"Life has made me hard," Susan said. "Life, and that family. I was so happy when we came home that I didn't mind the refugee part even. We all carried morphine and cyanide—"

"What-t?"

"When we left Paris, I mean. We carried it to kill ourselves with if we were captured, only I never meant to take mine, no matter what. I meant to come on to America. Somehow. It's been okay, too. I took a business course, much to Louis's disgust, got a job, worked in a canteen, and then met Bill."

"What became of the cyanide and morphine?"

"Oh, that." Susan knitted her brows. "I don't know. Mother took it, I suppose. We had a lot of fun with Daphne, about the stuff, Dick and I did. It was about the only fun we did have on that jaunt. She always carries saccharine and every time she dropped a tablet into her coffee, Dick would make death rattles and such." Susan laughed gaily. "Nobody thought it was funny but us kids, though."

Susan plied her spoon for a minute, then said, "People you and Mother's age are dumb." I recoiled, in horror, thinking that twenty-seven was bad enough, but it wasn't, after all, thirty-eight. "You waver so."

"Do we?"

"Sure you do. You let things rule your lives. You don't know what it's all about. I'm not like that. I know what I'm doing, and I've done it."

"That's what you think," I said, imitating her tone.

"Why not?"

"You're in love, aren't you? Or are you? Maybe you're not capable of falling in love, Sue. Come to think of it, maybe that's your trouble. Poor old Bill."

That got at her. Slightly. "I'm in love all right, but I'm not going to get married." Susan eyed me. "I propositioned Bill. He hit the ceiling."

"Bill's a good guy," I said. "You're lucky. Or rather, you were."

Susan watched me over her glass. "Well, he needn't have gone off his nut the way he did. He didn't understand it, either. He said I was more like the people he met around our house than he had thought, because I suggested such a thing. He was shocked. He left Mother out of the insults. Like everybody else, Bill thinks Mother is a saint. I don't agree."

"Don't you?"

Susan's smile was superior. "I admire Mary Kent. She's hard. She doesn't let life make her into a—a nothing, like my mother."

She dived into the malt again, scraping the bottom of the glass.

I said, "It seems to me a funny time to start worrying about your future children when you don't even know when his boat leaves if you'll ever see Bill again." I was hitting below the belt. Her face tightened. She lifted her spoon more slowly. "This isn't Germany, Sue. You aren't required to breed here." She put down the spoon. "If he happens to get put on the Arctic route, it's tough going. Why don't you think about things like that instead of about yourself, for a change?"

Sue began to cry. "You're a dirty dog, Jean. You're being mean on purpose. You're a skunk."

"What are you? Worrying Bill like that?" I didn't like Sue much now. I would hate to talk to Dick like that.

"Well, I'm no skunk. What I do is for the best."

"You're dumb, Susan, my pet. You've got a superiority complex, too. Bill is wasted on you. Someday he'll realize that—if he lives."

She wiped her eyes and blew her nose.

"On top of all the rest, you aren't even bright," I said. "You are putting on this beautiful act without even knowing what it's all about. You don't know what ails you, if anything."

"I do know. I asked Dr. Seward—"

"That fat quack!" I stood up. "I'm wasting a lot of good time," I said. I picked up the checks and fished out my change purse. "It's a good thing all our girls aren't as selfish as you are, Susan. We'd lose this war."

I paid for the drinks and walked out. At the door I looked back and almost changed my mind and got nice to her, she looked so abandoned and so rosily pretty, but I kept my chin up and went on. I didn't feel too sorry for her though. I honestly didn't like her. I didn't like Louis. I didn't actually like Dick much, and I had no intentions of weakening and really liking Ellen. I got a taxi. It toddled back to the Rexley in the thick wetness. The immediate past rose up and taunted me. Here you were, just a couple of people, with problems of your own, walking in the dim-out. A cab rolls up. A boy stumbles out. A woman opens a door. Then a woman lies dead in the areaway. Then another lovely woman lies gracefully dead on a sofa. Your whole life, which should never have touched on these things, is changed.

At the hotel there was a message in our box from Daphne Garnett saying not to forget her dinner. Time, seven. Place, The Green Flower, on West Forty-eighth near Eighth Avenue. I groaned in prospect. I looked around the lobby, and then peeked into the Grill, in quest of Patrick. He wasn't there.

But Dr. Seward was there. He loomed impressively behind an impressive stein of beer. I decided I had something to ask him.

CHAPTER TWENTY-TWO

When I think of the way I went after Dr. Seward and what I wanted to know I am sure that it must sound as though marrying into the detective business has made me rather bold and crafty. Perhaps it has. Not that I cared one small hoot how it seemed to Dr. Seward. So smug and fat—in that Alpine chair, with its little cut-outs shaped like hearts,—so self-satisfied behind his big stein of beer, he looked actually designed for being prodded. "Good afternoon, Dr. Seward," I said. I smiled down at him. With the maximum of physical exertion, he got on his feet, those beautifully shod feet which were too small for him now. He smiled. That is, he did something on that order with the features in the middle of his face, but he obviously didn't know me from Eve.

"Ah-h. Why good afternoon," he said. He was no flirt. He was instantly on his guard.

"Have you seen my husband about, Dr. Seward?"

"Why-a—"

I said, "I'm Mrs. Patrick Abbott. We met you at Mrs. Bland's."

"Oh, quite. That detective-fellow, eh? Quite. No, I haven't seen him." He cast a rueful glance at the beer from which I had so rudely disengaged him.

"May I wait for him at your table, Dr. Seward?"

"Why-a—but certainly. Quite. Of course."

He held my chair. I sat down. I took off my gloves and arranged my left hand, with the emerald, so the doctor couldn't miss it. He saw it and offered me a drink. He looked gratified when I had tea. If a rich patient came in, I thought, the doctor would rather not be seen buying an unknown young woman a cocktail.

Conversation languished pronto, and to get it under way I mentioned that we were staying in the hotel and did our loafing in this grillroom. The doctor re-marked that it was one of the nicest places in the neighborhood to drop into for a drink. He said it reminded him of Paris. The place was so deliberately Swiss that even I, who had never been to Switzerland, could practically see Alps, so I recorded his remark as an example of the doctor's remarkable inaccuracy. It goes to show, though, how everybody these days thinks about Paris.

Time was precious. The doctor might leave. Patrick might come in and queer my plans. I decided to get right to the point. Viz, what was the Bland family's taint?

I said to start, "I've just been talking with young Susan Bland."

The doctor's face went melon smooth. "So?"

"She's in a state, Dr. Seward. About something that she doesn't even know. She thinks she will inherit some ailment."

"She's hysterical," said Dr. Seward, in his plushy tone.

"She's in love," I corrected him.

The doctor's eyebrows quivered.

"Nonsense. She's too young for that."

I did a little fibbing and said, "I feel sorry for her, Dr. Seward."

"Yes. She'll be grateful, however, that we have used our heads, for her sake. Some day. It's not only that she's so young. The match is unsuitable. Nobody knows anything about the boy. Comes from one of those far western places. Kansas it is, I think."

"Have you been in Kansas, Dr. Seward?"

Dr. Seward hastily gulped much beer.

"Oh, dear, no."

I dislike the odor of beer. But I wouldn't even let my nose quiver and let him find it out. Too much was at stake. I even refrained from defending Kansas.

"Dr. Seward," I said, getting right to the point, "just what is wrong with Louis Bland?"

If I had jabbed the good doctor with a pin he couldn't've looked more startled.

"My dear young lady?"

"I simply have to know, Dr. Seward."

"But really? And what business, if I may ask, is it of yours?"

"None. Also much," I said. Probably confusingly. Then I said, "It must be wonderful to be a doctor. You know so much. You do so much good." The doctor leaned back and eyed me darkly. "You can make so many people so happy, I mean." The word happy made him suspicious. "I'm thinking about those kids. Bill and Sue. I love to see kids happy. They can be so utterly happy, that's why. When you're my age, twenty-seven, you aren't so completely happy as they are, there is always something getting in the way a little—you think too much, I guess—and when you get older I expect you get more so,—but they're really happy, those kids. I mean, they *were*. Of course, I can see your point, Dr. Seward. If Bill is from one of those fine healthy Kansas families it would be too bad if he married somebody in one of these old New York families, tainted with epilepsy maybe."

Dr. Seward was shocked.

"Just what *are* you talking about?" he demanded.

"The Bland taint. Maybe it's leprosy," I said. "It must be pretty bad, to be worth making two young people so unhappy, Dr. Seward."

He was now speechless.

"Or maybe Louis Bland's a drug fiend. They say you can inherit that tendency. Oh, dear. I believe that's it, though. Things are left around by somebody or other—hypodermic syringes—every time there's a murder—"

"Murder?" Dr. Seward exploded. "What on earth do you mean?"

"Don't you know that the police think Anna Forbes was murdered?"

The doctor got blustery.

"What nonsense! Who would murder her?"

"They don't know. But didn't you suspect they'd investigate? Didn't they send somebody to help with the autopsy?"

One of the doctor's plump pink hands waggled.

"Matter of routine. Good Lord! What a tempest in a teapot! Police in this town haven't enough to do, and don't do what they should even so. Waste of public money. Woman of no importance. Died a natural death—so to speak."

"Didn't they tell you about the hypo?" I quizzed. The doctor didn't answer. "Didn't they mention the wood particles they found in her hair?"

Dr. Seward drank some beer. He didn't reply.

"Is Mrs. Mary Kent one of your patients, Dr. Seward?"

He seemed glad of a different subject. "Yes, of course."

"Did you know her husband?"

The doctor looked cagy again. "Naturally. I attended him during his last illness. His death was very sad. He had everything in the world to live for—money, social position, a beautiful wife. He died suddenly."

"Ptomaine poisoning, Dr. Seward?"

"My dear Mrs. Abbey! All the detective stories young people read these days, and that sort of thing, make a lot of business for the psychiatrists. And, of course, in your case, married to a detective. . . ." He broke off. He observed me. He went on. "If you were my patient, I would advise you to consult a psychiatrist. Your curiosity is abnormal, to say the least. Mr. Kent died of pneumonia—double pneumonia, after an illness of only twenty-four hours. It is contrary to professional ethics for me to give you confidential information about my various patients, Mrs. Abbey, but I assure you that Louis Bland's affliction is neither shocking or even very serious. You must excuse me—been awfully nice seeing you. Really."

"Thank you. May I tell Susan Bland the taint isn't serious?"

"You keep out of this!" Dr. Seward said.

He beckoned the waiter, paid for the drinks—after another thoughtful glance at my emerald—after all, people in hotels do need doctors sometimes—said good-bye and departed. I had got strictly nowhere. And my tactics had been both crude and inadequate.

I felt awful.

Patrick came in before I finished my tea. He carried a small green-and-white-checked hatbox. He offered it rather meekly, for him, and said, "Bought you a hat."

"Darling!" I was thrilled and terribly excited. I could hardly untie the tapes, in my excitement. He had never done such a thing before.

Patrick sat down. "I went upstairs first, Jeanie. You weren't there. Worried me."

"It was all my fault, darling. Our brawl."

"No, it was mine. I was sunk. I always get nasty when I'm sunk."

"No, you don't, dear. You're sweet."

"You're pretty wonderful, darling."

"You're the wonderful one. Buying me a hat!" I got the lid off and lifted out some tissue paper and then the hat. It was a perfectly delicious creation in emerald green straw wreathed with yellow green grapes and a spot of stiff emerald green French veiling. I adored it. "It's a dilly, darling. Oh, that word slipped out. It's swell. Think of having a man who can pick hats!"

Patrick lit a cigarette. "Well, I didn't exactly pick it, chum. But I knew you wanted a green hat and I was passing that Chez Hortense shop and went in. Hortense is quite a gal. I described you and she remembered you and she said she had designed a hat specially for you, and this is the hat."

"It's perfect." I thought of something. "She didn't hold you up, did she?"

Patrick considered it, and said, "No."

I sighed with complete abandon and kept the hat in the box but where I could look at it. Patrick ordered a Scotch. "That Howe woman Dorn took me to see is a thoroughly silly old maid. I always distrust homely women. She's been in bed all day from shock, and meanwhile she has cooked up quite a tale. When we went to see her, Dorn had no real notion of arresting Hank. When we came away he was debating whether to hold him on suspicion or wait for some real evidence. Honestly, the thing that's holding him off is his having his mind so set on Ellen's being the one. I guess you were right about Mrs. Gilbert, Jean. She was nuts about Hank, collected his belongings as souvenirs—pencils he had used, a handkerchief, clippings about him, various office memos, not one of them meaning one damn thing. The police had collected that stuff already, but hadn't attached much significance to it, until this Miss Sarah Howe comes through with a romantic tale about how Mrs. Gilbert was a martyr to unrequited love. When we left her, Dorn was purring like a cat. You should see that apartment!"

"Mrs. Gilbert's?"

"No. I saw that too, though. It's a colorless place. But she had clothes, quite gorgeous for a working gal—the police piped that, too. No, I meant Miss Howe's apartment. She's about fifty, and twittery, and everything in the place is very hearts-and-flowersy. Pretty tough luck for Hank Rawlings, I say. The old girl even knew about Ellen—didn't know her name but believes that some rich divorcée was the reason Hank hadn't fallen for Mrs. Gilbert."

"Will they arrest Hank?"

"Not yet, I think. But it's not Miss Howe's fault. She did her worst."

The waiter brought the Scotch. I was still sipping my tea. I told Patrick then about Dr. Seward. He grinned. I told him about Sue. He said he didn't think Sue was as hard as she pretended. He said she acted like that in self-defense. I didn't press the point. I was too happy about the hat and having the quarrel over to do any point-pressing. I told Pat about Mrs. Kent's husband dying of pneumonia, in the care of Dr. Seward, and about the morphine and cyanide the Blands and their friends carried when they fled from Paris, which made him look grim, and finally I remembered that Daphne Garnett had phoned to remind us of her party.

"She called Ellen, too," Patrick said.

"Ellen?"

"I stopped to see Ellen on my way back from seeing that Howe woman."

"Oh." I felt uneasy. "Ellen didn't go with you to get the hat, did she?"

"No. I picked up the hat on my way to Ellen's."

"Oh. Did you ask Ellen if and where she went last night?"

"Yes. She said she did go out and she walked east as far as Madison, then walked south a block and then went back home. The detective saw her return to the house. She didn't notice him, however."

"Why did she go out?"

"She didn't realize that Susan leaving the house was Susan. She admits now that she heard Susan leave the house last night, but she—Ellen—thought it was Dick, and she hurried out to try to catch him. She didn't see either of them. Then this morning, it turned out to have been Susan who went out."

"But Dick left the house, too, Pat. Dorn said so."

"Ellen says he didn't."

"What do you think?"

"Policemen have been known to make mistakes, Jeanie. Oh, another thing, Hank's alibi isn't too good after all, I'm afraid. There is no one who can swear that he stayed in the bus all the time he was in the station, except when he made the phone call. Dorn concocted that story in order to get under my skin and make me tell anything I knew, if I did know anything. But he was pretty close to what could have been the truth. I don't mean that Hank killed her. The very idea is ridiculous. You can't even imagine old Hank flitting out of the station and over to her apartment and bashing in her head and planting a hypo—and the hypo is the hitch, of course. Ellen is the one who Dorn thinks leaves hypos." Patrick looked grave. "Dorn's out for a kill, though. If he can't get Ellen he'll settle for Hank."

"How can he? If neither did it?"

"Circumstantial evidence, you know. That fool *Pink Umbrella* picture counts against Hank, too. The police distrust artists. Of course the fact that Hank never painted but one picture helps some."

"Did you see it, Pat?"

"Yes. It's nice. Hank could have been a painter, if he'd wanted to enough. Goldberg, by the way, advanced the idea that the girl's dead body being so artistically arranged hinted strongly that an artist had arranged it."

"For heaven's sake, Pat."

"Ellen was terribly depressed. Sue had telephoned, but I suspect she was unpleasant on the phone, and Dick was fidgeting about, and the new maid was snooping for dear life, so I had Ellen pack a few things and move here."

"Here? What about Dick?"

"He came too," Patrick said happily. "The police will tag along, but it won't be so hard on them here, and I'll be around, too."

I said, very sweetly, "I hope you found them rooms near us, dear?"

"Yes, I did. They're just a few doors along, on the same corridor," Patrick said.

"Oh," I said. Just oh. I put and kept my mind firmly on my new hat.

CHAPTER TWENTY-THREE

We drove to The Green Flower with Ellen and Dick Bland. They seemed very lighthearted. Dick and Pat talked nonsense. Ellen sat listening, which she did so very well. She seemed tranquil. How could she be, really? I didn't understand her. I never could.

She wore over her black dress—one of the two I had always seen her in—a black cloth coat. Her hair was drawn up from her face, with the two slim white strands shining like ornaments. Her little black hat was perched like a crown. I was conscious in the cab of her perfume. It was a faint fresh scent, rather apple-blossomy. It would only be very definite, I thought, in an enclosed space, or when freshly applied. It was modest. It seemed to suit Ellen.

She was such an enigma to me that I would find myself taking every little thing pertaining to her to pieces, examining each item, and pondering its meaning. Like the perfume.

Why had she gone out last night? Why had Dick gone out? Or had he? Had she again lied? Why had she twisted the fact of Susan's leaving the house? What all was she concealing? Why? The questions streamed through my mind under my new green hat. All the answers I conjured up, and they were many, continued to be unsatisfying.

The Green Flower occupied two basements in two old brownstone houses in a neighborhood overborne by somber warehouses. Even without a dim-out the vast unlighted buildings would make the area gloomy. The rain had stopped, but the air was cold and wet on the face as we left the cab. You could smell the river.

A black iron lantern ornamented with a green glass flower indicated the restaurant. There was no awning and no doorman, no pretense of any style. We walked down three stone steps and entered a wide low-ceilinged room furnished with crude wooden tables and chairs. Gingham curtains were drawn over the windows, but there were no tablecloths. Madame Sabin, the proprietress, sat behind the cash desk, like an enthroned black-eyed queen. Her greeting was in French. The lighting was pleasant and the smells of cooking delicious and Patrick and Ellen agreed with mutual satisfaction that the atmosphere seemed truly French. In one corner of the restaurant a sort of grotto had been contrived with a stage where three musicians, in Basque costume, played Basque music on a violin, a viola and a cello. Beside the grotto was a small dancing space.

Daphne had a large table reserved near the grotto. It had places for twelve. With the exception of Louis Bland and Mary Kent, we were the last to arrive.

I loved the restaurant but those twelve places were discouraging. That made too many people, for one thing, and it was such a mixed lot. Our clothes alone were a motley. Daphne wore a rose-colored embroidered crepe dinner dress, very queer with her red hair, and a flowery evening hat. Ellen was in black. Susan had come—and in her brown tweeds. I had on my same black suit and the emerald green hat. A porcelainish woman Daphne introduced as Mrs. Carrington wore a fluffy low-necked evening dress. Mr. Carrington, who reminded me of a biscuit with a Boston accent, wore a dinner coat. Clint Moran was in his old brown suit, Patrick in his navy worsted, Bill Reynolds in his ensign's uniform, Dick Bland in his gray flannels. When Louis Bland drifted in, in a white tie, and Mary Kent in a long-sleeved, sapphire-blue gown that made her eyes look like della Robbia plaques, the sartorial confusion was complete.

Daphne blamed herself. "I just kept asking everybody and told no one anything," she said. "But there you are." The fact that we might not be too congenial didn't trouble Daphne. "Clint, darling, Madame Sabin asked you to wear your dinner jacket," she complained. "It's in hock," Clint replied. Quite a long statement, from him. Daphne fluttered wildly and tried to cover it up by talking. "Clint plays first at half-past-eight. He's got a surprise for us. Ellen, darling, I hope you don't mind my having asked Louis and Mary?" (This was before they arrived, of course.) "Of course you don't. Why should you? Mary asked me if they might come. What could I do?" Ellen said, "But why should I mind?" Susan said, "Anybody ought to mind." Dick said, "Nice going, Sue!" Daphne fluttered some more and spilled her saccharine tablets. "They won't like it, either," Daphne complained. "It hasn't enough style. It hasn't any, in fact, but it's French. These people are from Bordeaux. The food is delicious." Mr. Carrington remarked, in a biscuit-like voice, "They know their food in Bordeaux, n'est-ce pas?" Mrs. Carrington sighed and said she was homesick for Paris. "We lived among them so long we are really of them," she sighed. She was a dilly. They both were dillies. But when Louis and Mary Kent came in, the talk about France took another, unpleasanter, tone. Mrs. Carrington told Mary Kent that she had a letter from Paris and that it was amazing how they kept up their courage. Mary Kent replied, enviously, "But why not? The

Germans don't interfere with the people who have money, you know. They say Monte Carlo never has been so gay, and Cannes is too utterly marvelous!" Their talk about France was like a homesick record, played over and over. But the food was beautiful and so was the wine and when they started talking about Maxim's and the Crillon and the old Foyot's, I thought I would die of sadness if I never got to see Paris myself.

For a time there was nothing too awfully wrong with the party. Sue and Bill were so happy at being back together that, by ignoring us, even they enjoyed the affair, and we got all the way to coffee without a really serious jar.

Mary Kent then said to Mrs. Carrington, "I suppose you keep up with your murders, don't you, Marjorie?"

"Murder?" trilled Mrs. Carrington.

"Hank Rawlings's secretary, I mean. Somebody murdered her last night."

"That engineer fellow?" Mr. Carrington asked.

"He didn't really live in Paris," Louis Bland hastily corrected him. "He was hardly more than a tourist." He looked at Ellen. "Seems he's in pretty deep."

"Aw, nuts," Dick Bland said.

With his beautiful hands, Louis fitted a cigarette into the holder. "How splendidly you use the English language, Dick. I congratulate you, my boy."

Dick retorted that he didn't use it to be nasty, at any rate. The quarrel raged across me between father and son, and was short-phrased and bitter. Dick was angry and uncontrolled. Louis was deliberate and malicious. Daphne hastily summoned champagne. Susan and Bill got up and danced on the little dance floor. Ellen was silent, and Mary Kent looked on with ironic amusement and the Carringtons looked down their little noses. Clint ignored it.

When the quarrel languished, Mary Kent said, "Seems the woman was both beautiful and too too devoted to her work." Dick said something under his breath and looked as if he was about to jump up and choke her. I asked him if he wouldn't like to dance. He got up and followed me on the floor. "I can't dance," he said then, "and I know why you asked me to." He marched me around. "I'm sorry. I just can't hang on to myself when they start doing their stuff."

"I wouldn't mind your beating them both up, Dick. Only, don't do it at the party."

Dick stepped on my foot, and excused it.

"She came here deliberately to say what she said, Jean. She's like that. She just waited for her best chance, then pounced. I hate her. I hate them both."

"Why is she like that, I wonder?"

"She was born that way," Dick said. "She's naturally mean. So is Louis. I wouldn't care if they were both dead. We'll never have any peace till they are. We'd better go back to the table, hadn't we, Jean? With me away, they'll pick Mother to pieces."

"Pat will look after her, Dick. He's a slow starter, but thorough when he gets around to it. Listen, where did you go last night?"

"Nowhere."

"Were you at home all night?"

"No, I wasn't." He was silent a minute then said, "I had to go out for a little while, but no one saw me go and I didn't think anybody knew. Mother must have heard me, and told Pat. Yes? She knows everything. But don't speak about it to anyone else, will you not?"

I promised. "You do know you're watched by the police?"

"And how! That's why I don't want it discussed. I eluded them, see." He grinned at the memory. "I like Hank. And I'm sorry I got so crazy mad, Jean. They made me sore. I like Hank an awful lot but I would have stood up for anybody, even somebody I didn't know, if they started talking like that. It's awful."

"Murder is terrible," Mrs. Carrington was opining when we got back. "New York is such a brutal place, *n'est-ce pas?*"

"People think nothing of murder here. It was so different in Paris," said Daphne.

Patrick said, "Now, Daphne, you do the French an injustice. No one can do murder so fascinatingly as the French." Daphne shivered.

"But they have such wonderful laws, Pat!"

"Also the guillotine," Patrick observed.

Daphne spilled her saccharine again. Mary Kent fixed her round eyes upon Patrick and said, as her cared-for ugly hand crept into her golden bag for a cigarette, "I'm afraid I started something."

"You don't say so?" Susan sneered.

Ellen frowned at Susan. Louis Bland drawled, "Besides, murder is shoptalk for the Abbotts. I'm sure they find it tiresome." It was an insult. Patrick let it go by.

"Let's dance, Bill," Susan sniffed. "You can't hear them then for the music."

Louis looked after her with something akin to admiration. Then his dark handsome eyes shifted to Bill and clouded.

The talk got easier, turned to clothes again, and perfumes. Mrs. Carrington asked Ellen what hers was. A common drugstore staple, Ellen said, and named it. Patrick asked Ellen to dance and Mr. Carrington stepped out with Mary Kent. Dick said, "Struggle with me?" There wasn't really room to dance. We kept to the edges. When there was a break in the music, Patrick and Dick changed partners, and it gave me a chance at last to say a little say. "Let's leave," I said. "It's not going to be any pleasanter. We can take Dick and Ellen and go some place else. Ellen will want to. Dick's drinking too much champagne."

"We have to wait till Clint plays, don't we?"

"Oh." Yes, that was necessary. "I guess so."

"Besides, I'm learning things."

"What?"

"Little bits, to fit into the puzzle."

I sniffed. "I'm afraid if the party keeps on much longer, people tomorrow will be reading about the multiple murders at The Green Flower. Your little bits will be too late."

"Pat," Daphne cried, when we got back again, "you must decide. Which of us would make the best murderer?"

"Mr. Carrington," Patrick said.

Mr. Carrington's biscuit face turned red.

Louis Bland said, "I vote for Ellen."

Daphne gasped. Ellen's face didn't change at all. Dick looked murderous. Patrick said easily, "Ellen is too rational. She's got the guts to do murder but she has far too much sense."

"Oh, indeed?" Louis Bland said.

"Well, you couldn't do it," Dick told him angrily. "Did you hear what Pat said? It takes guts."

Their brawl was on again, sharp and bitter.

Then, at last, it was time for Clint's number. He got up and slouched along to the tiny piano at one side of the grotto. The musicians had retired from the little stage. The lights were dimmed.

The surprise was the singer. She was old, forty at least, her cheeks very raddled and coarsely made-up with an ugly, dry-looking rouge. She was dressed in the shabby silks and feathers of the traditional stage prostitute. She came on when Clint eased out of a medley of current hits into a French song called *La Chanson des Rues*. She sauntered in, swinging her hips in the usual fashion, and sat down on a chair under a spotlight. It seemed old stuff until she sang.

She had a very deep contralto. It was low-pitched at first, resonant, achingly sad. Then a harsh wild note entered her voice and she sang a couple of stanzas with a spine-chilling violence. She subsided into the low unhappy tone and finished diffidently and sadly, as she began.

She was stunning. Before she finished we had all left our darkened tables and had gathered closely around the grotto.

Clint got up and went to our table and fetched his champagne glass. He set it on the piano and started an encore. After the encore, the audience wanted *La Chanson des Rues* again. They repeated it. When the singer left the stage, the lights came on, we went back to our table, and Clint stayed at the piano, doing his usual stuff. Only at our table, I suppose, would we appreciate the sly digs he gave in the shape of "The Last Time I Saw Paris," or the sad splendid *Tristan* motifs he tucked in among the cowboy tunes, the tangos, and the jive.

Patrick dropped down beside me when we returned to the table. He picked up the glass in front of him, set it down as he recalled it wasn't his, then picked it up again and got up and wandered over to the cash desk. Then he started a conversation with the proprietress. He came back with the glass empty.

While the woman sang, Bill Reynolds had left the restaurant. Sue was sulking. Dick was drinking too much. So was Sue. Louis was winding up for more trouble.

He had just learned about Ellen and Dick's moving to the hotel. "Naturally, I can't force your mother to stay in the house I provide for you, but I can force you, Dick," he said.

"Try it," Dick said.

Patrick said, "You can blame me, Louis. They seemed to be rattling around in that big house—"

"This isn't your affair, Abbott."

"You're darn right it isn't," Patrick retorted. "If it were, I'd sock you one. I happen to dislike men picking on women."

"We must be going," I said. I stood up. "It's been lovely, Daphne."

Ellen said, "Will you mind if Dick and I come along with you?"

I did, but Patrick was delighted.

Susan refused to leave. Daphne said she would drop her at the girls' hotel. Ellen appeared to hesitate, because of Sue, then came with us.

At the hotel the Blands went directly upstairs.

Patrick had an errand to the drugstore where we had the coffee last night and I went along for the walk. "Why do we go here?" I was asking, at once. Then we were outside again in the damp mist-gray night.

"Something funny about that champagne. Smelled like almonds."

"Mine didn't."

"I believe—hope—it was only the glass I picked up when I sat down next you. After we'd been listening to the singer. Madame Sabin gave me a clean cream bottle—got it here in my pocket. I noticed a sign in that drugstore last night which said analyses were made there by a registered chemist."

"Almonds? That means cyanide, Pat!"

"Might."

"They all know about cyanide. They carried it when they fled from Paris. Who did it? And why pick on you?"

"That was Louis Bland's glass," Patrick said.

CHAPTER TWENTY-FOUR

The analysis couldn't be had till tomorrow morning, when the chemist returned to work. Patrick put the little bottle back into his pocket. We left the place and started walking around the block. The air was colder and clearer, but all the same, the dim-out made the night peculiar. We walked very slowly. I slipped my hand through Patrick's arm and said I would never get over the feeling you had in a dim-out that somebody was creeping up behind with the idea of socking you in the back of the head. He grinned, but as he lit our cigarettes he quietly looked behind us.

We seemed to have lost our sleuths. Neither the mousy man in the raincoat nor the solid citizen in the brown suit had been around this evening.

My heart was beating anxiously because of Patrick's narrow escape from being poisoned. He laughed it off. He would never have tasted the stuff after smelling it, he insisted.

"What will you do with it?" I asked.

"Turn it over to Dorn. He can get an analysis made in the police laboratory at once. No time to waste, maybe."

"Why?"

"There might be another murder."

"Louis?" I asked.

Patrick moved his shoulders. "I sat down in his chair. The glass was his."

"But who would do such a dreadful thing?"

"Which of them wouldn't?" Patrick qualified it. "Except Ellen."

I thought back. "They were all there. Every one of the people at dinner—except those Carringtons—were in and about the house when Anna Forbes was murdered. Any one of them could have put the poison in the glass. They all hate him—all except Mary Kent. And Daphne, who doesn't hate anybody." Patrick said nothing, so I said, "That saccharine's suspicious-looking, though. If you wanted to carry poison and habitually carried saccharine, that little enamel box would be a cute place to carry it. Don't you agree?"

"Might be risky. Might get taken by mistake by yourself."

"It was just a crazy idea," I said. "Anyhow Daphne would have no reason to poison Louis, Pat."

"No."

We strolled along.

"Unless she did it for Clint's sake?"

"Yes."

We turned left on Fifty-sixth. "Daphne adores Clint, Pat, in a sort of enveloping maternal fashion. She must worry about him a lot." I kept on thinking, out loud. "If Louis died, Clint would get some money, they say. And money is something Daphne would think people can't do without. Daphne's not so silly as she sounds either. She thinks, in a way. I listened to her talking to you last night, there at the drugstore, and a lot of her prattle made sense. Of course, I can't imagine her actually doing the deed—but if she did do it, she is the kind that would certainly use poison."

"I think you might have something there," Patrick conceded. "But what about the other victims? What about Anna Forbes and Laura Gilbert? Why would Daphne murder them?"

I admitted then that I couldn't see how she could do those two murders, anyhow, both of which had required physical strength. "Maybe somebody else killed them. Daphne would only kill Louis."

"Oh, Daphne's husky enough to do the job," Patrick said, going back to the previous statement and speaking in that over-casual tone which always made me think he was keeping something back. "I've got a few ideas about those murders, Jean. To start with, I'm sure that the Anna Forbes murder was not a calculated murder. Laura Gilbert, however, was murdered deliberately, in cold blood."

He stopped talking, so I said, "Maybe Clint killed Laura Gilbert and left the hypo to throw suspicion directly on Louis himself?" I instantly saw my mistake. "No—Louis would have no reason to kill Laura Gilbert. He would want her to live, if he thought there was a chance of Hank's being snatched away from Ellen." I sighed. "I feel so sorry for poor Clint, though. I hope he didn't do it. Still, I do think you really have something there, Pat." I mentioned the repetition of the Tristan music, wondering if that music really did foreshadow death as it did in the opera, though, if so, it was a shame to give Louis Bland such a beautiful motif. "Of course, Clint could have got the cyanide, somewhere. They all know about cyanide after that refugee experience—poor things."

"Here's Reuben's," Patrick said. "Let's get a cup of coffee and I'll ring up Dorn and arrange to pass along my almond-flavored champagne. This time, Dorn can't accuse me of concealing material evidence." He grinned. "Not that I didn't try." We went in and Patrick left me at a table to the right of the wide door from the cocktail room into the main dining room while he telephoned Dorn. He came back and we ordered ham sandwiches and coffee. We didn't want the sandwiches, but there were so many on the menu that it seemed the only thing to do.

"Dorn's coming to the Rexley in half an hour. He'll meet us in the Grill. Wants to see me about something else, he said." Patrick looked grave. "You mentioned cyanide. Anybody can get the stuff, you know—always makes me see red. There was a jar with a glass stopper labeled potassium cyanide in plain view in the mirror of that drugstore last night."

"Clint Moran hangs out there, Pat."

"You're suddenly harping on Clint, chum."

"I'm sorry. I hate it, too. And why pick on Clint? They all detest Louis, Dick loathes him. Dick's an emotional, uncontrolled creature. Sue would kill her father without a regret if—if she found out he had lied to her about that taint—she is so cold and deliberate."

Patrick stopped me, snapping his fingers and looked extra-solemn. "I just happened to think of something that spoils the whole idea, Jeanie."

"What?"

"Louis isn't dead!"

I giggled.

"So, after all," he continued, "the poison may have been meant for me."

I considered that, calmly now.

"No. Because it was dropped in the glass while we were clustered around the grotto listening to the woman sing. Whoever did it wouldn't know that you would go back and sit down, just by chance, in Louis's chair and pick up his glass.

Listen—that reminds me—Clint went back to the table during the applause after their first number. He brought his own glass back and set it on the piano. Oh, Pat, he did it! Of course, he did."

"And the other two murders—I mean, the real murders? Did he do them, too?"

"Do they have to be connected?"

"We can't have two homicidal maniacs floating around at the same time," Patrick said. I agreed. Patrick murmured, "Shush!" Talk about angels! There stood Clint, in the door between us and the cocktail bar. His opaque green eyes quested the room. They lit on us and rested there with no change in his dull loose-fleshed face.

"Hello, Clint. Come have a drink," Patrick called.

He came, sat down, and accepted a gin and tonic like a robot taking it from other robots.

"Your show over?" I asked. It couldn't be. It wasn't ten yet, and he was supposed to play a second time, for the supper club. He shook his head. "This your recess?" I asked.

Clint said, "Permanent one, I hope."

Patrick said, "The singer was swell, Clint."

"Sure. We'll team up, maybe get a spot in a real nightclub."

"But what about Daphne, Clint?" I asked, thinking how she would worry.

His whole face tightened. "Nobody asks Daphne to horn into my affairs."

Patrick changed the talk to something trivial about nothing particular and let Clint down the drink and have a second before he asked, "Was Sue at the restaurant when you left, Clint?"

"Yeah. Throwing her weight around. Nobody there then but Daphne and Louis and his lovely. Never saw Sue drink before. Sue ought to marry that guy Bill."

"Louis stopped it, I believe."

A turgid gleam flicked in and out of the eyes, but Clint did not comment.

"What's wrong with Louis?" I asked, ignoring Patrick's tiny frown, because I asked it.

Clint said, "What isn't?"

"I mean the family taint," I said. I felt embarrassed the minute I had, Clint being in the family.

Clint grinned. Definitely. "You remind me of the police. They flocked to that flophouse I call home and stayed three hours the first time—yesterday—and two hours the second time, today. Yapped considerably about hypodermics. Have spent my life among nuts, but never met a nuttier one than Detective Dorn."

Patrick said, "The police may make things difficult for Ellen, Clint."

"Never," said Clint.

"I mean, if you know anything that will be useful to Ellen—" Patrick began. Clint put in, "Listen, Pat, Ellen's okay. No jury would convict her of anything."

"I've no intentions of letting it get so far as a jury, Clint!"

All at once Clint emitted a peculiar giggle.

"I thought it was me they were after, Pat. They good as accused me of murdering that Gilbert woman—when I forgot myself enough to admit I had talked to her."

"You knew Laura Gilbert?" Patrick's voice was quiet but incisive.

Clint glanced at Patrick and for a second or two his heavy face seemed rumpled from indecision. It smoothed out. He retired wherever it was he stayed most of the time and stayed there. Except when I asked him, in spite of Patrick's wanting me to lay off the family affairs, why he played the Tristan music. He grinned and said it made Louis sore. I watched him out of an eye-corner and thought about him. His heavy-lidded green eyes seemed to see very little. The ears heard abnormally much, like those of the blind. His hands—which were as light and skillful on a little cottage piano as they had been on the great Steinway in Ellen's drawing room—were big, white, clumsy-looking and thick-fingered. Clint roused the mother in me, but in a painful sort of way. There was something painful in the way Patrick felt about him, too. I could tell by his voice when he spoke to Clint. Why did we feel like this? What had Clint done to deserve the sympathy he roused in people? He had had money and more opportunities if lumped together than come perhaps to a thousand ordinary men. He must have squandered his money. He was still squandering his health, and his talent. What sort of life did he lead when he wasn't eating or playing? A flophouse was one of those places where you got a bed for a few cents by the night, a bunk in the same room with a lot of other down-and-outs. It couldn't be that bad, could it? If it was, why didn't Daphne or someone get a good room for him and pay for it? The price of one lunch the way they lived would rent a clean room for a week. Maybe he wouldn't accept it. Maybe somebody with a clean room wouldn't want Clint. . . . There was a special note in his voice when he had talked about Ellen. He was another who was devoted to Ellen Bland. That was odd, too. You wouldn't think him capable of devotion. Maybe he hated Louis so much that he was drawn to Ellen merely because Louis had done her wrong too. . . . Anyhow, I would hate, I decided, to have anyone as amoral as Clint Moran hate me. You'd hardly call him completely sane. . . . I thought of Daphne. He resented her hen-like hovering. His resentment had been sharp and definite.

I glanced at Patrick. He was smoking indifferently. But his eyes met and stayed on mine in one of those deep exchanges that make you think the other person knows what you are thinking and is himself thinking the same thing.

Clint just sat and drank and said nothing.

The drinks didn't seem to affect him, other than having given him, perhaps, a talking phase.

He said, abruptly, "I should have stopped Ellen from marrying him in the first place. I knew what he was, if she didn't." That was all. It went back a long time, at least nineteen years. He had a memory, then.

"We've got to push along," Patrick said a little later. Clint said nothing. Patrick paid the bill and we left Clint staring at his glass.

"He's one dilly!" I said, when we were in the dim-out again and meandering towards the Rexley.

"He likes Ellen."

"He hates Louis, and Daphne irritates him."

"He knows plenty behind that dumb-looking facade, Jeanie."

"Can't you make him talk, dear?"

"How?"

"Oh—deprive him of music, or something."

"Not bad, Jeanie! Only, it would take time, and I doubt if the Marines—"

"The Marines!" I exclaimed. I had forgotten the Marine Corps entirely. I said, "So he knows Laura Gilbert? Maybe he did do it, dear?"

"Motive? She wasn't robbed. He couldn't have been interested in her, I think. I mean, for himself. He's never cared about women. He's fond of Ellen because she stands by him, won't let him starve—even when he had money coming in regularly, in Paris, he was broke half the time and Ellen fed him. He is mad at Daphne because she is ambitious for him when he himself has no ambition. Time, to a man like that, is something which just rolls along—if it exists."

"I do feel so sorry for him, darling."

"You're pretty sweet, dear."

We walked along to the Rexley, thinking of poor Clint.

CHAPTER TWENTY-FIVE

We walked under the awning outside the restaurant entrance and the doorman in the mulberry-colored uniform opened the door for us. We sat down at our favorite table. There weren't many people in the place. Music which seemed to issue from the pillar where the beer steins stood on the encircling shelves was at the moment the sweet music from *Show Boat*. Lieutenant Dorn hadn't come in.

"One thing sure," Patrick said, after he ordered Scotch for himself and an Old-fashioned for me, "Clint is all out for Ellen. I'm glad of that." I felt a twinge.

I said, modulating my voice to hide any trace of that twinge, "If you were about to be thrown in the clink on suspicion that you'd brained your beautiful secretary, I wouldn't be sitting around all cool and calm the way Ellen is darling."

"Of course you wouldn't. That's why I married you, dear."

"You didn't marry me. I married you. And I meant what I said, Pat. She's too cool to make sense."

"Exactly what I meant, baby. I like being made a fuss over, which is why I picked you instead of Ellen."

"She was already picked when you met her," I said. "Are you working for them officially, Pat? For Hank and Ellen?"

"No. Ellen can't afford a detective and neither could Hank, I guess." Patrick was being modest. He either worked for nothing or asked outrageous fees. It was about time for one of the latter, with the Marines ahead—oh, I didn't mean to say that. We had enough. Yet we did have expenses—an office, a secretary, a home, an impish dog and an arrogant cat. "Dorn's not fooling, Jeanie. I couldn't just sit around and let him trap them, could I?"

"What makes you think he won't?"

Patrick looked troubled. "Don't say it, darling."

"I'm sorry. Have you any idea who really did it—them, I mean?"

"Ideas. That's about all. How can I prove it? That's the trick."

"It would be just *too too utterly* satisfactory if it turned out to be Mary Kent," I said.

Patrick grinned slantwise. "Motive, dear?"

"I know. That's just it." I set my teeth in my lip. "If only it were Ellen who was dead—"

"God forbid!"

"But it isn't. Two other women whom Ellen would probably be happy to get rid of are dead."

"You sound like Dorn," Patrick said.

Dick Bland came in, saw us and came over. He sat down. "This is luck," he said. "At last. I've been haunting this place, hoping you'd show up." His eyes were abnormally bright. He turned down a drink, saying he hadn't time for it. "I told Jean while we were dancing about leaving the house last night. It wasn't anything, Pat. I wanted a drink, see, so I finally slipped downstairs. There wasn't a thing in the house. Louis's crowd had evidently cleaned out our supply the night before— So I left the house and started to find a drink. Then I got ashamed of myself. So I walked it off. I walked miles, I guess, until I was so tired all I could think of was getting back to bed. There was a detective loitering along outside our house and it wasn't much of a night to loiter—in that soup. He saw me go. To-night when Jean asked me if I left the house I said, before I thought, that I had and it worried me, because I didn't mean to tell anyone and I don't want it to get back to Mother. I'll tell her myself, eventually. After all, I didn't do any drinking."

"Okay, Dick," Patrick said. "Glad you're being careful."

"It's easier if you lay off everything. That darned champagne tonight! Then, when Louis starts in on me—aw, skip it."

"Just watch yourself, kid."

Dick had something else on his mind. He turned it over, you could almost see him doing it.

Dick said, "There's another thing I should tell you, Pat. The night they found Anna I went back to the house, I don't know at what time exactly, but nobody was there. I went up as far as Mother's room, then peeped into Sue's, then I decided to go and get another drink. The drawing room door was open slightly. I snapped on the lights and looked around. Nobody was there, so I went on down and out of the house."

Patrick concealed excitement. "You turned on the chandeliers, didn't you, Dick?"

"Yes. I saw the light streaming out the open window a minute later when I left the house. I didn't go back. I was pie-eyed, and anyhow I didn't remember about the dim-out regulations."

"Where did you go, then?"

"To a place I know on West Forty-ninth, just off Broadway. Dive."

"Is that where you saw Clint?"

"Clint? I didn't see Clint that night—oh, yes, I did, but earlier, along about one o'clock. He was playing in another jernt, that one's on Lexington near Fifty-second. I relate these facts with proper shame, Patrick, because that phase of my life is over." Not entirely, I feared.

"You didn't leave your key in the door when you left the house, did you, Dick?" Patrick asked.

"Key?" He grinned. "Why, yes, I did. Why?"

"I just wondered. There was a key."

Dick said, "I haven't told any of this to Mother. I feel like a jerk, going into that house and then leaving it when, if I had stayed, I might have saved Anna's life, even though it wasn't worth saving. It's bothered me a lot."

"Anna was dead when you were there, probably. If the window was open. You couldn't remember the time?"

"I didn't look. I remember what I do when I drink—I told you that—but I seem unable to do anything about what I do. I ought to have gone to bed that night when I got there. I ought to have gone back to turn off that light. I know I left the key, but I didn't go back to get it. I knew I'd drunk too much already, but I went out and drank more. That's me. I beg your pardon—*was* me."

Patrick grinned at the boy. "That's the stuff, Dick."

When he was gone, I said, "First it was Ellen's key. Then Louis's. Now it's Dick's."

Patrick made no comment.

A few minutes later, Lieutenant Jeffrey Dorn walked in, softly, like a cat. He looked smug enough to have a pocketful of hypos. He sat down with us and ordered rye and appropriated Patrick's specimen of champagne very matter-of-factly. As he dropped it into his pocket, he took care to keep it top up, but otherwise he was fairly uninterested.

Dorn smiled the smile. "Why did Mrs. Bland and her son move to this hotel, Mr. Abbott? That's what I want to see you about."

"Probably because I proposed it. Lieutenant."

"You weren't trying to interfere with the police?"

"I know I couldn't do that, Lieutenant Dorn. But the house was unpleasant after what had happened. There was a new maid. Mrs. Bland suspected her of snooping—"

"Mrs. Bland seems to think everybody snoops."

Patrick ignored it. "She caught the girl going through her personal correspondence. You can't expect her to overlook that?"

Dorn said, "No, I suppose not." (Pretty clumsy work on the part of the lady-police detective, I thought.) "I can see your point, Mr. Abbott. But they should have got police permission to move."

"I don't suppose it occurred to them. It didn't to me. They aren't under arrest, are they, Dorn? They weren't under orders to stay in the house, were they?"

"No," Dorn admitted. He took out his cigar. "No, they're quite free. Naturally."

Patrick spoke softly. "To walk into your traps?"

Dorn smiled. Patrick held a match for his cigar.

"What about the kid, Mr. Abbott?"

Patrick said, "I haven't seen enough of the boy since he was only a very small boy to hold an opinion of any kind about him. Mrs. Bland, however, wouldn't do murder."

"So you said. A very broad statement, Mr. Abbott."

"Not in her case, Lieutenant Dorn."

"You don't care for the boy, I take it?"

"You're wrong. I love that kid. I'd be sick as hell if I thought he was involved in this mess."

Dorn drew on his cigar. "Well, don't be sick, Mr. Abbott. The kid's out. The girl, too. We've got the case sewed up, as a matter of fact." He drummed on the table, his sky-blue eyes watching Patrick. "It would be pleasanter for Mrs. Bland if we arrested her at night, wouldn't it? She'd hate to walk out of a place like this under police escort in broad daylight."

"I'd hate to have her subjected to it at any hour, Lieutenant—aside from the good long horselaugh I would laugh later on when you discovered your mistake."

Dorn smoked placidly.

Then he said, nicely, "We have several new bits of evidence. They're a little puzzling, Mr. Abbott. One concerns a character named Moran. His full name is Clinton Tulane Moran. Tulane is Bland's middle name too, incidentally. You probably know that. They're first cousins, mothers were sisters. Moran did a peculiar sort of errand today, possibly at the request of Mrs. Bland. More about that later. The fellow lives in a cheap rooming-house on Third Avenue—also peculiar because he seems on intimate terms with his rich relatives. We've questioned him twice, once after the Anna Forbes murder and again today about the Gilbert affair. Frankly, we couldn't get a thing. Can't dope him out, don't know if he's stalling or merely feebleminded. So I put a tail on him and have kept him there—"

"I beg your pardon," Patrick put in. "You didn't suspect Moran at first of knowing anything about the Forbes murder, did you, Lieutenant?"

"No. Questioned him as a matter of routine. He is in and out of that house a lot, apparently. Now about that peculiar errand of Moran's. He didn't know he was being watched, of course, and yesterday afternoon, after I'd been working on him myself, Moran went to the Shandon Building, went in a booth in the lobby, made a phone call, then lit a cigarette and hung around near the side entrance. After a few minutes this Mrs. Gilbert came down from Rawlings's office upstairs. She was the one he had phoned to, you see—our man got that much. Moran knew her, but she didn't know him—he had to introduce himself. They went to one corner of the lobby and had a long talk. The woman got mad. Moran was evidently very firm about whatever it was, he didn't talk much but stood his ground. Finally she stamped her foot and said she'd heard enough and started for the elevators. 'Okay, sister,' Moran called after her. 'You've had fair warning.' Then, last night, she was murdered."

Patrick looked shocked. "Holy smoke, Dorn! What do you make of that?"

"What do you, Abbott?"

"I think he bears watching, to say the least."

Dorn said, "Tell me all you know about him, Abbott."

Patrick spoke only after what looked like determined resolution to see an unpleasant duty through.

"I got acquainted with Clint Moran, like the others, a few years ago in Paris. I think I might say I ought to know him better than the others, because I saw more of him. When Clint ran out of money he visited his friends, and as a new friend, I was subject to considerable visiting because he could count on new friends buying drinks. I frankly found it worth while. He is not only a very entertaining pianist. He's also a peculiar human being. I was very curious to know why, or how, he ticked. I spent a good deal of time studying him, but I can't say I know much about him even yet."

Dorn was leaning forward, but trying to conceal his eagerness.

"Like you, Lieutenant, I am certain that Clint knows more about these murders than he lets on. Clint is thoroughly familiar with the Bland house, practically grew up in it. He is there a good deal. There was considerable liquor on the tray the maid brought up the evening we were there, which was the evening before she was murdered. Only Clint of these present was drinking. Yet there was no liquor in the house the next day." Dorn didn't ask and Patrick didn't explain that he had only just heard this from Dick. "Mrs. Bland doesn't drink. I know myself the boy wasn't drinking yesterday." Patrick dropped his voice even lower, for emphasis. "Why couldn't it be possible for Clint to have stayed on drinking that evening after the others left the house? Night before last, I mean. Maybe he has his own key. Maybe he came back and drank up the liquor. Maybe he got drunk and hid in a closet and Anna Forbes found him in the small hours of the night and started bawling him out and he pushed her out the window. Maybe he didn't know what he was doing. He's sometimes a mean customer, when drinking."

Dorn said cagily, "The woman was killed by a blow from the picture, Mr. Abbott."

"I can tell you how the picture happened to be in the drawing room. Daphne Garnett—"

"That silly one, eh?"

"Right. Daphne said Louis Bland brought the picture downstairs and they were looking at it, when they stopped in early in the morning. They left it on the coffee table near the fireplace, thinking the housekeeper would put it back where it belonged in the morning. The murderer probably used it because it was handy."

"Ah," emitted Lieutenant Dorn. It was a nice ah.

He looked cynical again. "Did you question Moran yourself?"

Patrick's nod was full of gloom.

"I tried. It's like talking at a lump of dough."

Dorn nodded sympathetically.

"It's hard to understand, though, why Moran would kill Mrs. Gilbert. He would only have done it because Mrs. Bland asked him to do it, Mr. Abbott. He had no personal quarrel with the woman, he didn't even know her—at least she didn't know him. She had never set eyes on him till they met in the lobby of that office building. He has a doglike devotion to Mrs. Bland. We've found that out anyway. That woman seems to hypnotize people—some people. Fortunately the lady has no such effect on me. She's just Suspect Number One to me, Mr. Abbott. If Moran did it, it was because Mrs. Bland egged him on to kill both women. One word to that sort of moron—Moran, moron, ha, ha." The detective laughed! I stared at him in horror. He was bad enough when he *wasn't* being funny. "I meant to say, one word to a guy like that and anything can happen. If that's how it was, we'll hold her for first degree murder just the same."

Patrick looked sad and resigned.

"Mr. Abbott, I congratulate you," Dorn said.

Patrick looked beaten.

"I haven't understood you entirely," Dorn said. "I wasn't quite sure what you were up to, Mr. Abbott. I'll admit it now. I thought you knew more than you were telling and were covering up for Mrs. Bland. That woman seems to hypnotize people— Pardon, I said that before. Not the women, though. What do you think of Mrs. Bland, Mrs. Abbott?"

Patrick said, "My wife doesn't care for her."

I felt my eyebrows meet. Patrick avoided my glance.

They talked now like buddies.

"What are you doing about Rawlings?" Patrick asked.

"Keeping an eye on him. That's all. Got a man tailing Rawlings and another after Mrs. Bland, and a third on Clint Moran. Called the others off. Needed them on two other jobs, as a matter of fact. Rawlings didn't do it, Mr. Abbott. We're sure of that, though he may know more than he's telling—he's another that's taken in by that woman. Figured you were, too. Don't mind telling you so now."

"You don't know my husband," I said, with an icy glare at Patrick. Whether I liked Ellen or didn't, she was his friend. "He never lets sentiment interfere with business, Mr. Dorn. Would you believe it, he even stood me up at our wedding! We had to wait till he solved a few murders—and the murderess was a lovely creature, but that didn't stop Pat's turning her in."

"You mustn't blame him too much, Mrs. Abbott. Our trade isn't always a pleasant one, but, if I may say so, it is invariably interesting."

"I'll say it is," I said. Very interesting. Poor Clint. Poor Ellen. Poor me, married to two-faced Patrick Abbott.

"Any more ideas about that phone call?" Dorn asked Patrick.

"The one I got, supposedly from Rawlings? Nope."

"Moran has one of those in-between voices, when he uses it, Mr. Abbott. He may have called and the operator may have mistaken his voice for a woman's."

Patrick looked admiring. "Yes. Never thought of that, Dorn."

"Moran had the opportunity. Seems that Miss Garnett started with him in a cab last night to that nightclub restaurant place where he was on the program and he stepped out on a red light at Sixth and West Forty-eighth and disappeared in the crowd. Miss Garnett went on to the place and apologized for him, said he was sick. They assumed he was drunk, but he's good when he does show up, so they let him come back tonight. We checked on all this. You understand."

Patrick lit another cigarette.

Dorn said smoothly, "Mrs. Bland happen to mention where she went when she left the house around midnight last night?"

"Yes. She said she walked west to Madison, down to Fifty-fourth, and back along Fifty-fourth and Park and on home."

"That's what she told you, you mean?"

I said bitterly, "Wasn't it confidential?"

Patrick looked down his nose. Dorn said, "Now, now, Mrs. Abbott. You mustn't take it like that. It's hard for a woman to get the right slant on these things, one reason I never married, I expect. Let's see, Mr. Abbott. At the time Mrs. Bland left her house, Clint Moran was in a drugstore at Fifty-fifth and Madison."

"So were we," I said.

Dorn smiled a smile which would make a poison dart look sweet. "I am aware of that, Mrs. Abbott. My men make careful reports, I assure you. To get back to Moran. He left the drugstore a moment ahead of Miss Garnett. Maybe he saw Mrs. Bland outside, during that instant. Our men didn't note it, but the two who happened to be on that job just then didn't know Mrs. Bland by sight. This is theory, Mr. Abbott. Well, if Mrs. Bland and Moran had an understanding about the Gilbert woman it would take only a glance to make him act. Maybe he saw her. Maybe that explains why he stepped out of the cab."

"Nuts!" I said.

Patrick kicked me, secretly but hard.

Dorn gave me a sour look.

"Did he leave ahead of Miss Garnett, Mr. Abbott?"

"I'm afraid he did. She kept after him to go, then he got up and went suddenly, and she finished something she was saying before rushing after him."

Dorn reiterated, with satisfaction, "If it was prearranged between them a glance from Mrs. Bland lurking somewhere outside would be all it would take."

Abruptly, he reached for his hat. He started to rise. He sat down again, to do more pondering.

If he had a wife he couldn't keep her, I thought. He would bore her to death. In no time at all you would know exactly how he ticked, which was something I could never say about Patrick—the hell with Patrick, just the same.

Dorn said then, "Thank you for your help, Mr. Abbott. Thank you again, I mean. But one good turn deserves another. Am I mistaken in thinking you would like to know what poison was contained in those hypos?"

Patrick's eyes gleamed, gratefully. "I guess you know that, Lieutenant."

Dorn made it dramatic.

"Both hypodermics were filled with a solution of the venom of a South American snake. The deadly *fer de lance*."

CHAPTER TWENTY-SIX

Patrick sat smiling softly after Dorn was gone.

"Snake poison!" I said. "How horrible!"

Patrick laughed.

I said, with ice, "I hope you are amused." I felt bitter. It's a terrible thing to sit by and watch somebody you're crazy about pulling a low dirty trick. I said, with acid, "You look like the cat that swallowed that well-known canary."

Patrick laughed harder. He whooped. People looked.

"You threw poor Clint to that Dorn wolf, Pat. Don't you realize the awful thing you've done?"

"Maybe I threw the wolf to Clint, pal."

"Don't pal me, dear."

"But can't you imagine old Dorn blundering around in the impenetrable maze which is Clint?"

"I don't care anything about that. The thing is, why did you? You don't think Clint—did it, do you?"

"He talked to Laura Gilbert. He threatened her for some reason or other. His departure from the cab in which Daphne was taking him to the nightclub has obviously not been satisfactorily explained. Clint will keep our Dorn busy for a while and gain time for Hank and Ellen. Dorn won't arrest anybody now until he has more thoroughly explored Clint."

"Walked around and around the outside of Clint, you mean. Poor Clint. You've got a lousy profession, Pat."

"Yeah." Pat sighed. "But it has its moments, you must agree."

"Snake poison!" I felt a wave of nausea. "How dreadful! I mean, to carry it around like that. Louis is a freak."

Ellen came in from the lobby. She was dressed as she had been at dinner, in her trim black coat and little hat. She looked distinguished and elegant as she crossed to our table. Patrick rose and seated her, and, refusing anything to drink, she said, "I'm here to bother you again, Pat. Susan left that restaurant almost an hour ago but she hasn't returned to that hotel where she's staying. I'm worried. I thought of calling Bill, but—"

Patrick said, "Don't call Bill, Ellen. An hour or so isn't long in New York. Maybe she went to a movie, or maybe she's visiting with another girl."

"There are thousands of girls in that hotel," I said.

Ellen nodded soberly. "I thought of phoning Louis but it would give him an excuse to come here. I expect you're right. But I am anxious." She looked brighter. "You two do make me feel good. You've got so much sense."

Patrick said, "Now will you have a drink?"

Ellen thought it over, but declined.

"It was a marvelous thought, having us move here, Pat. You've no idea!" Her head was tilted. "I had got so used to my misery in that house that I'd stopped noticing it. That's a fact. Now I have a room of my own. I can sit down and relax, go to bed and not feel that someone is prowling in the rooms downstairs or in the halls. It's wonderful."

Patrick smiled paternally. "It's my duty, Ellen, to warn you that you aren't as alone as all that. Dorn suspects everybody, more or less, and he's not going to lay off watching you just because you've come here. He may lay it on a little thicker."

"I realize that. But that's not the same thing, Pat. We aren't guilty, Dick and I. So let them snoop. We have nothing to conceal. I'm not worried about professional police snooping. It was the kind Anna did that drove me wild. A kind of prying into your very soul." Ellen flung out her hands. "There. It's finished!"

"Right. By the way, we've just had a chat with Clint, Ellen."

Ellen's straight black brows went together. "Clint? Did you go back to The Green Flower?"

"No. We stopped at Reuben's and Clint came in. He's walked out on his job."

Ellen said, "Daphne ought to let Clint alone. She wants to help him, but it's no good."

I said, "He's a queer creature, Ellen."

"Yes. He is. But there's no use trying to peg him in anywhere. Clint can't function in any of the accepted patterns." Her eyes filled with pity. "The people like Clint who can't buck life, specially the talented ones, and let it destroy them—

oh, I feel so deeply sorry for them always. There is only one thing to do for Clint, and that's to take care of him. I've said that a thousand times to Daphne, but she doesn't agree."

Patrick said, "And to Louis too, no doubt?"

"Oh, yes. Over and over. Louis has far more money than he needs. His father would have provided for Clint regardless of what he did, and Louis should, too. He's our job. I do what I can. He was always welcome at that house, at least to a meal. Not a bed—Anna wouldn't permit that. I kept the piano tuned on his account. The liquor in the house was there mostly for him, I thought it better for him to drink there than in cheap dives. Naturally, it would be better if he didn't drink. He is an incurable alcoholic, I think. The battles I fought with Anna, because of Clint."

"He would do almost anything for you, Ellen." I slipped a look at Patrick. If it was double-talk, his face gave no sign.

"Yes. I think he would. Except stop drinking."

Patrick said, "Ellen, why would Clint go to Hank's office-building and call Mrs. Gilbert on the telephone and have her meet him in the lobby and stand there and talk to her?" Ellen sat staring. "Clint knew her by sight, Ellen. But she didn't know him."

Ellen said, "But how odd. How did you know about it?"

"Not from Clint. My source thought Clint was threatening Mrs. Gilbert."

"Clint wouldn't threaten anyone, Pat."

"He might use force, if angry. Mightn't he, Ellen?"

"Yes. He might. On the impulse. But why would he be angry with poor Mrs. Gilbert?"

"Because she was vamping Hank. In other words, for your sake, Ellen."

Ellen said, "We must ask Hank Rawlings about it, Pat."

"He probably wouldn't know about it. The girl wouldn't be likely to tell her boss she'd been accused of vamping him, specially if she had hopes of hooking him, and I'm afraid she had the hopes, Ellen."

Ellen turned pink.

She asked, "How did you know this, Pat?"

"Dorn told me. That's between ourselves. They had a tail on Clint. He couldn't hear what Clint said, but as Mrs. Gilbert left him he shouted out something about having given her fair warning. That night near the time she was murdered, Clint left the cab in which Daphne was taking him to the nightclub and what he did from then on till he got back to his rooming house in unaccounted for."

"But perhaps—they wouldn't actually accuse him of killing Mrs. Gilbert, would they, Pat? I mean arrest him?"

"They might."

Ellen's face went very taut. Her hands worked.

"Pat, he wouldn't. I'm sure Clint knows nothing about that. I can't say why.

Haven't you felt that way about someone? Though you had no proof?"

"Don't let it worry you, Ellen. Suppose they do arrest him. A night in the jug won't hurt Clint, won't be much different from his own digs, if they are as bad as Dorn seems to think."

Ellen said, in a low tone, "Oh, they are. It's a dreadful place. He didn't do it, Pat. He didn't!"

She seemed very sure and very alarmed. Patrick didn't ask any more questions. We had a moment of silence.

Ellen spoke first. "Pat, I know now that I'll never shake off Louis as long as we both live. It's haunted me for days. I'm just fooling myself to think he will marry Mary Kent." She had a funny look in her eyes. "When we were running away from Paris all I could think of was my regret because I hadn't married Hank. Of course, I kept reminding myself, if I had I wouldn't have got the children. But we were going to die anyhow, I thought. Even after we got on board a ship, we hadn't much hope. We thought it would be torpedoed. I made up my mind when we got here, if we ever did, and Hank still wanted me, nothing would stand in the way. But something did. Hank turned me down." She moved her shoulders. "I told you about that."

"Can't say I blame him, Ellen."

"It's Dick," Ellen said. "Dick hasn't a chance—if I fail him. Hank went to Washington then, and a few months ago, Louis started getting definite about Mary Kent, so we kept waiting. But something very queer is happening—I was so sure they would marry—now I am sure they won't—I don't understand it—Anna's death did something to Louis. He's clinging to us as he never did before."

She cut in on herself. "I'm becoming one of those vague fluttery women," she apologized. "But if it isn't one thing it's another. I have to take time out from fretting over Dick to fret over Sue and now it's Clint."

"It's a very bad habit, Ellen. They'll all be all right. Listen, what do you use for money?"

"Money?"

"I don't want you to worry about money, that's all. We're right here, remember."

Tears came suddenly in Ellen's eyes. "How like you to think of that, my dear! But I have plenty of money. I saved quite a lot after I was married and bought an annuity with it, and now I have a little income, have had for more than a year. Sue has her own income now from a trust fund her grandfather arranged for her, so I even have somebody to borrow from, if I should need to."

"It was just an idea," Patrick said.

With an abrupt movement, she straightened her straight back and turned her head a little in the direction of the street door into the Grill. I followed her glance. Hank Rawlings came in. I saw his face when their eyes met. I saw the long tender look. I saw him stop seeing anything but Ellen. Their glances clung together in joy and devotion. When he got to the table, their hands joined involuntarily. There was a perceptible interval before they even remembered we were there. I felt ashamed of myself. Whatever else, they loved each other deeply. This was the real thing, the kind you read about.

I glanced at Patrick. He was watching me, also tenderly, if a little smugly, too, because he loved seeing me finding out that he was right.

CHAPTER TWENTY-SEVEN

I intended to ask Patrick more about the snake poison but it skipped my mind. First because of Hank and Ellen, afterwards because of something that happened as we took the elevator upstairs.

Hank left after a couple of minutes. He'd stopped in to ask Patrick about Ellen. On running into Ellen herself he promptly took himself off lest the police think their meeting was planned—which would make difficulties, he feared, for Ellen.

Patrick stopped at the newsstand for cigarettes and the late papers. I bought a book, a great collection of world masterpieces for twenty-five cents. Not that I expected to read it, but I never feel entirely equipped without a book, particularly when it's everything ever written for only two bits. When we caught up with Ellen, who was waiting near the elevators, Louis Bland was there.

He stood looking down at Ellen, and apparently asking some favor. He seemed humbled, which wasn't his style at all. There was a whining note in his voice, but we didn't really hear anything he said. Ellen's eyes were averted and her mouth was hardened from intense repugnance.

Patrick said in my ear, "That Kent dame certainly has her work cut out for her, snaring Louis."

When Louis saw us he looked bored and departed pronto. Then Ellen went pale all at once. Patrick took her arm. She needed it, too. In the elevator she said harshly, "No one will ever know how I despise Louis Bland. Look at my children! Sue's bitterness! Dick's weakness! Look what he's done to me!" She recovered her self-control. By the time we had reached our floor, nothing unpleasant might ever have happened. We told her good night at her door. That was why the snake venom went out of my mind at that time.

In our room I tossed my masterpieces at a table, fell into my nightgown without even gloating on how elegant heavy pale yellow real-satin crepe feels against your skin, and blacked out on hitting the pillow. I woke suddenly wide awake. Patrick was gone!

His pillow was cold. The spot where he had slept the same. That meant he had been gone some time. The radiolite dial of the traveling clock said twenty minutes to three.

I snapped on the light. A note tucked into the silk shade said, "Gone to find Sue.

You look sweet asleep so couldn't bear to wake you. Back soon. Love, Pat."

I was furious. What a dirty trick, walking out on me like that! I grabbed the telephone. "How long since Mr. Abbott left the hotel?" I asked the clerk.

"Twenty-five minutes, Madam," he replied. He must be keeping a record, to be so exact.

"Thank you," I said.

I got my book thinking how funny it was I had got it so soon before needing it. I opened it at random and landed on this: *"For he seems to have laid it down as a maxim that the best person to murder was a friend; and, in default of a friend, which is an article one cannot always command, an acquaintance; because, in either case . . . suspicion would be disarmed. . . ."*

I closed the book.

Had something happened to Sue? Where would Patrick look? What might happen to Patrick?

Ellen Bland would know—of course she would—at least something—and she could hardly be asleep, for anxiety. I reached for the phone and asked for Mrs. Bland.

The clerk said, "Mrs. Bland left the hotel five minutes ago, Madam."

"Oh. By herself?"

"Alone, Madam."

"Oh. Give me Dick—Richard Bland, please."

"Mr. Richard Bland is not in the hotel, Madam."

Something terrific was certainly going on. I got up and dressed, getting into my suit and topcoat and the felt beret. It was no time for my new hat. A high wind was picking at the blinds. I closed the windows. I put my change purse in my pocket and left my bag. I didn't want to be bothered with a bag. I didn't know exactly where I was going but I might have to walk and the bag would be a nuisance.

I thought the clerk might know more than he'd said on the phone. He declared he didn't. His jaw dropped when I came down—he asked in a polite hotel-clerk-style where the fire was—but all he knew or chose to tell was that Dick, Patrick and Ellen had gone out separately, and in that order, each alone.

Patrick, he said, had turned right from the Fifty-fifth Street entrance. To me, that meant he had gone to the Bland house. I was dead sure of it—rather dumb on my part.

The wind was blowing a gale. It moaned high up around the tops of the sky-scrapers and fell into the narrow street in stiff small whirlpools. It caught at my skirt and swirled it above my knees. I grabbed skirts with one hand and settled my beret deep on my head with the other.

Everything has a reason. That felt beret bought on an impulse from a French *modiste*, and largely because Mary Kent's selfish behavior had made the woman miserable, was to save my own life.

I lowered my head against the wind and hurried east along our usual beat.

Some people see sights in New York but all I had got to know really was a couple of long blocks on East Fifty-fifth Street.

There was no one about. Fifth Avenue was dark and vacant. Only a few distant red and amber lights animated the famous street. Stars shone above skyscrapers. The dimmed light of the street lamps made long shadows, and came back feebly, when at all, from dead-looking shop windows. There was no noise save that made by the wind, and my own footsteps. My heels made too much. I tried to walk softly.

I was afraid. I had that feeling of being watched and followed which I always got from the dim-out. It was worse because the hour and the wind had emptied the streets. I imagined a lurker in every dark doorway.

I hurried as fast as I could, for the wind. All at once I heard a flat dry scraping against the pavement. My back crawled. *Something was following me.*

No, I was meeting it. It was nothing but a scrap of crumpled paper brushed along by the wind. It fastened itself upon a hydrant and flapped viciously. I informed myself that such silly fear was childish. But you couldn't argue away the strangeness of such emptiness bounded by so much dark tallness. I was scared.

So I walked faster. Two cabs with blurred interiors wheeled slowly south along Madison, one behind the other.

A lighted cab went north. It was more disturbing than the others, because inside, two soldiers and two girls in flowery hats laughed and talked like puppets pantomiming in a moving case. The windows were closed and their voices silenced by the wheeze of tires and the rush of the wind. It was uncanny. I ran as fast as possible against the wind.

Then a group of gay people came out of a nightclub just beyond Madison and suddenly everything was fine.

Park Avenue was wonderful in the high wind, because there was room enough for it. It was arrogant and arrowy. Beyond, the block with the old houses was by contrast peaceful and quiet as a cove. I saw the white house with the black railings well ahead and noticed with a feeling of success a slim pencil of light between drawing room curtains not quite closed.

I was breathing hard. To recover my breath, I waited at the top of the steps before ringing.

Then I heard slow padding footsteps like those of a policeman. Patrolman Goldberg? I pictured that heartshaped face, petrified with suspicion, when he spied me. Here again, and at this hour. I reached to try the door knob. The latch wasn't caught. The door opened at my touch.

I stepped inside, closed the door carefully and picked my way through the hall to a spot I thought beneath the hall light. I swung my arm around to catch the chain. I felt exultant at escaping Goldberg. It seemed deliciously exciting. Patrick would laugh! I couldn't find the chain.

I moved forward, still groping in the air, then paused with my arm held up, to listen. That same slow tread was mounting the marble steps.

Deliberate fingers were feeling with a key for the lock. Goldberg was coming into the house. So they were watching the house!

He would find me here. That would not be funny at all. I went stiff with fright. What could I do? There was no time.

My arm descended—gravity no doubt doing its stuff—and touched wood. It was the door of the clothes closet under the stairs. I found the knob, opened it and backed in, sinking against yielding clothes on hangers and smelling shut-in wool and rubber.

The front door opened. Dick Bland's gangling shape, not Patrolman Goldberg's, showed against the moonlight-paleness of the dim-out.

Dick closed the door cautiously and felt his way to the stairs. He went up in the dark. He walked like a tired old man.

It didn't occur to me to speak up. I thought—if I did think—he was drunk. And my own position was so compromising.

At the second floor, Dick turned and climbed directly on to the third.

I stepped out of the closet and went on groping.

Then a queer thing happened. *There were two sets of footsteps.*

As Dick went up the front stairs to the third floor, *someone else was coming from the third floor to the second down the back stairs.*

It was just then I got the first whiff of Ellen's perfume. A wave of the fresh blossomy scent dipped down into the inert air of the first floor hall.

Dick passed the third floor by and went on to the top floor.

A door—the rear door into the drawing room—opened, less silently than Anna might have opened it, but still on silent hinges. I caught only the faint rustle of the latch. I did not hear the door close. Now I was petrified with indecision. I knew definitely that Patrick Abbott was not in this house. What was happening was too creepy for that. What should I do? Grope again and find the light and then announce my presence with a shout? Or step back outside and ring for proper admission? I waited. I took my time, as though I had some, to decide. I decided. Yes, that was the thing to do. To go out, to ring, and be invited in. I dreaded Ellen's calm eyes if I didn't. If she should find me here! She would think me silly. Suspicious. Even jealous! Tsk, tsk!

I took a short step in the direction of the vestibule.

The rear drawing room door closed. I stopped dead.

Someone was coming on down the back stairs. Fast.

Skirts rustled but the flying footsteps hardly sounded on the carpet. I couldn't go now. She would see me against the outdoors as I had seen Dick. Silhouetted in the door. She would think I had been snooping. Mrs. Bland thinks everybody snoops, Dorn had said. She was now in this hall. She came swiftly. The scent of the perfume was strong. I must step back in the closet. No, there wasn't time. She would hear me.

I stood still.

They say that blue eyes can see better in the dark than brown ones, and Ellen's eyes were blue.

CHAPTER TWENTY-EIGHT

The gloomy droplight shone in my eyes. I was flat on the floor. Patrick was stooping over me and feeling my head. "Ouch," I said.

Patrick said later that "ouch" had never been one of his favorite words but it sounded beautiful then.

"Something hit me, Pat."

"Um-m. A Chinese metal vase. If you hadn't had your new French beret on you might have got a skull fracture."

I said, "It was Ellen."

Patrick said, "How did you get here, Jeanie?"

"The clerk said when you left the hotel, you went east."

Patrick made a little sound in his throat. "He told me the same thing. That was why I came here. When I got back, and you'd gone, I came running."

"They say the married get so they think alike. What time is it?"

"Twenty-five past three."

"I haven't been here long anyhow," I said. I sat up. Patrick helped me. I put on my beret, which Patrick had removed, and then, with his help, got onto my feet. I sat down at his suggestion on the chair near the newel post. "Take a step," I said. Meaning a stairstep. "I never expect to regain consciousness."

"How *do* you feel, pal?"

"Awful. My soul aches. My stomach still has butterflies. Hold my hand tighter, please. Dick came in too."

"Dick? . . . Here? . . . When?" His voice sounded staccato.

"Right after I did. He went upstairs. All the way up. At the same time Ellen came down. The back stairs. She didn't speak to Dick. Wasn't that queer? She sort of slipped out. She can see in the dark." Patrick gave me a cigarette and held a match. "You see, there was a light in the drawing room when I got here and I thought you had found Sue and were here, for some reason—did you find her, Pat?"

"No. She hadn't got back to her hotel. Bill doesn't know where she is either. He's fit to be tied."

I said, "The front door lock wasn't caught, see. That's how I got in. I heard somebody coming along the street and thought it was Patrolman Goldberg. I couldn't face all that propriety. Then, it was Dick."

"Dick," Patrick said. Ineptly, like an echo. "Listen, you sit here and I'll have a look through the house—"

"No. I'll come with you!"

"Okay."

Patrick put an arm around me and I leaned against him going upstairs. I didn't need to, really, but it was very solacing. On the second floor, he found the chain and turned on the hall light. He opened the drawing room door. Now the place was dark. He flicked a switch. The lamps swam out all over the elaborate room. He flicked the other switch. The chandeliers blazed. "My God!" he said.

I saw what he saw. A slim foot elegantly shod in a man's evening shoe showed near the fireplace. We crossed the room. I hung onto Patrick's hand. Louis Bland lay in a heap between one sofa-end and the hearth. The satin-lined tails of his evening coat fanned out gracefully, as though arranged so after he had died. The handle of that Florentine paperknife, whose blade unsheathed was slim and darting as a stiletto, jutted from the back of his neck. His eyes were sunken and staring. His jaw had dropped. His long yellow teeth yawned out and made his handsome face hideous.

Gleaming on the rug between the sofas was another hypodermic.

Patrick looked at it wryly. "It didn't do him any good after all," he said.

He picked up Louis's beautiful dead hand—with his other hand that I wasn't hanging on to—and his fingers explored for an absent pulse. It was the left hand. The right was hidden under his coat. Patrick laid the hand down gently and peered down at the paper knife.

"I'll call Dorn, Jean. You wait here—"

I said quickly, "No. I'll come along."

I went ahead into the hall. "What about Dick, Pat?"

Patrick stopped to think.

The front door opened and someone entered. "Who's here?" Ellen Bland called up the stairs.

"We are, Ellen," Patrick said. "Come up."

"I saw the drawing room light," Ellen said, as she hurried up the steps. "I had a last-minute notion that perhaps Sue had come home, so I came here. You must have had the same idea?" She had on her hat and carried her bag. She was somewhat disheveled from the wind but still, I thought, when she came close, tidier looking than other people. No, elegant was the word. It was the way her head sat so elegantly on her neck.

She saw our faces then, and said, her hand flying to her heart, "What is it? What has happened? Something is wrong."

She was a good actress, wasn't she! But why had she returned? "Explain that later, Ellen." Patrick said. "Don't go in that room. Louis is there. He's dead."

Patrick reached for Ellen's arm. But she didn't need his support. She drew back, frowned, and said, "Louis, dead? Maybe you're wrong, Pat. I'll run and call Dr. Seward."

"It won't do any good."

"I don't believe you," Ellen said. "I don't think he's dead. And I also know what to do. If you'll call the doctor, I'll—"

She started for the drawing room door.

"Jean will call him, Ellen. I'll go in here with you."

I didn't like the task, but I performed it while they went back into the drawing room. Dr. Seward grunted when I told him Louis Bland was dead in this house, then roared out that he would be right over. "Don't call the police till I get there!" he commanded. When I got back upstairs Ellen and Patrick were coming out of the drawing room. Ellen was wiping her eyes. Her perfume was faint now, the wind had blown it away. It smelled stronger when she put her handkerchief into her bag.

"The doctor said not to call the police till he got here," I said. "What about Dick, Pat?"

Patrick shook his head at me. Too late. Ellen's glance moved between us.

"Dick?"

Patrick said, "He may be upstairs, Ellen."

Ellen's face went paper-smooth. "I'll go see. No—let me go alone."

"All right, if you want to. But watch the dark corners," Patrick said. Ellen was already up a flight. Patrick said, "I'll go phone Dorn."

"But the doctor said—"

Patrick's answer came dry. "I don't think the doctor can call this one an acci-dent, Jean. You wait here and—"

"No—I'll string right along. Darling—*Ellen did it.*"

Patrick made no answer.

While Patrick was dialing Lieutenant Dorn, we heard a noise in Anna's room. Patrick reached for the door knob and hung onto it while he reported Louis Bland's death to the police detective. He hung up the receiver, opened the door a crack, and switched on a light. It was a bright ceiling light. It glared on Clint Moran, who lay face down in his dirty brown suit across Anna's clean white bed. The stale air of the closed-up room was pungent with the juniper odor of gin.

Patrick turned off the light and shut the door. "He'll keep." He turned towards the back stairs.

Ellen was coming down, hurrying.

We waited.

"Dick's so sleepy he can't wake up. I must make some coffee. Oh, Sue's here, Pat. I glanced in her room, and there she was. I woke her. She's dressing."

That made a quorum, I thought. The whole family. Ellen. Dick. Sue. Cousin Clint.

"Did you tell me Clint had a key, Ellen?"

"I don't know. But he does have. Why?"

Patrick jerked his head at Anna's room. "He's in there. You'd better make plenty of coffee."

Ellen's eyelids faltered, then swept down.

"Yes, of course." She looked up. "Couldn't we get him out, Pat? Before—before the police get here? Dr. Seward will take him away, perhaps."

"I've already telephoned Dorn, Ellen."

Ellen stopped breathing. For once she looked really scared. She said, "Oh." Then she cried out, "But why did you do it, Pat? You had no right! The doctor said not to. Why—"

"I know. But this isn't the doctor's case. Louis was murdered."

Patrick asked, "Ellen, what was Louis saying to you tonight? There by the elevators?"

"Nothing important," she answered.

Ellen went on down to the basement kitchen. Patrick went towards the front of the hall. He picked the Chinese vase up, with his handkerchief protecting it, and set it in the clothes closet.

Dr. Seward arrived, breathing hard from too fast walking for a fat man against a head wind. He risked apoplexy by puffing right on upstairs when told where Louis was. He halted beside the heap and stared hard. He stared at the paper knife. He stooped with much grunting over the body. He reached out to touch the knife. He drew back his hand. He felt the pulse at the wrist, the throat, the temple. He said, "Less than an hour certainly." He closed the eyelids and the jaw. Now Louis Bland was beautiful again.

It was ten minutes to four.

The doctor struggled to his feet and stood looking at the hypodermic on the rug. He started to pick it up, then waved his pink hands and left it. "It did him no good after all," he said.

Patrick had said the same thing!

Patrick stated, "He was a hemophilic, Doctor."

"No, he wasn't!" Dr. Seward barked. He glared at Patrick, from habit.

Patrick said, "Why did he carry the viper-venom solution then? Why did he say what he said to Sue?"

The doctor emitted a heavy sigh.

"He wasn't a real hemophilic. Bleeder," he added, as if he had to explain it. "But it's true that his blood didn't coagulate normally. I doubt if he could have survived any major operation without a fatal hemorrhage. Louis spent his whole life in dread of bleeding to death. He carried the snake venom for that reason—it's a coagulant, if used locally, as you apparently know. But he wasn't a true hemophilic because there is no family history to that effect, which is necessary to confirm it. He had no right to say what he said to the girl. After he was gone, her mother and I would have told her the truth."

"Sue had cause to murder him, Doctor," Patrick said.

"Fiddlesticks! She wouldn't do such a thing. I know that girl."

Ellen came in by the rear door.

"Well, Ellen, it happened after all," Dr. Seward said. "But not the way he feared. His spinal cord is probably severed, and there was probably little or no bleeding." The doctor sighed his heavy sigh. "Anyway, we kept his secret."

"Who all knew it?" Patrick asked.

"No one now but Clint, Dr. Seward and I. And probably Mary Kent. People knew he carried the hypodermics but they didn't know why. We never told. We'd promised."

"Anna knew, didn't she?"

"Yes."

Dr. Seward said, "Anna kept a hypodermic about her just in case. I think she was disappointed in never getting her chance to save Louis's life."

Ellen broke in, "Listen, Dr. Seward! Clint's in Anna's room. He's drunk. We've got to get him out of here before the police come."

"We can't do that, Ellen," Dr. Seward said, shaking his head slowly. "This was murder."

Ellen looked frightened. And determined.

CHAPTER TWENTY-NINE

Law and order is navy-blue. It arrived on the heels of Lieutenant Jeffrey Dorn in the shape of a flock of uniformed policemen. In no time at all several large solid-looking patrolmen managed to be everywhere, looking very navy-blue. This being indubitably murder—Louis Bland wouldn't be likely to stick the knife in the back of his neck, just like that, anyway—there was no pussyfooting as in the Anna Forbes case. Experts swarmed like ants, taking pictures, fingerprints, poking the dead man, this and that. One expert found Louis's black cigarette-holder behind the sofa near which he'd fallen. The cigarette had burned a tiny brown hole in a valuable rug. Another lifted Louis's coattails and discovered his other hand grasping a perfumed handkerchief. The name embroidered on the handkerchief was *Ellen*. Others searched the house, and us.

One expert did nothing but stand around with a swathed flat package which turned out to be *The Pink Umbrella*.

It was very impressive. It was also dull.

I could see myself what ailed it. It was just too efficient. Dorn didn't do his own poking and sniffing, he had others do it for him. Maybe he thought he had to keep them busy. He formed *his* judgments on *their* opinions. Tsk, tsk. Maybe that's why he turned out not so bright as I feared. Even though Patrick still insists Dorn is both a good guy and smart.

Anyhow, it was soon over. Many hands at least make quick work. The experts filtered out. Louis Bland was removed in a basket, which he would have found most distasteful, to be carved up at an autopsy, a huge indignity to his person which would merely prove what the preliminary investigation surmised, that he had died from the stab in the back of the neck. His mother had bought the knife as a souvenir in Florence when there on her honeymoon, before Louis was even thought of. I found that fascinating. Dorn didn't.

The chased handle of the knife had been wiped clean of fingerprints. The blade, the doctors opined, and the autopsy confirmed, had severed the spinal cord.

All fingerprints had also been wiped off the hypodermic which, like its predecessors, had not been employed in the murder.

Dr. Seward and the medical examiner's doctors talked with Lieutenant Dorn about coagulating time, plasma, hemophilia, fear, the imagination, and viper venom. They discussed the relative merits as coagulators of rattlesnake, Russell's viper, and *fer de lance* venom. Patrick hung on every word but I stood away and shivered. It was a queer thing, I meditated, as fact was piled on opinion and opinion on fact, that a man's coagulating time being a little longer than that of other people should make him a nagger who bullied everybody connected with him ceaselessly all his life.

Then the body and the experts were gone. We all had coffee. One of the patrolmen had taken over that job from Ellen, Dorn being apprehensive of mass murder from coffee flavored with cyanide. (The report from Patrick's champagne had corroborated his suspicions.)

The patrolmen remained, strategically spaced. Patrolman Goldberg, in reward for having been in on the ground floor of the murder sequence, was assigned the drawing room. Lieutenant Dorn, in his well-tailored gray suit and another becoming necktie, sat at a table drawn near the front door of that room. A detective-sergeant named Herschel Pepple took notes in shorthand—there had been other note-takers with the experts.

The remainder of us faced Dorn, in two rows made with chairs and sofas.

In the front row from left to right were Ellen Bland, Dr. Maxton Seward, Dick Bland, Clint Moran, Susan Bland and—because he wouldn't sit elsewhere—Bill Reynolds, then Patrick and I. In great contrast to the rest of us Bill and Susan looked radiantly happy. They were making wedding plans, now that Susan was convinced she wasn't a social menace. In the second row, in order, were Louis's lawyer, who looked it, Mary Kent, appropriately garbed in grayish tweed and a gray felt hat, Daphne Garnett, ornately frazzled, and—a little apart—the two house servants, and finally Louis's valet, a Briton with a long melancholy face. All had been sent for by the police.

Dorn's sky-blue eyes were very round and very innocent. He was not smiling.

This was not a formal examination, he said. That wouldn't come until the murderer was formally accused.

This sounded to me like a kind of trap.

"I believe that I myself am somewhat to blame for this dastardly murder," Dorn said. That smacked of the trap, also. "The exigencies caused by the dim-out plus a current epidemic of local crime has put a great strain on the Force. No man can be two places at the same time."

"He's got something there," I whispered to Patrick.

He nudged me, scowling.

Among other things, Dorn said that when we had all got back to our respective abodes last night he had called his sleuths off because they were needed elsewhere. After our extreme activity on the previous two nights Dorn didn't think we would start anything again last night, everybody, even murderers, needing their rest. He had been in error. That was why he blamed himself, so to speak, for Louis's murder.

He began the direct questioning with Daphne Garnett.

Daphne said flutteringly that she knew absolutely nothing about anything. Louis Bland had been her guest at dinner last night, along with other people. He had left with Mrs. Kent, around eleven, she thought. She could not swear it, however.

Did she know that cyanide was put in his champagne last night at that dinner?

"Why, how dreadful!" Daphne cried. She forgot her French as she declared, "Well, I myself wouldn't've done it, Officer. I didn't even invite them. They asked to come. If I had been going to try to murder Louis, I would have invited them, wouldn't I?"

The etiquette of the situation gave Dorn to think.

"There you are," Daphne said.

Dorn asked her if she knew who killed Louis.

"It must have been a stranger," Daphne said. "Everybody who knew Louis simply adored him."

With this glorious lie, Daphne ended her contributions to the solving of the murder.

Mary Kent's eyes were red, but she had chic even in grief.

"Louis and I left Daphne's party shortly after eleven o'clock. We went on to El Morocco."

"Directly, Mrs. Kent?"

She hesitated, then said, "No, on the way we stopped for a moment at the Hotel Rexley. Louis wanted to talk to Ellen—Mrs. Bland. I waited in the cab. He was gone only a few minutes and came back very much disturbed."

"Did he say why, Mrs. Kent?"

She avoided the question. "He soon recovered his usual high spirits. He dropped me at my hotel at ten minutes past two. I noticed the time by the clock in the lobby as I entered. He said he was coming to this house to see if his son and daughter had returned, as he had requested, then on to his hotel, the Jacques." Her voice lowered. "That's all."

Dorn asked carefully. "Did he say anything about expecting the former Mrs. Bland to return to the house as well as the children?"

Mary Kent said quietly, "I'm sorry."

Dorn let it pass. Everyone—you could tell—felt that Mary Kent was being very decent to Ellen.

"Did anyone see you return to your hotel, Mrs. Kent?"

"But definitely. There was a night clerk at the desk when I asked for my key and two elevator men were at their cars. I spoke to them and told them good night."

"Good," Dorn said. "Thank you, Mrs. Kent."

Dorn asked the lawyer next how much money Louis had been worth, and who would inherit. We learned nothing.

"He was in my office yesterday arranging some—an allowance," he said. He was sorry he said it, and refused to say more.

Dr. Seward reiterated the snake-venom false-hemophilia business and said it was absurd to think anyone would *deliberately* murder Louis Bland. To be sure he was sometimes annoying, but always generous about money. The doctor was entirely irked. He thought Dorn ought to designate the murderer pronto, so everybody could go home.

Susan Bland said she came home last night because she had drunk too much champagne which made her feel sick and she was ashamed to go back to the girls' hotel. "I couldn't face being given the once-over in that condition by five thousand dames," she said.

"Are you accustomed to drinking, Miss Bland?"

"God forbid," said Susan. "It's a filthy habit."

She glared at Dick, who winked back, rather limply.

"You recently quarreled with your father, didn't you, Miss Bland? That was why you left home, was it not?"

"Sure. Everybody quarreled with Louis. But he always started it. Every darn time," Susan said, warming up.

"Don't you regret it?"

"No," Susan said defiantly.

Dorn pressed his lips tight. "What did you do when you got to this house last night?"

Susan looked aghast. "Must I tell everything?"

"Why not?"

Susan considered it. "Well, for a while I was sick as a horse. I erped, so to speak, then I was terribly sleepy and fell into bed. The next thing I knew Mother woke me and told me to get dressed."

Bill Reynolds said he knew nothing to tell. In his blue uniform he looked rosy and fresh and very disapproving.

Dick's downy dark-eyed face was twisted with distress. He was much more affected than the others.

"I came home for a very silly reason. Any port in a storm, see. I was just too darn tired, so to speak, to walk on as far as the hotel."

"You had your key?"

"Yes, sir."

"Well. Speak up!"

"There isn't anything to tell. I managed to stagger up the steps to the door and unlocked it, and thought thank God there is nobody to wake in this dump so I won't have to take my shoes off and went on up and fell on a bed and blacked out. I guess it wasn't such a terrific idea, at that."

"You didn't undress?"

"No, sir. Couldn't. Didn't even turn on the light."

"Drunk?" Dorn snapped.

Dick drew himself up. "Certainly not! That was why I was tired. I walked it off, see. Walked off the urge."

"Where was your mother?"

"I don't know, sir. At the hotel, asleep, I guess."

"You guess," Dorn said thoughtfully. "You didn't come in this house and go out again, did you, Dick? Something didn't happen here that you felt you had to go out and walk off? Something that made you very, very tired?"

The lawyer popped up. "You needn't answer that, Dick."

Dorn smiled the smile. "No. He needn't. That will do for now, Dick."

Dick sat down. Clint Moran was next. He said gruffly that when he got to his rooming house somebody was already in his bed and so he exited, then took a Lexington bus and came here. "Thought nobody would be in the old house and I'd have a good bed for a change."

Dorn's voice was very casual.

"Why did you choose Anna Forbes's bed?"

"Well, it was handy. First floor. Kind of tickled me, too, thinking how she'd feel if she knew it."

Ellen shook her head at Clint. Dorn took note. His eyebrows stirred. He remembered where he was and controlled them.

"Were you intoxicated, Mr. Moran?"

"Drunk as a skunk, Sarge," said Clint.

Sergeant Pepple looked up from his shorthand and stuffed back a grin, at that Sarge.

"Perhaps you were not in a condition to know just what you were doing, Mr. Moran?"

Clint yawned. "Could be."

"What time did you get here?"

"Good God, how would I know? I told you I was blotto. How long does this inquisition go on, anyhow?"

"For some people it will continue for some time," Dorn said. "You may sit down."

The valet said he had no idea what was in the hypodermic syringes which Louis

Bland had several of, it not being his business to know, only to keep them neat and see that his master always had one in his pocket, and, on occasion, take them to Dr. Seward—why he could not say, because it wasn't his business to know. Yes, though perhaps he should not say so, he had several times given Mr. Bland an injection of the liquid, once when the master cut himself with a piece of glass, another time when he was scratched by a rose-thorn.

"You know how to use a hypodermic, do you?"

The long face got longer. "Dr. Seward very kindly instructed me, if I may say so."

"Do you mean to say you had no curiosity about the contents of those hypos? When you handled them all the time?"

"Indeed, no, sir. It was not my affair."

"Do you know if Mr. Bland was afraid of anyone or anything in particular?"

The valet thought it over.

"It was none of my business, sir, but, though perhaps I shouldn't say it, he was terrified of sharp objects, sir."

"Mary Kent's fingernails," I muttered, at Patrick.

"Shush."

Patrick was next. He had nothing to say, save that he found the body because he had come to the house in the night looking for me. "It was my fault that my wife came here," he said. "If I had left word where I had gone, she would not have left the hotel. Being uncertain, and distressed by the tragedies which have accidentally involved us, she became alarmed and ran over here, believing I would come here to look for Sue." It sounded very dignified, put like that. He didn't say one word about my outsize curiosity.

Dorn said, very deadpan, "Too bad you don't know about our Missing Persons Bureau, Mr. Abbott. You needn't have gone out to look for Miss Bland yourself, you know."

Patrick gave him a slanting glance.

"I hated to put you to any extra bother, Lieutenant," he drawled, western fashion. "Knowing how busy you are."

I should have said before that we had made short statements previously to Sergeant Pepple, which Dorn had read and considered, so that no full statement of everything we had done was necessary now.

Dorn let Patrick go. I was the next.

I told about entering the house. I omitted the terror part—that I had thought that tread, which must have been Dick's, was Patrolman Goldberg's. I could feel the patrolman watching me now. That heart-shaped face probably had a heart-shaped brain behind it with a special crease in it because Goldberg never would believe that I was legally married to Patrick Abbott. San Francisco had confirmed his official inquiry, but what good was Frisco's—as Goldberg called it—word? That uncivilized place! Look at the movies.

"Do you know what time you arrived here, Mrs. Abbott?"

"It was two minutes past three when I left the Rexley. Maybe it took me ten minutes to walk here, because of the wind."

"The door was open?" He sounded skeptical.

"The door was closed. But the latch hadn't caught. I accidentally rested my hand on the door and it opened."

"You didn't ring?"

"No."

Dorn's voice was supersmooth. "Why didn't you ring?"

"I—I don't know."

"Come, come, Mrs. Abbott."

"All right. I was scared. The street was so spooky, in that wind."

"Indeed?" What sarcasm! "Continue, Mrs. Abbott."

"Well, I was trying to locate the light-chain when I heard somebody put a key in the front door lock. I stepped into the hall closet."

"Why?"

"I was scared. Why must I keep saying it? I was jittery."

"You thought your husband was upstairs, didn't you? I should think you would have called out, if you were scared."

"Well, I didn't," I said. "Then I saw Dick come in. He went straight up to the top floor, just as he said he did."

"You didn't speak to him?"

"No."

"But why not?"

"Well, I felt such a fool, that's why. How would you feel if somebody caught you lurking in a closet?"

"Continue, Mrs. Abbott," Dorn said crisply.

"I decided then to go back outside and ring and come in the right way."

"What was your impression of Dick, Mrs. Abbott?"

"I couldn't even see him, you see, except his silhouette. I had just come in. My eyes weren't yet adjusted."

"How did he sound?" Dorn insisted.

"He walked as though he was tired."

"Maybe he was carrying a load," Dorn said. "On his mind," he added, succinctly.

I saw Ellen's face. It went white.

"No, he just sounded weary," I said quickly. "I'm sure Dick told you the truth, Mr. Dorn."

Dorn smiled the smile, "Go on!"

"Well, I didn't go out and ring as I planned because just then somebody came slipping down the back stairs and about the next thing I knew the light was on and Pat—my husband—was there."

The lieutenant produced the Chinese vase, still swaddled in Patrick's handkerchief.

"Was this what you were struck with, Mrs. Abbott?"

I said, "My husband said so."

"Do you know who did it?"

I could feel Patrick's eye. But I didn't look at him.

All the same, I couldn't say the word which would accuse Ellen.

"No."

"Man, or woman?"

"I—I don't know."

"Perhaps it was Dick, going out again?"

"I— No, I think not."

"Why?"

"There were two people. I am sure I heard two. Dick and somebody else. The second one was more careful. It wasn't Dick."

Dorn said, "Your husband remarked that you have a keen sense of smell, Mrs. Abbott. Did you smell anything?"

"Yes. Wool and rubber, in the hall closet. The whole house was stuffy, rather."

"No perfume, Mrs. Abbott?" His voice was very cunning. I said nothing. I just couldn't.

He produced an envelope and held up the handkerchief found in Louis's dead hand. It gave off a faint ripple of that blossomy scent. "Don't you recognize this perfume, Mrs. Abbott?"

I thought it over. "I think my husband exaggerated my ability."

Dorn shrugged disgustedly. From another envelope he set out a small vial. "We took this from a handbag," he said. "That will do, Mrs. Abbott. I'm afraid we're just wasting everybody's time. Mrs. Ellen Bland—if you please."

Ellen stood up. There was a rustle. There always was, spiritual or otherwise, when she came into the picture.

"This is your handkerchief, Mrs. Bland?"

"Yes. It is."

"How did it happen to be in Louis Bland's dead hand?"

"I do not know."

"He saw you at that hotel tonight?"

"Yes, for a moment."

"What happened to upset him?"

Ellen said, "I think it had nothing to do with his murder."

The lawyer popped up. "This is not a formal inquest, Mrs. Bland. You needn't answer—"

Ellen said, "I have nothing to conceal."

Dorn said, "You're very sure of yourself, aren't you, Mrs. Bland! That's very interesting. Yes. You're very sure. That's the word. If you wanted to stick a knife in a person, Mrs. Bland, you would be very sure to choose the best place. You were a nurse. I daresay you studied anatomy?"

Dorn's words spun out sharp and venomous.

The lawyer rose, waved his hands, sat down.

Ellen kept silent.

Dorn said, "I have here the brief statement you made to Sergeant Pepple just after we arrived here tonight. You say you walked from the time you left the hotel, until three thirty-five, when you arrived at this house. We know at what time you left the hotel. We also know when you got to this house—according to Mr. Abbott. You had an hour, Mrs. Bland. Why don't you tell us what really happened?"

The lawyer coughed.

Ellen said, "I really did walk almost all that time, Officer."

"That's absurd! At that hour? In such wind?"

"I liked the wind. Very well, this is my story. At ten minutes past two I had had no word from her hotel about Susan. I had called there shortly before midnight, and had asked that a note be put in her box, asking her to ring me when she got in, regardless of the hour. Susan never drinks. I was concerned about her at dinner. But she dislikes interference, so I let it go. It worried me. I couldn't sleep. So, at ten minutes past two, I got up and tapped on the Abbotts' door, very lightly, thinking that they might be asleep. I didn't call on the telephone, which would be sure to wake them. Mr. Abbott heard me and came to the door. He said that Mrs. Abbott was asleep but he hadn't been and for me to go back to bed and he would go out and find Susan. I heard him go out five minutes later. But I couldn't rest. Then I discovered that Dick was not in his room, either. Our rooms adjoin. The door between was closed but not locked. He had left without my hearing him. So I dressed and went for a short walk."

Dorn restrained a sniff. "Walk?"

"I always walk when I'm disturbed, Officer. Well, I walked to the hotel where Susan had stayed the previous night. I didn't think Pat—Mr. Abbott—would go there, thought he would think it useless. I felt that a personal call might do what the telephone hadn't. Or she might be ill and not answer the phone. But she wasn't at the hotel. So I started back to the Rexley. Suddenly, it occurred to me she might have come here. I finally got a taxi and got here to find—well, you know the rest. I didn't even phone the hotel to see if Mr. Abbott had returned because I didn't want to wake Mrs. Abbott."

"That's a lot of walking," Dorn commented. His glance went to Dick. "You like walking, too. Like mother, like son, eh?"

Ellen's eyes blazed. "You are unfair!" she said.

Dorn ignored it. "We are again wasting time. You quarreled with your husband last night, Mrs. Bland. Luckily we have a record of that quarrel, since it took place publicly, in the lobby of the Rexley, near the elevators. He begged you to return to this house. You refused. He said it hurt his pride to have his children moved out from under his own roof like that. He said he was on his way to a nightclub, but afterward he would come to this house and, if the children, at least, had not returned, he would stay here till they did."

"Sit-down strike, yeah?" said Clint. Dorn gave him a glare.

Ellen said, "It was his custom to get his own way, even though he put himself out considerably to do it."

"You admit that you knew he was coming here then?"

Ellen did not answer.

Dorn picked up the vial of perfume. "If you took a taxi to your daughter's hotel, instead of walking, you had time for everything. Bland came here after he dropped Mrs. Kent at her hotel. You knew he was coming. Maybe he knew the girl had come in, maybe not. The boy may have been in and out. Anyhow, Bland waited."

Dorn took a deep breath. "This little bottle of perfume, which is the same as that on the handkerchief, is the only perfume of the kind in the house or on the person of anyone present. One of my men took it from your handbag this evening. Ellen Bland, you murdered Anna Forbes, Laura Gilbert and finally Louis Bland. Clinton Moran and Richard Bland, I order your arrest on suspicion of willfully aiding and abetting this cold-blooded woman in these outrageous murders. Take them into custody, Goldberg."

There was a brief pandemonium in which everybody behaved according to type. Patrick sat. I enjoyed a deep prickle of gladness because anyhow I hadn't told on Ellen. I never would.

Dorn gloated. His face radiated success.

Goldberg and Pepple restored order.

Patrick stopped relaxing and went over and started a whispered talk with Dorn, who shook his head to start with, then finally gave in, as if yielding to a childish whim.

"Sergeant Pepple, please take Mr. Moran into the hall and keep him there," he said. "Goldberg, see that the furniture is put back where it belongs. You help," he said, to the cook and housemaid.

Very quickly the room was back in order, the sofas facing across the fireplace, the chairs and tables placed. "Please, no smoking for just a few minutes," Patrick said, as Mary Kent's hand snaked towards her bag. "Put the picture on the coffee table," he said to its keeper.

The man unwrapped *The Pink Umbrella* as though it were a priceless treasure and laid it face up on the table.

It was a nice thing. It was no masterpiece, but it glowed as though it itself were happy.

It's the pinks, I thought. Two pink-cheeked kids on pinkish sands under a rosy-pink umbrella. The pink in the umbrella was gorgeous. The kids were happy. The painter had been when he painted it, too.

One joint of the heavy frame gaped. That corner was blunted.

Ellen sat on the sofa with its back to the windows. So did I. I saw her handkerchief steal to her eyes. Then she was calm again.

When everything was ready, Patrick turned the lights out and left the room. We sat in the darkness. Our eyes began to adjust. I saw Dorn standing near the light switches and Goldberg near the piano.

Patrick came back and stood leaning against the mantel. More minutes passed.

Then the rear door opened without a sound and a solid gray figure padded stealthily across the room to the middle window. Without disturbing the drapes it turned the catch and opened one panel of the window which, swinging inward, carried the drape with it.

A lean path of light, like pale moonlight, streamed across the room. It fell on Mary Kent.

She let out a gasp. She stared at the window. Her hand stretched for the picture. She remembered herself. The hand curved back towards her bag.

Patrick stooped and took the bag. Mary Kent swore angrily. Then she was quiet.

I glanced at the window. Anna Forbes, in her gray robe, seemed to be standing there.

Patrick said, "The light was brighter that night, Mary. The fog blended with the streetlight made a kind of glow. Anna saw you more plainly than we do now."

"I don't know what you mean!" Mary Kent said hoarsely. "Give me my bag, you—!" It was an ugly word. It shocked me. Patrick went on, in a graveyardy tone, "You sat here in the dark. Waiting. She came in. You were not waiting for Anna, Mary. So you sat very still. You didn't want her to see you. She would tell Louis. You didn't want Louis to know. You were waiting for Ellen. You came here that night to kill Ellen, because it was your only chance to get Louis, and you were at the end of your rope, with all your money sunk in German munitions, and Germany losing the war. Not winning, as you had counted on."

Mary Kent let out a scream. "Daphne Garnett, if you told on—"

Patrick interrupted her, and still talking in that doomful tone, said, "You were pretty tense, weren't you, Mary? Naturally. It isn't easy to sit and wait to kill. So when Anna spied you sitting there, silent, and lashed out at you in her fashion, you picked up the picture, which was so handy, and hit her in the head, and then, when you realized she was dead, you bundled her out the window to make it look like a fall."

With sudden resignation Mary Kent said, "I didn't mean to kill her."

"No. You meant to kill Ellen."

"Ellen spoiled my life."

"You killed Laura Gilbert, who did you no harm whatever. You killed Louis Bland, who treated you with more kindness than, I think, he ever showed anyone else."

Mary Kent was silent.

"The first hypodermic," Patrick said, "fell from the pocket of Anna's bathrobe. When you learned that the hypo cast suspicion on Ellen you planted the others to trap her. You killed Laura Gilbert simply to throw more suspicion on Ellen. You killed Louis for two reasons. First, you were bitter because, after all you'd sunk to, to get him, he was going to stand you up." Patrick turned to the lawyer. "You said that Louis Bland arranged an allowance yesterday. Was it for Mrs. Kent?" The lawyer nodded. Patrick said, "Did you kill him because it wasn't enough? Or because you thought he'd wriggle out of paying it, if he lived?"

"Give me my bag!" Mary Kent said.

Patrick asked, "Have you more cyanide in your bag? I think I'd better hand it over to Sergeant Goldberg, Mary. Cyanide is too easy a way out, for you."

The Tristan and Isolde music Clint elected for Louis Bland suddenly started rolling from the piano. Lieutenant Dorn yelped and snapped on the lights. Clint was playing, still in Anna's gray robe.

CHAPTER THIRTY

A few hours later Patrick and I sat breakfasting in the bay of our bedroom. It was a lovely day. Sunlight streamed in and glorified the silver and porcelain and glass, orange juice, toast, bacon and eggs, the precious brown coffee. We had had some sleep and baths, and our letters had been sent up.

One of them was from the Marines. Patrick had to report in five days. That was wonderful. Five days—I wanted to see the sights of New York, and Patrick was glad because he wanted to take plenty of time over Ellen and Hank's and Bill and Susan's wedding presents.

I nibbled toast and said, "Of course, it is *too too utterly satisfactory* that she was the one, but how did you guess it, dear?"

"I didn't guess it," Patrick said, reproachfully. "Not entirely, anyway."

"Then how?"

"I couldn't've but for you, pal."

"No fooling, dear."

"I'm not kidding. It's true. You found Hortense."

"Hortense?"

"It could have been done without Hortense, if there had been plenty of time, but she expedited matters. She told me, without knowing it, that Mary Kent was broke."

"Broke?"

"Put every bean in German munitions. I suspected it all along. All of them raved on about Paris—God, who doesn't? The light, the sky, the food, the cafés, the people, the specialness which is Paris—the flowers near the Madeleine, the tiny tots in kid gloves rolling hoops in the Luxembourg—"

"But Mary Kent? Remember?"

Patrick frowned. "Please go away and let me dream. That's a pal."

"But I don't see how you thought it all out. I suspected everyone more than Mary Kent. I thought Daphne did it, so Clint would get the money. I thought Clint did it, for his peculiar kind of fun. I suspected Susan, trying to involve her father, with the hypos. I ached for Dick, thinking he'd done it for his mother's sake. And I suspected Ellen all along. How did you do it, really?"

"Child's play, in this instance. Nothing to it. They were all nuts about Paris, and why not? Except the kids. America spells paradise to kids the world over. Ellen didn't want to live in Paris because her heart was here, with the kids, and with Hank. Daphne, Clint, Louis and Mary Kent hankered after Paris. Clint not too much because it took effort, but—"

"Poor Clint."

"Rich Clint. He's coming into a fat slice of dough, after the government's satisfied. Well, Daphne was pretty verbal about her disappointment over putting money in German munitions. She hadn't it to spare, she said, like Mary Kent. That set me thinking. There was something awfully urgent in Mary Kent's longing to go back to Paris. Too urgent. She didn't care if the Germans were there. They didn't bother people with money, she said. I puzzled it.

"You had told me about going to the hat shop. I thought about Hortense. An ocean voyage must have affected French finesse, I decided, if a *modiste* had lost her Parisian touch to the point of risking an old and rich customer by arguing with her. Something was cooking. And who would know more about a chic lady than her chapeau-maker? I called on Hortense."

I felt suddenly flat. "Oh. Then you didn't go just to buy me a hat?"

"Good Lord, woman! I wouldn't have the nerve to buy you a hat. The woman had it, waiting for you. Yellow eyes and black hair—she asked me when I mentioned a green hat—a type, she called you."

"What did it cost?"

"Forty dollars."

"Pat, you idiot! She held you up!"

"Oh, I don't know. It was no time to let her know I wasn't rich myself, chum. What she told me was worth a lot more than forty dollars. I managed—with consummate art, if I must say so myself—to worm out of her that Mary Kent was desperate about money."

He got on with the solution.

"All the time Mary Kent was the only one of them with the character of the cold-blooded murderer, but there had to be a reason why she did it. Why?

"I kept on puzzling it. What had Mary Kent's desperation to do with Anna Forbes? Why would Anna's death matter one way or another to Mary Kent? There had to be that reason why.

"I decided soon that the Anna Forbes murder was probably unpremeditated.

The use of the picture as a weapon confirmed it—though I had believed, to start, that she had only been pushed out the window. The area was deep. The fall could have been enough.

"I decided, then, that Mary Kent had done it and that it was Ellen she had been after. That was why I finally persuaded Ellen to move to this hotel. I knew that Mary Kent had gone to that house that night to kill Ellen. Mercifully Ellen was out—at Reuben's, with Clint. To kill Ellen was Mary Kent's only real chance at getting Louis. To have Ellen entirely out of the way. Louis would take her to South America. They would get to Buenos Aires, and back to France. If Louis balked, Mary would snuff him out, too, and thus be a rich widow, with money on both sides of the Atlantic. On top, whoever won the war. Louis was a dead duck, Jeanie, whichever course events took. It was only his money Mary wanted.

"That was my theory. It made sense. But to prove it!

"Well, swinging a hatbox with a green hat in it, which no self-respecting detective would do, I ambled along from Chez Hortense to the Hotel Dijon. Like so many New York hotels its service entrance also served as a fire escape and was respectably invisible from the front lobby. It would be no trick at all to go in and out without attracting notice by using the broad enclosed cement back stairs. Specially, late at night. That took care of that item. You took notice that Mary Kent told Dorn about telling the clerk and elevator men good night. She would take that precaution, with what she had in mind.

"Let's go back to the hypo. The first one was old Anna's. Dr. Seward told us that she carried it, hoping to give first aid to Louis, probably ecstatic over the very thought. But Dorn jumped at the conclusion that it was Ellen Bland's. Dorn himself gave Mary Kent the idea of planting the second hypo when she murdered Laura Gilbert, because he let her know he suspected Ellen.

"Mary made a full statement to Dorn this morning—you know that—when there was no longer hope of lying her way out—hoping thus to get herself clemency. She said she took cyanide along for Laura Gilbert. She was waiting in the hall, upstairs, when Laura Gilbert came in. She told her who she was and said she had come to talk to her because Ellen Bland was wronging them both. Mrs. Gilbert was tired. Mary Kent urged her to get into something comfortable. It gave her a chance to size up the apartment, think out her attack. She saw the bookends, and a box of matches nearby. Mrs. Gilbert came back and sat down on the sofa. Mary Kent rose to get a match for her cigarette and then bashed in the back of Laura Gilbert's skull. One blow in that area did the job—she would otherwise have dealt more. She left the hypo as a false clue to plant suspicion on Ellen.

"Laura Gilbert was killed within a few minutes after Hank left her. Mary Kent phoned the Rexley from a drugstore at Lexington and Forty-second, and left that message for me to call Hank. She didn't ask for me, just left the message. She called me instead of the police because she was more afraid of the police. She thought Hank would have an alibi, his train, and the hypo would hook Ellen. Then she got in touch with Louis and came with him, you remember, to the Rexley Grill for a nightcap—we saw them come in. She meant for us to know she was here.

"Meanwhile something was happening to Louis that she hadn't anticipated. He was more affected by the death of his old nurse than he himself would have imagined. Louis was sentimental under his peevish disposition. Anna was a prop, too, and Louis always had to have props. His children and his former wife suddenly became more necessary to him than ever. He didn't want to go away.

"He probably had all sorts of imaginary new fears. And he wanted Ellen back at any cost. Louis never believed Ellen guilty, really. He knew she wouldn't do it. No doubt Mary Kent egged him on in accusing Ellen, but his motives were what I said—he wanted her accused so that he could rescue her. He had plenty of money. That would protect Ellen. Money can do anything, so people like that think.

"Mary got more restive each moment. Then Louis made a deal with her. I suspected this, but didn't know what it was till the lawyer said, this morning, that Louis had been in and had arranged an allowance for *someone*. The allowance was for Mary, on condition that she release him from his promise of marriage. But Mary didn't trust Louis. She was bitter with defeat. So she dropped cyanide in his champagne glass. It misfired. So, knowing he had asked Ellen to come to the house, she changed her clothes, used the back entrance of her hotel, followed him there, and planted the knife in his neck. She bought the perfume—which was discussed at dinner—and after killing Louis she went up to Ellen's room and got the handkerchief. You smelled it strongly in the hall because she was then applying it to the handkerchief. She heard Dick coming in, and used the back stairs. She put the handkerchief in Louis's hand and left the house, again by the back stairs because, should anyone else come in the front door, it gave her the best chance to hide. And then she saw you—those amazing eyes—and tried to polish you off à la Laura Gilbert."

"Her error." I said. "Bronze vases bounce right off my thick skull. Want to feel the bump again?"

I had to sit on Patrick's lap so he could feel the bump. A couple of minutes went by before I got back to murder.

"How did she get into the house, Pat?"

"Key."

"All those keys!"

"They worried me at first. It's quite simple, however. Louis left a key in the lock when he went in with Mary Kent and Daphne Garnett. Mary Kent saw it and took it, meaning to use it to come back and have things out with Ellen. Louis had other keys, remembered he had left it, forgot it then. The key Ellen found in the lock was Dick's. Dick came home, as you know, while Ellen was with us, turned on the chandeliers in the drawing room, and left the house again."

"Why didn't Dick see the body?"

"He was blotto, darling. Also, on his way out, when the lights were on, he would keep to the right of the steps, away from the areaway."

"Oh."

"I felt sure that Mary Kent had come to the house alone the second time. Louis smokes continuously. But when we came into that room, at the time Anna's body was found, there were no stubs in the ashtrays, though Louis had admittedly been there, with the two women, for fifteen or twenty minutes—Daphne said this later—not long before. That indicated that Anna had heard them come in and, after they were gone, she went up and emptied the ashtrays, left them shining, as you know. Perhaps she put the stubs in a paper, which she dropped in the incinerator downstairs. Before she fell asleep Mary Kent returned to the house. Anna heard something, was puzzled, got up and went upstairs again, but didn't see Mary Kent, who was cautiously not smoking just then, until she opened the window and looked back."

I nodded admiringly.

"You were marvelous about the hemophilia, Pat."

"Child's play, dear. Everybody knows they use snake venom to stop bleeding these days."

"But you didn't know what ailed Louis, dear."

"I did, sooner than I said. When a taint jumps a generation it can be that particular taint. Bland got after his daughter, not his son. It is carried by the female—if Bland had the disease, his grandson through Susan would have it, but Dick would not be affected. Red ink marked items in his college scrapbooks about himself only when there had been bleeding—a tooth extraction, a blood-transfusion. Ellen dropped the remark that he might burst a blood vessel, and then quickly covered up—they can bleed to death internally, you know, too. Things like that added up to hemophilia. I didn't know it wasn't the real thing, though, till Dr. Seward said so. And I didn't know which special viper venom was in the hypos till Dorn told me—*fer de lance*— I guess Louis preferred a snake with a French name."

"So you suspected Mary Kent all along?"

"Yes. She had it in her to do murder. She was so selfish, Jeanie. She took your hat, when she didn't really want the hat. When she was told that Anna was dead, her first concern was that she might have relatives who would sue Louis. She was so envious of Ellen—of her friends, her lovely kids, the men devoted to her. She is a very mean hunk of female."

"I wish Ellen hadn't lied so, Pat."

Patrick said, "She was constantly in a state of terror because she thought Dick had committed the murders. Dick adores her so. You yourself were afraid Dick had done them, for his mother's sake. And knowing something about drunks Ellen knew that they don't always know what they've done, afterward."

"And you never suspected her, at all, dear?"

Patrick's arm tightened about me. "So help me, I did. Do you remember how I made the crack, there in the drawing room the first time we were there, about its being a long drop to the area? Just then she came into the room. I asked myself over and over if I had given her the idea. Then, that same time, Anna came into the room when Ellen was talking about Hank and saying they were going to be married, at last, and I wondered if the old girl had jumped onto her about it later on, and if Ellen had lost her head and struck her. I even thought that she came to the hotel that morning knowing already that the body was in the area. But the lights left on in the room, with the window still open, didn't make sense. Ellen wouldn't have left those lights blazing. Who would? Surely no one, except a drunk, or a maniac, after killing a woman. The light would be sure to attract the police who would promptly discover the body. So, of course, I thought—when I concluded that Ellen didn't do it—that Dick had, and that Ellen knew it, and was lying to protect him. Any more coffee?"

"Tsk, tsk. You know there isn't. Well, everything's settled, darling. Sue and Bill and Hank and Ellen are getting married and Dick will join the Marines. So shall I. They need typists. I like the green uniform."

Patrick held me away and glared.

"No, you don't. I'm not going to have my wife—"

"Tsk, tsk. Don't hog the Marines, darling."

"Well, the more Marines the sooner we'll see Paris." Patrick looked superior. "You can't, at that. You're married to one."

"I'll join something," I said.

THE END

About the Rue Morgue Press

"Rue Morgue Press is the old-mystery lover's best friend, reprinting high quality books from the 1930s and '40s."
—*Ellery Queen's Mystery Magazine*

Since 1997, the Rue Morgue Press has reprinted scores of traditional mysteries, the kind of books that were the hallmark of the Golden Age of detective fiction. Authors reprinted or to be reprinted by the Rue Morgue include Catherine Aird, Delano Ames, H. C. Bailey, Morris Bishop, Nicholas Blake, Dorothy Bowers, Pamela Branch, Joanna Cannan, John Dickson Carr, Glyn Carr, Torrey Chanslor, Clyde B. Clason, Joan Coggin, Manning Coles, Lucy Cores, Frances Crane, Norbert Davis, Elizabeth Dean, Carter Dickson, Eilis Dillon, Michael Gilbert, Constance & Gwenyth Little, Marlys Millhiser, Gladys Mitchell, James Norman, Stuart Palmer, Craig Rice, Kelley Roos, Charlotte Murray Russell, Maureen Sarsfield, Margaret Scherf, Juanita Sheridan and Colin Watson..

To suggest titles or to receive a catalog of Rue Morgue Press books write 87 Lone Tree Lane, Lyons, CO 80540, telephone 800-699-6214, or check out our website, www.ruemorguepress.com, which lists complete descrip